HAPPY EVER AFTER AT PUDDLEDUCK FARM

DELLA GALTON

B
Boldwood

First published in Great Britain in 2024 by Boldwood Books Ltd.

Copyright © Della Galton, 2024

Cover Design by Alice Moore Design

Cover Photography: Shutterstock and iStock

The moral right of Della Galton to be identified as the author of this work has been asserted in accordance with the Copyright, Designs and Patents Act 1988.

Every effort has been made to obtain the necessary permissions with reference to copyright material, both illustrative and quoted. We apologise for any omissions in this respect and will be pleased to make the appropriate acknowledgements in any future edition.

A CIP catalogue record for this book is available from the British Library.

Paperback ISBN 978-1-83518-523-0

Large Print ISBN 978-1-83518-522-3

Hardback ISBN 978-1-83518-521-6

Ebook ISBN 978-1-83518-524-7

Kindle ISBN 978-1-83518-525-4

Audio CD ISBN 978-1-83518-516-2

MP3 CD ISBN 978-1-83518-517-9

Digital audio download ISBN 978-1-83518-518-6

Boldwood Books Ltd
23 Bowerdean Street
London SW6 3TN
www.boldwoodbooks.com

For Angie Parkhurst, my favourite sister-in-law. With my love.

1

A wonderful sense of peace filled the Puddleduck Farm kitchen on that Sunday evening in January. Frost sparkled on the trees outside, but the kitchen was toasty warm. The Aga belted out heat and the air smelled deliciously of cinnamon apple crumble and custard, a pan of which still sat beside the hot plate. Three dogs curled up on the warm flagstones in various parts of the kitchen, but the room was huge, so you could have comfortably fitted in several more without tripping over any of them. An Irish Wolfhound, a black Labrador and a half-grown dalmatian were a breeze.

Phoebe Dashwood and her grandmother Maggie, whose kitchen it was, sat opposite each other at one end of the old farm-house table. It seated twelve at a push so there was plenty of room for them to spread out. The remains of a cheese ploughman's supper and a crumble dessert were scattered across its wooden surface, wood which was polished smooth by years of dinners and dozens of family memories.

'I should get this lot cleared up,' Maggie said.

'I'll do it in a sec,' Phoebe promised. 'There's no rush. Nothing ever happens on a Sunday evening.' She eyed her grandmother speculatively across the table. 'I'm not expecting a call-out tonight.'

She thought fleetingly of Sam, her other half, who'd stayed at home, while she'd nipped over for a girlie supper with her grandmother. She hoped she could head straight home to him rather than via a chilly stable on that cold January night.

Phoebe owned and ran Puddleduck Vets from a converted barn on her grandmother's land, which in its heyday had been a dairy farm, but was now an animal sanctuary. Puddleduck Pets – not to be confused with Puddleduck Vets – was home to a selection of cats, including a half-feral ginger tom called Saddam, a kennel full of dogs, several ducks, three donkeys, and any other animal in need of care and protection. Puddleduck Vets shared out-of-hours emergency work with Marchwood Vets, another local practice, and it was Phoebe's turn to cover the night shift.

She yawned and looked at her phone, which remained comfortingly silent. It was just after 8.30 p.m. 'I'll probably head home soon,' she told her grandmother. 'Although I do appreciate you making me supper. The cinnamon apple crumble was amazing.' The kitchen still smelled deliciously of the latter and Phoebe sniffed the air appreciatively.

'It was, wasn't it?' Maggie looked smug. 'It's a new recipe I found online.'

'Online. Get you! Since when did you go hunting for recipes online?' Maggie was well known for her aversion to all things technical, despite the fact Phoebe and the rest of her family had been trying to get her to use a mobile phone – or even a landline, come to that – for years.

'Since Eddie showed me an easy way to do it. I'd have picked it up ages ago if someone had shown me properly before... instead of just rushing through things at top speed. Eddie's got patience.' Eddie was her new husband and despite the fact they'd known each other forever, they were still in the honeymoon stage of their marriage, and he could do no wrong.

Maggie clicked her tongue and gave Phoebe a look that dared her to comment – either about Eddie's patience or her newly acquired technical skills. 'I've been on-lining loads lately, I'll have you know. I'm an expert on-liner. I could probably write a guide for it. You know, for beginner on-liners and old people. Eddie said I took to it like a pro.'

'Good for you.' Phoebe suppressed a smile. She was way too content and replete with food to call Maggie out on this one.

Her grandmother was in her mid-seventies. Not that she looked it, with her brown hair still barely touched with grey and her sparkling eyes – hazel brown, the same colour as Phoebe's. She still had the kind of energy that made Phoebe, who was thirty-seven, feel breathless and exhausted sometimes.

There was a tiny silence, and then before either of them could speak again, the blare of Phoebe's mobile broke it.

She reached for it, seeing immediately a number she didn't recognise. A client after all, then.

'Hello, Puddleduck Vets, can I help you?'

The woman's voice came in gasps. 'Oh! Thank goodness, I've got a person. Not an answer machine. I'm sorry to call so late, but I don't think it can wait. I'm so worried. It's Primrose, my little dog.'

'What seems to be the problem?' Phoebe shifted in her chair. The concern in the woman's voice made Phoebe straighten her back, and she switched automatically into professional mode.

'We think she's got something terribly wrong. Something internal. My husband thinks it might be bladder cancer, or even kidney cancer. She's got all the symptoms, you see. She's peeing blood. She's not in season, she's been spayed. We're so worried. She's so little. My husband Googled it...'

It wasn't just grandmothers who could become 'expert on-liners', Phoebe thought wryly. The internet made everyone an authority, these days.

Phoebe interrupted gently, 'Please don't worry. What kind of dog is Primrose and how old is she? Is she registered with us?'

'She's a cocker spaniel. Only three... we're so worried. And yes. We usually see lovely Max, Mr Jones, at the practice.'

'And what's your name, please?'

'Amy Lydford.'

Lovely Max was Phoebe's junior vet. He was a favourite with all her female clients because of his charming manner and meticulous care. His Hugh Grant voice and rugged good looks didn't go amiss either!

'I'm Phoebe Dashwood, Max's boss. I'm on call tonight. Would you be able to bring Primrose into the surgery? Does she seem well enough?'

'Yes. She does. I will. Oh, thank you so much. Shall we come now?'

'If you can, that would be great. And please...' Phoebe had been about to say, 'don't worry,' but the call had already disconnected. She turned to Maggie, who'd been listening to the whole exchange with interest and was now leaning forward, her eyes curious.

'That sounded serious.'

'Yes, I think it might be.' She relayed what the woman had said, and Maggie nodded thoughtfully.

'Bless you. So much for a quiet Sunday, then, huh!'

Phoebe nodded. 'It's most likely a urinary infection. But they're panicking, bless them.'

'I expect they've been doing the tippy tappy dance, haven't they?'

'Tippy tappy dance?'

'Eddie calls it the tippy tappy on-liner dance.' Maggie rolled her eyes. 'When folk do the tippy tappy dance and find things on the worldwide webby.'

'Right,' Phoebe said. It was a whole new world – or at least a whole new language – but then as Eddie was pretty deaf and he and her grandmother mostly communicated in a mixture of British Sign Language with their own made-up bits thrown in for good measure, it wasn't entirely surprising they had different names for things than most people.

'And now they think they're expert on-liners,' Maggie added.

Phoebe nodded. Her grandmother clearly saw no irony whatsoever in this situation. She was thinking of a tactful answer when Maggie continued, 'Some people will do anything to get out of the washing up.'

'I'm not getting out of the washing up. I can do it now before I go.'

'No need. You go off and perform your veterinary magic.' Maggie gathered the plates, clinking the cutlery, and the three dogs woke up as one and started looking interested in case there were leftovers. Tiny the wolfhound and Buster the old Labrador didn't bother getting up, but Roxie, Phoebe's six-month-old dalmatian, stretched and came eagerly across.

'Go on, off you go.' Maggie waved her hands at Phoebe. 'I'll look after Roxie while you sort out the spaniel. I'll put the plates in the sink to soak. Eddie can do them when he comes back from seeing his son. One of them's his, anyway.' She smirked. 'He took off at lightning speed as soon as he'd polished up the last scrap. Thought that would get him out of the washing up. Huh! Men!'

They both smiled. The warmth in her grandmother's voice told Phoebe she didn't mean a word of it. Maggie would be washing up as soon as Phoebe left the kitchen. Independent and feisty she might be, but she loved looking after people and of course animals. She'd loved looking after her husband, Farmer Pete, when he'd been alive, and she loved looking after Eddie now – no matter how much she pretended to complain about him.

'Good luck,' Maggie called after her.

'Thank you.'

* * *

Amy Lydford and a man who looked every bit as fretful as his wife arrived twenty minutes later. They rushed into the surgery reception, where Phoebe had just put on all the lights. The man was carrying Primrose wrapped in a tartan blanket and Phoebe's heart sank. Oh, goodness. They clearly hadn't been exaggerating about their little dog's condition if she needed to be carried.

'Let's get her up onto the examining table and I can have a proper look at her,' she said, as Mr Lydford – 'Please, call me James' – lifted the little dog up and unwrapped the blanket.

'Hello, little one, are you not feeling so good?' Phoebe petted the spaniel's head. She was brown and white and to Phoebe's relief, now she could see her properly, the little dog's eyes were bright and alert. Apart from the fact she was panting slightly, which was no doubt caused by the stress of her journey and her clinical surroundings, she seemed absolutely fine.

Phoebe checked her over carefully while Primrose submitted patiently to her ministrations. There was no sign of anaemia. No temperature, no disturbing swellings anywhere. Nothing that looked abnormal at all. Phoebe frowned, slightly puzzled, and then wished she'd kept a poker face when Amy Lydford jumped to conclusions.

'Oh my goodness. It's serious, isn't it?' She wrung her hands together. 'What are you thinking?'

'Yes. Please tell us,' James added, his eyes anxious. 'We need to know the worst. We have insurance.'

'I'm thinking we should do a urine test before we jump to any conclusions,' Phoebe told them both. 'So what I'd really like to do is to collect a sample now from Primrose, and then we can start ruling things out.'

'Is there a medical way of doing that? Or do we have to wait for her to go?' Amy asked.

'The least invasive way is to wait for her to go. I'll just get a scoop and we can pop outside?'

A short while later, the three of them were outside in the pitch black of the yard, following Primrose around with a torch and a sterile container and leaning forward swiftly every time it looked as though the dog was going to squat.

It was a moonless night, low cloud obscured the stars, but it was freezing, and Primrose was obviously in no hurry at all to oblige them. She was far too interested in all the amazing new sniffs she had found. Dogs, cats, donkeys, people – the yard must be a sniff heaven for dogs.

They had spent about ten fruitless minutes getting colder and colder – Phoebe's knees had actually gone numb – before Amy said, 'She doesn't like going on concrete. She'll never wee on the concrete at home, it has to be grass. Is there any grass anywhere?'

'Yes, of course. We can take her up to the small paddock.' Phoebe puffed out a clouded breath of relief. 'Good idea. Maybe we should give her a drink as well. Would that help?'

Both Amy and James nodded emphatically, and Phoebe rushed back into the surgery to get a bowl of water and a bigger torch, terrified Primrose would perform before she came back again.

Luckily Primrose didn't. She was way too excited about the prospect of a night-time walk to stop long enough in one place for a wee. She wasn't even that interested in the bowl of water or the hypoallergenic treats Phoebe had collected. She tugged on her lead and danced about.

'She doesn't much like going in public either,' Amy mentioned suddenly. 'Have you noticed that, James?'

'I have. Yes.'

'Maybe there's too many of us. Maybe if just me and the vet go up to the paddock.'

'Sure thing. I'll go back and wait in the surgery.' James sounded relieved as he put his hands in his coat pockets and turned back. Phoebe wished she'd thought to put on her coat when she'd left the farmhouse. She hadn't expected to be wandering around a field in the freezing cold. So much for nothing ever happening on Sunday evenings. That would teach her to tempt fate.

Carrying the bowl of water and the sterile container and flashing the torch to show the way, she walked alongside Amy and Primrose towards Maggie's small paddock, which was currently empty of animals, but once more, Primrose refrained from weeing.

Phoebe had a sudden urge to laugh. This would be comical if it wasn't so serious. She must not laugh. She wasn't sure Amy would be able to see the funny side. One thing she was 100 per cent sure about, though, was that if Primrose didn't go soon, her hands would be too numb to hold the flaming container.

'She's going to do it. She's doing it... Now...'

Phoebe leapt into action, and to her immense relief, her lightning reflexes meant she caught some of the precious liquid, even though Primrose had caught her off guard.

'Bingo,' she said triumphantly. 'Well done, Primrose. Right then, let's get this sample tested.'

'You can do that now?'

'I can, yes.'

They walked back in companionable silence. It was wonderful to be back in the relative warmth of the surgery, where Phoebe asked Primrose's owners to wait with their dog in reception while she did the necessary tests.

She'd been hoping this whole thing was a storm in a teacup. It certainly didn't look like there was much wrong with Primrose, except for the fact her urine was red. Phoebe could see that clearly in the lights of the surgery. No wonder the Lydfords had panicked. Phoebe would have been worried too.

But to her surprise, the urine dipstick test showed everything to be normal. Feeling as though she was in some surreal nightmare, Phoebe did a PCV test, grateful she'd recently invested in a centrifuge and could do them on site. There were no red blood cells present. Phoebe stared at the result with a frown on her face. Whatever was colouring the dog's urine certainly wasn't blood then. It was completely baffling.

2

Phoebe stood in the examining room of her surgery, racking her brains. There had to be some explanation, but she had no idea what it was. She'd been freezing outside, but now she'd thawed out, her fingers were tingling, her head ached and she felt hot with stress. What on earth was she going to tell James and Amy Lydford, who were sitting patiently waiting for her in reception on the other side of the door? She was going to have to say something. She couldn't just tell them that as far as she was concerned, there was absolutely nothing wrong with Primrose, other than the fact she had a rather odd shade of urine.

She stared hard at what remained of the sample. Could she Google it? Or maybe ask on the online vet forum she was on. There was bound to be someone up late. Hopefully they'd be a dog expert who specialised in urology. She thought of Maggie's expert on-liner phrase and her head throbbed with the irony.

A burst of laughter from the other side of the door stirred her from her musings. At least the couple weren't as anxious as they'd been when they'd arrived. Not if they were laughing. She could hear voices. More than two voices. The third one sounded like

Maggie. What was she doing over here? There was more laughter and... was that clapping she could hear?

Totally mystified, Phoebe opened the door and poked her head out. 'Is everything OK? Oh, hi, Maggie.'

'Hello, darling.' Maggie glanced at her with affection. 'I just came to check everything was all right. I saw lights in the field.'

'Sorry, that was us.'

'Yes, yes. So I've been told. Trying to collect a sample in the dark. Always tricky. Did you get anywhere with it?'

'Er... no, not really. Well, except to discover everything seems normal.'

'Ah, that's such a relief,' Amy said, 'if you'll excuse the pun.' With a grin, she glanced at Maggie. 'I think it was right – what you said.' She looked back towards Phoebe. 'Your senior vet had a theory on what might be wrong with Primrose. She's seen it before.'

'Has she really?' Phoebe looked at Maggie suspiciously. Yes, she'd been looking after animals for decades, but she didn't actually have any veterinary qualifications. Not that this had stopped her handing out advice when she'd done a brief stint for Phoebe as a receptionist in the early days of Puddleduck Vets.

'Yep, it's beetroot,' Maggie said confidently. 'It dyes your wee pink. Very alarming but completely harmless.'

'Granted, but dogs don't usually eat beetroot,' Phoebe said, although her heart had leapt in response to the suggestion. Maggie was definitely on to something. There were probably other foods that could do the same thing.

'Primrose doesn't eat beetroot,' James said. 'But, as we were just saying, she does eat Tyrrells vegetable crisps. She loves them and they have quite a bit of beetroot in them. We had some friends round for a finger buffet last night and I'd put some bowls of crisps out. I thought it was odd there were none at all left over.

The little monkey must have pinched them.' He stroked his dog's head and she wagged her tail from side to side. The slow wag of a dog who thinks she might be in trouble.

'It's OK, angel, it's fine. You can eat as many Tyrrells crisps as you like.' Amy dropped to the floor, grabbed her dog's head and planted a kiss on her soft brown head. 'Oh my goodness. What a palaver. All that worry and it was just beetroot crisps. Would you believe it?'

'Is that what you think it was too?' James looked at Phoebe hopefully. 'There's not a more sinister explanation?'

'There certainly doesn't appear to be. All the tests are normal.' Phoebe didn't know whether to feel massively relieved or slightly miffed she hadn't spotted the problem before Maggie had. Deciding it didn't matter, the main thing was the outcome was good, she smiled at the couple.

'Just keep an eye on her, but I think beetroot crisps are most definitely the root cause of the problem, if you'll excuse the pun.'

Everyone laughed at the weak joke. They were all high on relief. James was nodding his head. 'That's great news. We're sorry we've wasted your time. I'll come and settle up. I take it we won't have to pay for the second opinion?'

'No,' Phoebe said, before realising he was joking.

'All's well that ends well,' Maggie said, as they both waved the couple off a few minutes later with Primrose trotting happily beside them.

When the night had swallowed them up once more, Phoebe closed the practice door and turned to Maggie. 'Senior vet, huh?'

'I didn't tell him that. He just assumed. And I saw no point in correcting him. He thinks he's got a good deal now.' She raised her eyebrows. 'Two vets for the price of one. Great deal. Besides, I was right, wasn't I?'

'You were right. Thank you, Gran.'

'Can we stick to senior vet? I prefer that to Gran.'

'Senior vet and expert on-liner,' Phoebe said, sticking her tongue firmly in her cheek.

'Perfect,' Maggie said. 'Good grief, look at the time. It's gone ten. Where's that dirty stop-out, Eddie? Be off with you, junior vet.'

They both snorted with laughter.

Phoebe called Roxie and was waving goodbye when dirty stop-out Eddie arrived home again.

* * *

There was a lot of laughter the next day too when Phoebe reported the events of the previous evening to her staff in the gap between them starting work and opening the doors of Puddleduck Vets for the first appointment of the day.

Lovely Max was on holiday this week. He was seeing his family for a belated Christmas catch-up. It was the middle of January, but it seemed to Phoebe that lots of people had their Christmas festivities in the quieter first month of the year, these days.

Marcus, her receptionist, who was currently training to be an animal behaviourist, and Jenna, her vet nurse, real name Jennifer Aniston, but who called herself Jenna so everyone could differentiate between her and the famous one – at least that was her story – both gasped with relief and mirth when Phoebe told them about Primrose's visit.

'I bet your face was a picture when Maggie rocked up with her diagnosis,' Jenna said. 'Thank goodness she was right. It could have been tricky if she'd told them it was just beetroot and then you'd gone out and said there was a serious problem.'

'Yes, I know. I don't think they'd have believed me. Jeez.' The same thought had crossed Phoebe's mind. 'But I think they'd already told her Primrose had been eating beetroot crisps, so it wasn't a totally wild guess. The main thing is that she's OK. It was a happy ending.'

'We like happy endings,' Marcus said, glancing at them both, his face serene. 'We don't always get them, do we?'

'We get them as often as we possibly can,' Phoebe said happily. Marcus was currently going out with Natasha, who was Maggie's young pet sanctuary manager and adored animals almost as much as Maggie did. Marcus and Natasha were perfect for each other and Phoebe was hoping for a happy ending there, too.

'So what have we got on today?' she asked them.

'I'm doing the health check and nail trimming clinic,' Jenna said, 'and you're on appointments and whatever else crops up.'

Phoebe nodded and she went and turned the sign on the door from closed to open. 'Bring it on,' she said.

* * *

Mondays were always busy. Phoebe thought this was partly because people liked to get appointments done early in the week and partly because they held off from bringing their pets in over the weekend so they didn't have to pay out-of-hours charges. That Monday was no different. By the end of it, Phoebe had seen a cat with furballs, an injured chicken, a dog with a tummy upset, and a rabbit with an ear infection.

She'd spayed a cat in the afternoon, with Jenna's help. There had been no emergencies. Nothing unexpected, although she had a call-out on a farm to see a bull on the way home. Apparently Titus had a problem with sore gentleman bits – at least that's what the dairy man had told her.

Even in this day and age, some dairy men still didn't like to discuss the male genital problem of their animals with a female vet. They'd skirt around the subject and there would be long pauses while they did anything and everything to avoid saying the actual names of the parts in question. Phoebe had heard all sorts of phrases, varying from, 'He's got a wonky donger,' to, 'His lunch box is short of a tomato.'

It was usually less problematic when she got there because then they didn't need words. The dairyman could just point at the affected organ, which they seemed to find a lot easier.

To Phoebe's relief, when she arrived to see Titus, the dairyman had gone off duty and she ended up seeing the farmer instead, who was a woman and quite happy to discuss the problem in more detail.

'I think he's got an infection in his balls, bless him.' She raised her eyebrows. 'Occupational hazard. But we'll need to get on top of it pronto, so he can carry on getting on top of things pronto, so to speak.' She winked. 'Can't have young Titus out of action for too long.'

The farmer's diagnosis was correct. Phoebe administered antibiotics and a painkiller and left the farm, secure in the knowledge that Titus would at least be more comfortable now. Most of the dairy industry used artificial insemination these days, but of course they still needed a bull and the equipment needed had to be scrupulously clean, or there was trouble all round.

* * *

Phoebe finally got home to Woodcutter's Cottage just after 8 p.m. She was tired out already and it was only Monday, but thankfully she was no longer on out-of-hours call. She'd handed over the baton of twenty-four-hour call-out to a vet at Marchwood.

Phoebe knew she'd be forever grateful to the Marchwood practice, or more specifically to its owner, Seth Harding. She'd gone to work at Marchwood when she'd first moved back to the New Forest from London, and Seth had been a great mentor.

Up until she'd met Seth, she'd specialised in small animal practice, but he'd introduced her to the rewards and challenges of treating larger animals and Phoebe had found she loved that too. She wouldn't have liked to have given up either. The variety was what made her job so worthwhile.

Since she'd set up Puddleduck Vets, she'd treated alpacas, kunekune pigs, and a plethora of sheep and cows, as well as numerous dogs, cats, guinea pigs, hamsters and pet rats.

The oddest patient she'd ever been called out to had been a crayfish called Reggie, whose young owner had suspected he was dead, but fortunately he'd just shed his shell, as crustaceans needed to do when they'd outgrown their last one. This had been before she'd even worked for Seth – in fact he'd joked back then that it was her reputation for bringing animals back from the dead that had prompted him to employ her.

The oddest *client* Phoebe had ever had to deal with was more difficult to pinpoint. There had been Alice Connor, who called all of her male animals Boris, no matter what the species. Alice looked as though she'd stepped out of a 1950s film, despite being only in her mid-thirties. She hadn't been very keen on talking about problems of a sexual nature either, Phoebe seemed to remember.

Then there had been Mr B, the tall and gangly chef, who had point blank refused to give her his actual name because he'd been so paranoid about identity theft. He was also fixated on avoiding hidden cameras – not that Phoebe had any cameras in her surgery, hidden or otherwise. Mr B had been the owner of the kunekune pigs. He'd insisted he couldn't see any vet but her, which had been annoying when Max had been out to him already, but Phoebe had softened towards Mr B considerably when she'd seen how much he doted on his kunekunes.

Knickerbocker Gloria was a strong contender for the oddest client award too. She'd registered with the surgery last year and had told everyone who would listen that she'd been a pole dancer in her youth – Knickerbocker Gloria was her stage name – and she'd wanted to bring in her 101 guinea pigs to get their claws clipped. Having beaten Phoebe down in price because she'd claimed she was a poverty-stricken pensioner, she'd then turned up in vintage designer clothes, and clearly wasn't broke at all.

Phoebe loved all of her clients. Even the odd ones. She wouldn't have swapped her job for anything. In fact, she thought, when she finally unlocked the front door of Woodcutter's Cottage and stepped inside, she wouldn't have swapped any part of her life at all.

'Anyone home?' she shouted, knowing there was because the lounge light was on. Sam, her partner, soulmate, and long-term best friend, called a greeting from the lounge.

'Hi, love, you're earlier than I thought. How was the call-out?'

Roxie, who'd gone to work with Sam today, arrived just ahead of him to greet her. The half-grown dalmatian's tail was wagging so frantically that her whole body wagged with it.

Phoebe hugged them both, breathing in the faint smell of soap on Sam's skin – he'd obviously showered already – and the warm puppy smell of her dog.

'I must admit, it's wonderful coming home to you two. The call-out was fine. I saw a bull with sore testicles.'

'Stop there.' Sam put his hands up to ward off her words. 'I definitely don't want to know any more details.' He grinned at her and she smiled back into his gorgeous blue eyes and leaned forward to push back an unruly lock of hair.

'What is it with you men? I thought there were no taboo subjects these days.'

'There are definitely taboo subjects,' Sam said. 'Or icky ones anyway. Especially just before we eat supper. I made chicken soup and I got some of that cornbread you like from the supermarket. Hope that's OK?'

'You are the most awesome fiancé ever. Do you know that?'

'You're pretty awesome yourself. Shall I serve it up while you get a shower?' He glanced pointedly at her hands. 'After seeing the – um – bull.'

'I have washed my hands, you know.'

'Phew.'

'But I will have a shower.'

'Cool. Don't be too long.' Sam headed towards the kitchen. 'There are some things I want to talk through with you.'

3

Phoebe wondered what things Sam wanted to discuss as she stood under the shower, luxuriating in the hot water pummelling her skin. One of the things she really liked about Woodcutter's Cottage was its modern shower. It was probably the only modern thing about it, she mused, lifting her face to wash off the day.

Woodcutter's Cottage was a tiny two-up, two-down, seventeenth-century cob cottage with a thatched roof, tucked away up an unmade road, beside a woodland near Linwood, which was a stone's throw from Puddleduck Farm. It was incredibly handy for work.

It didn't belong to Phoebe. She rented it from Tori, who'd been her best friend for as long as she could remember. Tori, Sam, Phoebe and Frazier, Phoebe's younger brother, had grown up together and much of their time had been spent at Puddleduck Farm. It had been an idyllic childhood – growing up in the countryside, with the whole of the New Forest as their back yard.

Phoebe had left briefly to live in London, with another vet, Hugh, she'd met at veterinary school. More recently she'd even had a dalliance with the resident lord of the manor, Rufus Holt, but both of these men had turned out to be emotionally unavailable – to her, at least. Rufus had since got engaged to his son's live-in nanny.

Then Phoebe had finally noticed what was right under her nose – and what her friends and family had known for ages, that Sam Hendrie, whose mother, Jan, was best friends with Phoebe's own mother, Louella, was the perfect man for her.

They'd got together the previous July and Phoebe still had trouble believing just how amazing it felt to be with Sam. Although she'd been close friends with him for as long as she could remember, she'd thought there would be no chemistry. She had been so wrong. From the moment they had first kissed, the chemistry between them had grown and grown. She loved everything about Sam: his integrity, his love of animals, his perceptiveness, his thoughtfulness, his stoic nature, his straightforwardness and his utter reliability. She loved the fact he was a hard worker, and he was very family orientated too. He worked at Hendrie's Post Office and Stores, which was his mother's business in Bridgeford, a New Forest town on the banks of the River Avon on the borders of Hampshire and Dorset. He also worked as a riding instructor on the weekends at Brook Stables in the forest, which helped to pay for his own horse, Ninja, who was kept there.

On Christmas Day, Sam had asked Phoebe to marry him and since then they'd been living in two places because Sam owned a first-floor maisonette in Bridgeford, and although it had a garden, this wasn't connected to the flat's back door. It was harder work having Roxie there because it meant going downstairs with her and round to the back garden every time she wanted to go out. As well as Ninja, Sam also had Snowball, a black cat, so life was pretty full-on.

Maybe Sam wanted to talk about that. Living at two places was only a temporary measure. They planned to buy their own place together, and although they were in no hurry to set a date for their wedding, buying a house together would make day-to-day life a whole lot easier.

The sooner she finished her shower, the sooner she'd find out. Phoebe dried off quickly, dressed in comfy slob-about clothes and skipped downstairs. Woodcutter's was a great cottage and she suspected Tori would probably be willing to sell it to them, but it was very small. Ultimately the answer was to sell Sam's place and buy a bigger place together.

She stood in the kitchen doorway breathing in the delicious scents of chicken soup. Sam could cook too. That was another thing to add to the long list of things she liked about him.

She took an appreciative breath. 'Wow, that smells good,' she murmured, as he turned from the stove, brandishing a wooden spoon. 'What did I do to deserve you?'

'You must have been very good in a previous life,' he winked. 'And it is pretty good, if I do say so myself. Shall I serve it up?'

'Definitely.'

They ate at the little table in the small kitchen. More often they ate off trays on their laps in the lounge, but soup was definitely safer at the table, especially with Roxie around, who was inclined to try and jump on a lap if she could.

Neither of them spoke again till they'd emptied their bowls and Sam was wiping his clean with a hunk of fresh bread.

Then Phoebe leaned forward expectantly. 'So what's all this important stuff we have to chat about then?'

His eyes brightened. 'I thought we should start looking for a house. I know there's no rush, and there are a couple of things I want to do over at mine first, but there's no harm in seeing what's around, is there?'

'I couldn't agree more. What things need doing at yours?'

'Nothing major. A lick of paint to spruce things up. Maybe a better carpet in the bedroom. The kitchen's still all right. Dad and I did that when I bought the place.' Sam's father was a joiner and kitchen fitter.

'Can I help?' Phoebe asked.

Sam shook his head. 'You've got enough to do.'

'So have you, Sam. I don't mind wielding a paintbrush.'

'Let's see how we go.' His eyes warmed. 'This is my quietest time of year at Brook. Not many people bother with riding lessons in January. It's too cold.'

'I don't blame them. OK. Good plan. But I can still help.'

'Keeping Snowball and Roxie out of the way while I paint would be a help,' he said thoughtfully. 'And actually, I was hoping I might be able to drag Ma over for a night of painting and mother/son bonding. If I tell her I need a hand with the painting, I think she'll come. She's improved in leaps and bounds lately, and I think she'd feel safe at the flat.'

Sam's mother suffered periodically from agoraphobia, which had initially been caused by post-natal depression, and last year it had flared up again. Thankfully she was now having counselling for it and she was doing really well.

'That's a nice idea,' Phoebe said. 'OK, I'll keep Roxie out of the way when you do the painting. Puppy classes start next week – so that might be a good opportunity to get your mum over.'

'Brilliant. When are the classes?'

'They start next Thursday night in the Bridgeford Community Centre. I've got the details on a card Marcus gave me.' She rummaged in her bag. 'Here we are, Paula's Puppy Pals. It's a 6.30 p.m. start.' Phoebe turned the business card over in her hands. On the back there were three paw prints alongside a picture of a black Labrador.

'She's pretty experienced by the sound of it. She's been dog training for twenty-five years.'

Phoebe already had an image of Paula in her head, inspired by Marcus's description of a grey-haired maestro. She envisaged a motherly woman in her mid-sixties wearing a tweed blazer and possibly a trilby hat. She wasn't sure where the hat image was coming from.

She smiled fondly. 'We should probably have taken her to classes when she was a bit younger, for the whole socialising thing they're supposed to do, but it all got a bit hectic in December, what with Gran's wedding and Tori having the baby, not to mention Christmas. Anyway, she gets plenty of socialising with other dogs at Puddleduck. She likes other dogs. I'm sure she'll be fine, even if she is the biggest puppy there.'

Famous last words, Phoebe thought on the following Thursday night when she rushed into Bridgeford Community Centre, slightly late. She charged through the wide double doors that opened onto a foyer and bumped slap bang into a woman with a young black and tan German shepherd. She wasn't sure which dog was the most surprised, but the young shepherd was the most vocal. He pulled and strained on his lead, stood on his hind legs and barked loudly at Roxie.

Roxie, not to be outdone, barked back, and then threw in a couple of growls for good measure. The shepherd retaliated. The foyer had vinyl flooring where the slightest noise reverberated loudly so it all sounded much worse than it was. Blushing furiously, Phoebe hauled Roxie away across the slippery floor before there was a full-scale kick-off.

Before either she or the shepherd's owner could speak, a tall woman in jeans and a Barbour coat came rushing out of an internal door that Phoebe could see led into a big hall where some other dogs were all quietly behaving. Phoebe presumed the woman was Paula, although she didn't look like Phoebe had expected. So much for the smiley tweed motherly character she'd imagined. This woman was thin faced and did not look happy.

'Goodness me. What is all this row? Enough already. Pack it in this instant.'

To Phoebe's amazement, both dogs shut up immediately and looked at Paula with something akin to respect.

'Wow,' said the shepherd's owner. 'You clearly have the touch.'

'I should hope so after twenty-five years in the business.' Paula looked slightly less cross. 'What happened there?'

'I think the dogs were a bit startled to see each other. Bertie isn't used to other dogs.'

'It was my fault,' Phoebe apologised. 'I was rushing and I didn't realise there was another dog about.'

'Lesson one,' Paula said. 'Don't take dogs for granted. Always introduce dogs slowly and calmly. After all, we'd probably have something to say about it if a complete stranger charged up to us, full pelt, would we not?' She glanced at Phoebe. 'How old is your dalmatian?'

'She's five and a half months.'

'Hmmm, and you're just bringing her to puppy class now. She might be better in a class for older dogs.'

Taken aback, Phoebe said, 'I did mention it on the phone. We haven't been to a class before, and I think you said the puppy class would be a good place to start. She is still a puppy.'

'Ah. Yes, I do remember. You're the vet, aren't you?' Paula frowned.

'That's right.' Phoebe felt wrong footed.

'You'd better come in then. You're the last to arrive.' Paula held the door open. 'I'd really appreciate it if you could try and arrive on time in future.'

Phoebe and the German shepherd's owner exchanged chastened glances as they followed Paula into a large hall where Phoebe could see there were already four dogs with their owners, spaced at intervals, each of them standing next to a yellow fluorescent cone.

Did they all look smugly complacent? Or was that just Phoebe's fevered imagination? She decided she was being over-sensitive. Nevertheless, it was not a good start.

The evening didn't get any better either. Roxie, who had never barked at other dogs and loved everybody, had clearly been rattled by her earlier experience and Phoebe couldn't take her near to any of the other pups without her lunging and barking again.

To make matters worse, all the other canine participants, which included a cute brown dachshund, a yellow Labrador pup and two cockerpoos, were much smaller than Roxie, and their owners threw Phoebe reproachful glares, as she repeatedly hauled Roxie away, muttering, 'She's never done that before. I'm so sorry. She normally loves other dogs.'

It was obvious no one believed her and as the hour class wore on, and she was forced to leave a big gap between her and the other dogs, she felt more and more like a pariah.

The one area where Roxie did shine was when they learned their first exercise, which was 'Sit'. Roxie had been 'sitting on command' since she was a tiny pup and she was more than happy to plonk her bottom on the floor at top speed as soon as she was asked. Especially if there was a treat involved.

'Very good,' Paula said, when she came to check their progress. 'She's a natural.' She looked at Roxie consideringly. 'I am wondering, though, if you might be better off in my later class where there will be more dogs her age. They're bigger in that class too. Can you make 8.15 p.m. on a Thursday?'

'Possibly,' Phoebe said. 'Or if I can't, my partner may be able to. Is it OK if there's more than one trainer?'

'It's fine. In fact, I'd encourage it. Half the battle of dog training is continuity, so it really helps if everyone who has contact with the puppy is involved. Do you have kids? Ideally I'd like the whole family to come to training classes.'

Paula smiled encouragingly and Phoebe found herself warming to her a bit more. 'OK, thanks. And no, we don't have kids. But my partner, Sam, is very happy to be involved.'

* * *

'It sounds like fun,' Sam said, when Phoebe reported back to him later that night. 'And the later start would be better for me, it means I can nip in and sort out Ninja after work first.'

'We could both go,' Phoebe suggested. 'Paula said the more the merrier, as far as she was concerned.'

'Great. Let's play it by ear then.'

She nodded. The prospect of Sam coming along to the dog training class with her next Thursday was a cheering one. Moral support... Perfect.

* * *

The following week at Puddleduck Vets turned into one of the busiest weeks Phoebe could remember. Not only did there seem to be a surfeit of problems with their existing clients' animals, they also had four new clients register, two of whom had just moved into the area and two of whom had come via recommendations.

Phoebe loved it when new clients registered, particularly when they came via recommendation. It meant her business was a success, although she was aware that if they kept expanding their client base, they were going to need another vet. She'd been aware of this at the end of last year but hadn't had time to do anything about it yet. It was a catch-22 situation. The more clients they had, the more pressurised she felt to employ a third vet, but also the less able she felt to take any time out to interview one.

It was Max, back now from his leave, who came up with the solution.

'Jenna and I can cover the practice for a few days while you and Maggie do the selection process and interviewing,' he suggested.

'Maggie?' Phoebe questioned. 'I'm not sure. She's not really qualified.'

'Don't let her hear you say that,' Jenna said. 'It was Maggie who wanted you to employ Marcus, wasn't it, and he hasn't turned out too bad.'

Marcus, who was in earshot at the time of this conversation, although pretending not to listen, blushed scarlet.

Phoebe shot him a smile across reception. 'It wasn't just Maggie's idea. You came highly recommended,' she told him.

'Thanks, boss.' Marcus, who'd worn a suit to work when she'd first employed him, and had insisted on calling her boss, always reverted to formal mode when he was stressed.

'Will we be getting another receptionist too?'

'I'm not sure. Do you think we need one?'

At the moment, Marcus and Jenna covered reception between them and if they needed holiday cover, Maggie was happy to step in – or they could use a temp agency, which Phoebe tried not to do.

'I don't think we need anyone else,' Marcus said staunchly.

'If it's not broke, don't fix it,' Max added, flicking them both a glance.

'OK,' Phoebe said. 'I'll just look for a vet for now. We're not going to be doing longer hours so we can keep reception as it is for now. I'll speak to Maggie about the interviewing.'

Maggie, as she'd suspected, was delighted.

'Come to supper on Thursday night. That's Eddie's darts night. We can chat about it then. We could do the tippy tappy on-liner dance together, couldn't we? Don't they have online portaloos for vet staff?'

'Portals,' Phoebe said, giggling.

'That's what I said, isn't it?' Maggie winked. Sometimes, Phoebe was sure her grandmother deliberately said the wrong word just for its entertainment value.

Maggie was as sharp as a tack, despite all her fooling.

'The only problem with Thursday is it's dog training night. So I won't have much time.' Phoebe hesitated. 'Although Sam did say he was happy to go this week, come to think of it.'

'Problem solved then. Sam will enjoy some quality time with that pup, I'm sure.'

'OK, it's a date,' Phoebe promised. And on Thursday evening, when Sam called in to Puddleduck Farm to collect Roxie, she found to her surprise she was quite relieved at the prospect of not having to face Paula.

Sam laughed when she mentioned it.

'I'm sure Paula will be an utter pussy cat,' he said. 'But I will report back later. See you back at home.'

4

Paula of Paula's Puppy Pals was nothing like Sam had expected, he thought, as he strolled into the Bridgeford Community Centre early, having taken heed of Phoebe's dire warnings not to be late, and saw a tall blonde putting out what looked like traffic cones at strategic points around a large hall. It doubled up as a sports hall. It was marked out for badminton. Sam had a vague memory of playing here as a kid. Right now, he seemed to be the only one in attendance.

He cleared his throat from the doorway. 'Hi, sorry if I'm too early, but it's our first visit.'

The woman turned and Sam found himself face to face with the most stunning woman he'd ever seen. She had straight blonde hair, pulled back into a clip, chiselled cheekbones and amber eyes. Sam did a double-take. He'd never seen anyone with those colour eyes before. Maybe they were contact lenses.

'Er – are you Paula?' Phoebe hadn't said anything about the trainer looking like a glamour model. He thought she'd said she was sixty-something too. This woman couldn't have been older than twenty-five and she looked like she'd be more suited to a catwalk than a dog walk. Maybe she was Paula's assistant.

'No, I'm Destiny, I'm a colleague of hers.' She smiled at him, and those amazing eyes warmed. 'Paula can't be with us tonight unfortunately. She's broken her hip. I'm covering for her. We're friends as well as colleagues. It's all been a bit hectic, as you can imagine.'

'Yes – er – sure...' Sam blinked. 'I'm Sam, and this is Roxie. We joined the puppy class last week, but Paula thought as Roxie was a bit older and bigger than most of the puppies, we'd be better off coming to this class instead.'

'Yes, I think you're on the list Paula gave me.' She crouched down and stroked Roxie under her chin. 'You're rather gorgeous, aren't you, my love?'

Roxie fawned beneath her touch, wriggled her whole body and closed her eyes in ecstasy.

Fleetingly, Sam knew how she felt. Being in Destiny's presence was like being under a spell. It wasn't just how she looked, although that was undoubtedly part of it. It was her whole presence. Warmth and confidence exuded from her. He felt as though someone had thrown a golden blanket over the three of them.

'You don't see many dalmatians about these days,' Destiny continued. 'Gorgeous dogs. They used to be carriage dogs, I believe.'

'Yes, I think you're right.'

'But I think they were originally bred to be hunting dogs, guarding the borders of Dalmatia.'

'Really, I didn't know that.'

'There's a firefighting link too,' Destiny continued, standing up. 'In the days when there were horse-drawn fire engines, dalmatians were used to guard the horses who tended to get antsy at the scene of a fire. Very brave dogs.'

She looked back into Sam's eyes.

He gulped. He felt tongue tied. 'You, erm, really know your stuff.'

'I learned it when I did my animal behaviourism degree.' She smiled at him, causing dimples to appear in her cheeks. 'Knowing an animal's heritage and what they were bred for can tell us a lot about why they behave as they do today. I'm sorry. I haven't introduced myself properly.' She held out her hand.

'I'm Destiny Dolittle. I have my own behavioural practice. Animal Magic. It's lovely to meet you.'

'Sam Hendrie,' Sam said, managing to gather himself a bit as he took her hand. 'That's a really apt name.'

'It is. And no, it's not made up.' Those dimples appeared again. 'People often ask, but Dolittle is actually my family name, and...' She broke off and Sam heard voices at the door and realised they were no longer alone.

A woman with a whippet came into the room. She was followed by a man with a golden retriever. They were chatting animatedly and obviously knew each other. As Destiny turned to greet them, Sam took a step back. It looked as though his time alone with the glamorous trainer was over. Sam wasn't sure whether he should be disappointed or relieved.

Sam had never been to a dog training class in his life. But being an instructor himself, with a long-established reputation with riding pupils, he knew a good teacher when he saw one, and Destiny Dolittle was in a class all of her own. Even if that was a pun!

When she introduced herself to the group, it became apparent her reputation preceded her. One woman actually gasped when Destiny mentioned Animal Magic.

'Wow, I've been a fan of yours forever. You sorted out a dog for a friend of my cousin's. He'd bitten a postman twice and she was ready to put him on death row, but you rehabilitated him.'

'Royston the Rhodesian Ridgeback,' Destiny said. 'Yes, I remember the case. About two and a half years ago, wasn't it?'

'That's right. Oh my God. I can't believe you're actually training us.' The woman clapped her hands together in delight. 'What an honour.'

The class itself was a real eye opener for Sam too. While he hadn't had any real preconceptions, he'd assumed they would be teaching their dogs things like walking to heel, stay, and lie down, helped by some aptly placed bribery – Phoebe had told him the class was run around reward-based training, but it was on a different level to that.

Destiny had begun by telling them about the way dogs learned. 'One of the first things to remember is we are dealing with a species who don't speak English,' she began. 'It sounds so obvious, I know, but it's so easy to forget. Although it's certainly possible to get them to associate a certain word with an action, for example, sit means putting their bottoms on the floor, they will respond much more to our body language than a verbal cue. Dogs communicate via body language. They are much more visual than they are audio. If you can just take away that one fact from tonight, it would be amazing.' She paused to make sure they understood, but Sam could see that, like himself, the entire class was hanging on to her every word.

Even the dogs behaved. They sat quietly listening, as though mesmerised. After what Phoebe had said about last week, Sam had been slightly worried Roxie would snap and growl if he got too close to another dog, but she didn't so much as glance in another dog's direction. It was as though the whole class, both humans and canines, had fallen under Destiny Dolittle's spell.

The behaviourist went on to explain that shaping a behaviour first with the use of body language and treats was a much more effective way to teach canines than to speak.

'At least at first. We can put in the voice commands later, of course, if you wish. But for now, I'd like you to just humour me and forget everything you may have previously learned about dog training. Tonight I am going to teach you a method of loose lead walking, which you may not have seen before. Please be mindful of other dogs' space. Some dogs will certainly need more space than others. So don't get too close to each other. You can spread out. We have plenty of room.'

It was incredible how quickly the dogs responded to their owners' body language with not a 'heel' command in sight. By the end of the session, every dog in the class was walking happily on a loose lead with only the occasional transgression.

Sam was amazed.

When they gathered in front of Destiny again for feedback and questions, he was the first to raise his hand.

'Are they going to carry on doing that at home? Roxie has never yet walked on a loose lead.'

'You'll need to practise, of course,' Destiny replied. 'But as long as you remember the basics. Reward every movement your dog makes in the right direction, and withhold reward, including your attention, for every movement in the wrong direction. This is the basis for teaching your dog anything at all. There is no need to raise your voice. Your dog isn't deaf.'

She had dropped her own voice, not that it mattered. You could have heard a pin drop in the big sports hall.

When the class finished, Sam couldn't believe an hour had gone past. As he filed out with the other owners and their dogs, he could hear people talking about what they'd just experienced.

'I've never seen anything like that. It's amazing.'

'I'd heard she was good, but I had no idea she was that good.'

'Mesmerising,' was all the guy with the Staffie cross had to say. 'Absolutely mesmerising.'

Sam was inclined to agree with him.

He drove home with a tired-out Roxie in the back of his Subaru, feeling excited and enthused. He couldn't wait to tell Phoebe about the class.

* * *

Phoebe and Maggie had also had a productive evening. They'd been looking at CVs on a vet agency online.

Maggie might not be quite the expert on-liner she'd claimed, Phoebe thought, but she was certainly a lot more confident around computers than she'd ever been before, and Phoebe was thrilled. Eddie was good for her grandmother. In every way. Phoebe had suggested he might want to help them tonight, but Maggie had said he was going to the pub to play darts.

'We don't need to live in each other's pockets, darling. We're too long in the tooth for that. And besides, relationships are better if you can each pursue hobbies independently. It's different when you're working. But Eddie and I spend enough time together in the day. We both like being outside, see.'

That made sense. Back in the day when Puddleduck had been a dairy farm and Eddie had been a farmhand, they'd both have spent much of their time outside.

Maggie had always been brilliant with animals. Slightly less so with people, even by her own admission, Maggie was of the opinion that the world would be a far better place if there were more animals and fewer people in it, but despite this, she was incredibly observant and perceptive.

They had printed off the CVs of a handful of possible candidates and were now narrowing them down.

Maggie had just spotted something Phoebe wouldn't have thought was a red flag if her grandmother hadn't pointed it out.

They were looking at the CV of a forty-year-old vet who had worked in several practices around the country but whose longest job had been only nine months.

'She sounds a bit flighty,' Maggie said.

'Yes, but haven't you read her resume?' Phoebe showed her the page. 'Look, it says she loves variety and is gathering as much experience as possible.'

'Yes, but she's hardly going to fess up to the fact she's a pain in the neck to work with and regularly gets given her marching orders.' Maggie pursed her lips.

'Well, I suppose that might be true, but it's not a definite, is it? We'd only really know by talking to her.'

'Hmm.' Maggie looked sceptical. 'Have you noticed she never stays in the same area when she changes jobs?'

'That's not true. She's worked in two places in Hampshire and four in Devon.'

'Devon's a very big county. There are probably dozens of vets there. And look at where she went after that. Southend in Essex. No one ups sticks and moves to the other side of the country unless they have very good reason.'

'Mmm, I see what you mean.'

Maggie looked triumphant. 'By all means get her in for an interview if you like. You don't have to listen to what I say.' There was a meaningful pause. 'I just wouldn't want you to waste your time, that's all.'

Phoebe decided to play devil's advocate. 'You're probably right, but what if there's another reason? What if she's on the run from an abusive partner? And every time she gets settled he catches up with her and she has to move on again?'

'Your trouble is you've got a vivid imagination. But if she was on the run and he's chased her round all those places, there no reason to think he wouldn't chase her round the forest too. And you need her to be focused on her work, not playing hide and seek with her ex.'

'Poor girl,' Phoebe said, just as the back door opened and Sam appeared. 'We could be her last hope.'

'What poor girl?' Sam asked, looking from one to the other, as he let Roxie off in the doorway.

'Someone who is probably a figment of your fiancée's overactive imagination,' Maggie told him, stretching her hands above her head and yawning.

'Hi, Sam.' Phoebe glanced up as Roxie hurtled across to greet her. One of the things she loved about Roxie was that she was always massively pleased to see you – even if you'd only been apart for ten minutes. Let alone the eternity of an evening. Sam looked pretty animated too. 'How did it go? Was she good? What did you make of Paula?'

'She was an absolute angel,' Sam said. 'Roxie, I mean. I didn't meet Paula.' Following Roxie more slowly across the room, he smiled at Maggie and kissed Phoebe. 'Paula's broken her hip apparently, so she sent a stand-in. A woman called Destiny Dolittle.'

'That name sounds familiar. Was she blonde and very beautiful?'

'She was.' Sam looked at her in surprise. 'Do you know her?'

'No, but I have seen her. You have too, actually. She was at Rufus Holt's New Year's Eve party. She was talking to Marcus and Natasha. Don't you remember?'

'Nope,' Sam said, looking mystified.

Phoebe felt a little bit relieved about that. Her mind flicked back to the moment that Tori had pointed out Destiny Dolittle at the party. The stunning younger woman had been wearing a figure-hugging sequin dress and had been chatting with a circle of male admirers.

The thought of Sam spending an evening in close proximity with her made Phoebe's stomach twang a little with jealousy. Gosh, that was a new emotion for her. Jealousy wasn't something she felt very often.

Funnily enough, when Tori had pointed out Destiny at the party, her voice had been full of envy too.

'It's hard not to be jealous when someone's that beautiful and that talented,' she had said wistfully. 'And she's only twenty-seven. Mind you, I'd definitely like to be that slim.'

'You've only just had a baby,' Phoebe had reminded her, and the two friends had been able to laugh at themselves.

Annoyingly, Phoebe didn't feel very much like laughing now as she looked at Sam's animated face. He'd obviously had a great evening with the divine Destiny Dolittle.

'Did *you* think she was beautiful?' Phoebe persisted. She could hear a very slight edge in her own voice.

'I suppose. If you like that sort of thing,' Sam answered, and it may have been a trick of the light but to Phoebe's suddenly heightened perception he seemed to have gone a little pink.

'More importantly,' Phoebe said, catching herself, 'was she a good trainer?'

'She was an amazing trainer.' Sam's eyes misted over slightly and Phoebe felt the smidgen of jealousy take shape and grow into a prickly little spike. 'To be honest, I don't think I've met anyone as good.'

'She's the woman who owns Animal Magic,' Maggie joined in with the conversation. 'She has a very good reputation. She's only young, but she's a natural, so I've heard.'

'She sounds wonderful,' Phoebe said. 'The divine Destiny Dolittle.' Oops, she had meant that to be light and cheery, but it had come out as catty – oh, the irony. Phoebe became aware that both Maggie and Sam were looking at her rather oddly.

She put on her brightest smile. 'Ignore me. Sorry. I'm tired. But I'm really pleased Roxie's getting the best trainer. That's brilliant news.'

Sam looked reassured. 'Anyway, you can see for yourself next week. Paula's not going to be around for a while. Ms Dolittle will be taking the class for the foreseeable future.'

'Great,' Phoebe said. 'I'll look forward to that.'

5

As it happened, Puddleduck had another really busy week. Quite a few people, it seemed, had got kittens and puppies for Christmas, despite the RSPCA's well-publicised warnings: a dog is for life, not just for Christmas. The first week of February seemed to be prime time for vet checks and inoculations.

Phoebe was glad she'd made the decision to take on another vet. She and Maggie had narrowed the longlist down to a shortlist of three and they were interviewing in the first week of March.

The shortlist was made up of three very different candidates. There was Leonora Miles, a hotshot young vet who'd qualified at the London Vet School and was working at her first job in London but wanted to come back to the New Forest because that was where her family lived. This echoed Phoebe's own experience, which was one of the reasons she'd been drawn to Leonora.

The other two candidates with great experience were both guys. Tim Staples was currently working at a practice in Devon but wanted to come back to Hampshire because his elderly mother lived there, and Oliver Petworth was already local.

Phoebe had also run the CVs past Max and Jenna in case they

spotted anything she and Maggie hadn't noticed, but they'd both agreed they looked like good candidates.

Sam had nearly finished painting his kitchen, although his mother hadn't managed to make it over, apparently, and Phoebe was keeping her promise to make sure Snowball and Roxie were out of his way. They hadn't spoken much more about Roxie's dog training classes with the divine Destiny Dolittle – the name Phoebe had secretly given her – but Sam had showed her the heel work techniques they'd learned last week.

'So you can get in some practice before you go,' he'd said with a grin.

Phoebe had promised she'd practise, but somehow the week had gone by without her doing any, and before she knew it, it was Wednesday evening again. She'd had every intention of practising on Wednesday lunchtime, but an emergency appointment to see a cat with kidney failure had put paid to that and on Wednesday evening she had a long-standing arrangement to see Tori, which she didn't want to break. Tori was her best friend and they hadn't met since the New Year's Eve party. They'd spoken by phone and WhatsApp a lot; Tori's conversation was full of broken nights and breastfeeding, the joy and the difficulties of new motherhood. And her WhatsApp feed was full of pictures of Vanessa Rose, who'd been born at the beginning of December, but Phoebe wanted to catch up with them both in person.

Also, she knew Tori's partner, Harrison, was out. Phoebe had warmed to Harrison a bit since she'd first met him, but she still felt more relaxed when he wasn't around. She wondered some-times if this was because he was a man of few words and often looked grumpy or because he was best friends with her ex. Harrison also worked with Rufus Holt, or Lord Rufus Holt, as he'd been since his father had died and passed on the hereditary title. Whatever the reason, it was easier to see Tori when Harrison wasn't there.

Phoebe decided she would take Roxie with her and if the worst came to the worst then maybe they could practise in Tori and Harrison's big back garden. She seemed to remember they had outside lighting.

This plan was scuppered by the rain and the fact Tori opened the door in her dressing gown, even though it was only 7 p.m. when Phoebe arrived.

'Hi, lovely one. Excuse my attire. I meant to get dressed earlier but I didn't get round to it.'

'You've been wearing your dressing gown all day?' Phoebe tried not to let her surprise creep into her voice. Tori was usually very appearance conscious, not to mention a complete workaholic. She owned and edited the local free magazine, *New Forest Views*. Mind you, she'd be on maternity leave, technically at least, although Phoebe suspected she'd still be keeping an eye on things. 'Is it OK if I bring Roxie in?'

'Yes, of course it is. My God, she's grown. She's getting really big. And to answer your other question, no, just since lunchtime when I got my head down for a nap. Harrison was here for a while to take over baby duties. Vanessa Rose doesn't believe in night-time sleeping.' She beamed, but there were dark shadows under her eyes and her red hair was mussed up and unstyled. Phoebe hugged her.

'Gosh, you must be exhausted. Where is she now?'

'She's in her cot but I'm just about to feed her. Come in, come in. It's a foul night out there. Roll on spring, I say.'

The kitchen smelled of toast and percolated coffee. There was baby paraphernalia and mess everywhere, but there was also an amazing warmth. Phoebe cooed over Vanessa Rose and Tori clucked proudly as she lifted her daughter out of her cot and into her arms.

They sat on the couch at the diner end of the open-plan room and caught up on each other's lives. There was a lot to catch up on – Tori and Harrison were planning both a wedding and a christening this year. The christening was planned for June, although the date had yet to be finalised, and the wedding was planned for the last weekend in August.

'We literally got the last date the vicar had for the wedding,' Tori told Phoebe. 'The whole world wants to get married in August, apparently.'

Phoebe wasn't a bridesmaid because Tori wasn't having any. She'd told Phoebe in the early stages of planning that this was a political decision.

'There are quite a few kids in Harrison's family,' she'd explained, 'so if we had them all, we'd end up with about eight bridesmaids and five pageboys. We definitely don't want them all – we're still getting to know most of them to be honest. But we don't want to have to choose some and leave out others either – it's a minefield.'

'You didn't weaken on the bridesmaids then?' Phoebe asked her now. 'Last time we spoke you said there'd been some pressure from Harrison's family.'

'We resisted it. Why? Were you having an urge to be my maid of honour?' Tori enquired as she unfastened her nursing bra and settled Vanessa Rose in a different position.

Phoebe shook her head. There was something incredibly intimate about being with a new mother while she was breastfeeding her baby. She felt her own throat close as she witnessed the love on Tori's face, as she tended to her daughter.

'What's it like?' she asked softly. 'I don't mean the breastfeeding bit, although I suppose I do mean that as well. I mean the whole motherhood thing. Is it like you expected?'

'Yes and no. It's a lot harder in some ways, and in other ways it's easier.' She paused reflectively. 'Actually, the breastfeeding bit's much easier than I expected. I know lots of women find it too painful but we seem to manage OK on that front. The sleepless nights are the hardest.

'Harrison's great. He's a very hands-on dad. But I try to be the one who gets up in the night. I'm still on maternity leave but he has to go to work every day. I feel like I'm sleepwalking through my life. But there's also this other overwhelming feeling that's hard to describe. It's a kind of numbness but also an elemental earthiness that spreads like a protective warm blanket over everything. It makes it all possible. And the love. Oh, God, Phoebe, the love is overwhelming. It hurts but it's also glorious. I feel like I would die for this little bean.'

She looked down at the baby in her arms and then glanced up at Phoebe. 'It's crazy. I can't believe there was a time when I said I didn't want kids. Now she's here, I can't imagine there was ever a time when she wasn't here.' Her eyes filled up with tears and one rolled down her face. 'Don't worry, they're happy tears,' she explained. 'I think there must be shedloads of hormones still flooding my body. That and sleep deprivation.'

'Wow.' Phoebe blinked back a surreptitious tear of her own. 'Just wow.' The fact that she'd been contemplating doing heel work in Tori's back garden with her half-grown dalmatian puppy suddenly seemed ridiculous and awfully trivial.

Roxie was currently shredding a tissue. 'No, Roxie,' she said absently, getting up and taking it off her. She swapped it for a dog treat she had in her pocket – and felt fleetingly guilty. Some trainer she was, rewarding her dog for stealing.

'Anyway,' Tori said, giving Phoebe a direct look. 'This has all been me, me, me, so far. I want to know what's going on with you. How's Sam? How's work? Have you two found anywhere to live yet? Have you decided whether you're going to buy a house or a flat? Are you actually living together? And last but not least, do you fancy making some more coffee because I can't get up.' She dropped a kiss on Vanessa Rose's head and grinned.

'So many questions.' Phoebe went to sort out the percolator. Roxie followed her and Phoebe slipped her a piece of digestive biscuit she hadn't finished earlier and got a wag of thanks.

As they waited for the coffee, she told Tori about Sam's painting mission and about her decision to take on a new vet and then, without even realising the subject was still on her mind, she said, 'Do you remember that girl we saw at Rufus's New Year's Eve party? The glamorous one in the sequin dress? I think you said you interviewed her for the magazine?'

'Destiny Dolittle,' Tori said promptly. 'How could I forget a name like that? Yes, of course I do. Why?'

'It turns out she's Roxie's dog trainer.' Phoebe explained how that had come about and Tori listened carefully.

'That sounds perfect,' she said when she'd finished. 'Why are you looking so worried?'

Phoebe hesitated. She went and refilled their mugs and brought them back to the couches. 'This is so silly I'm not even sure I want to share it,' she said quietly.

'You can share anything with me. You know you can.'

Phoebe sipped her coffee and swallowed hard. 'It's just that Sam seemed so blown away by her. So completely under her spell. That is totally mad, isn't it?'

'The only mad thing is you thinking he might have his head turned by a pretty face,' Tori said lightly. 'He's completely besotted with you. He just asked you to marry him, didn't he?'

'Yes, I know. I told you it was silly.'

'No, hang on a minute. I didn't say the feelings were silly. Irrational maybe but definitely not silly.'

Phoebe bit her lip. She felt really stupid now and a little ashamed of herself. It sounded as though Tori was trying to backtrack, but it wasn't helping.

'Jealousy is such a horrible emotion,' Tori continued. 'God knows I've felt it often enough.'

'Have you? When?' Now Phoebe was really surprised. One of the things she'd always admired about her friend was that Tori never took anything too seriously. Or at least she hadn't until she'd met Harrison. She'd breezed through life, she'd been addicted to dating and she'd had dozens of relationships which she'd tired of very quickly and abandoned for the thrill of a new chase.

'Since I met Harrison and fell in love,' Tori said promptly. 'He goes to all these society-type occasions with Rufus and I know they're crammed to the hilt with beautiful young women, all of whom went to the same kind of posh public school Rufus and Harrison went to – most of them looking out for a partner. Why wouldn't he get tempted and realise he didn't have to settle for a common or garden journalist, who got pregnant when they barely knew each other?'

'You're not a common or garden journalist. You have your own very successful business. You're a huge catch. And he was already in love with you when you got pregnant.'

'Was he, though? Or did he think I trapped him into matrimony?' Tori shook her head ruefully. 'I didn't say it was rational. I said I understood jealousy.' She shifted Vanessa Rose in her arms and the baby opened her beautiful blue eyes and locked on to her mother's gaze.

'Frankly, if I knew Harrison was spending any amount of time with a stunner like Destiny Dolittle, I'd be pretty rattled myself.'

Phoebe released a breath she didn't realise she'd been hold-ing. 'Would you truly?'

'Of course I would. Any sane woman would be. I mean she's gorgeous, she's talented, she's wealthy, she's also really nice from what I remember when I interviewed her. Pretty damn bloody perfect. What's *not* to dislike?' She giggled.

Phoebe joined in. 'Thank you. I feel so much better now. Do you really dislike her, or was that just a turn of phrase?'

'A turn of phrase. I don't know her enough to dislike her. I'll tell you one thing though, Pheebs, I wouldn't want to be her. I bet she inspires jealousy wherever she goes. That's if it's possible to inspire jealousy,' she added, thoughtfully. 'Inspire referring to something positive and jealousy being such a negative emotion.' Tori was a wordsmith and hated to get things wrong.

'Yes, I guess you're right. That can't be very nice.'

'There's bound to be something she hasn't got. There always is. No one's life is totally perfect.'

'Maybe it's love,' Phoebe suggested. 'Do you know if she's single?'

'No, I don't. She didn't say when I interviewed her. We mainly talked about her business and why she'd started it up. We didn't really touch on her personal life.' She paused. 'Anyway, Sam's not going tomorrow night, is he? You are. So you can check her out for yourself.'

6

It had been brilliant talking to Tori, Phoebe mused. There were some things you definitely couldn't discuss with your partner, and irrational, unprovoked jealousy about another woman was one of them.

Her best friend had been right. Jealousy was such a negative emotion – especially when it was completely unfounded. It grew like a nasty little cancer from a couple of innocuous cells, spreading insidiously until it had wrecked everything. Phoebe remembered a girl at the London Vet School who'd been convinced her childhood sweetheart, back home in Essex, was two-timing her with her cousin. She'd worked herself into a right old state about it, even going as far as driving back to spy on them. It turned out he hadn't been two timing her at all, but in the end he'd been so fed up with her constant sniping and lack of trust he'd ended the relationship anyway.

Phoebe knew the only answer to jealousy was to stamp it out. Face it head-on, which was what she intended to do. Meeting Destiny Dolittle herself was the first step. All through Thursday, in between consultations, Phoebe found herself conjuring up little vignettes of scenes that might happen after dog training class.

In one of them, she was helping Destiny to clear up the cones after class and they were having a heart-to-heart. Destiny was telling her she had a childhood sweetheart who'd been a massive support throughout her meteoric rise to stardom – and she *was* a star, Phoebe had checked online – and they were getting married in the spring.

In the imaginary scenario, Phoebe was congratulating her and confiding that she too was getting married this year, not that she and Sam had any concrete plans yet, and before very long they were comparing engagement rings and swapping details about their dream weddings.

There was actually nothing online about Destiny having a partner and Phoebe couldn't see a ring on her finger in any of her publicity shots either. She'd studied a few. There were several training videos where she was working with a dog and Phoebe had managed to pause the video and zoom in to see if she could see a ring. She hadn't spotted one, but maybe Destiny took her ring off when she was training in case she lost it.

She was obviously a private person. There was very little about her personal life at all online. Even in Wikipedia. But this didn't deter Phoebe from her imagined scenarios.

In another imagined scenario, Destiny laughed uproariously when Phoebe asked her if there was a man in her life and confessed she was actually gay.

'I don't publicise it for Angelica's sake,' she confided, staring into Phoebe's eyes. 'Angelica's very private. So please keep it to yourself.'

This was Phoebe's particular favourite. Angelica was the perfect name for Destiny's made-up lover. Angelica and Destiny – the golden couple.

A rather pointed cough from Marcus jolted Phoebe back into reality and she realised he'd just asked her a question. She glanced at him.

'Sorry, what was that? I was miles away.'

'I noticed.' He raised his eyebrows. 'I know you're not supposed to be working tonight, but there are two call-outs. One's to a bitch whelping in Bridgeford, and the other's a call from Marchwood to see a parrot in Lyndhurst. They both sound quite urgent but they're in opposite directions. Max can't be in two places at once. I said I'd phone the parrot woman back. I could tell her we'd be really late, but I said I'd ask first.' He paused for breath.

'Of course.' Phoebe glanced at the clock, as she weighed up the options. It was just after five. There were no more appointments. The surgery closed at 5.30 p.m. Bridgeford was only fifteen minutes away and it was in the right direction for dog training. But if there were complications with the whelping, she might be there a while. Lyndhurst was in the wrong direction, and further away, more like twenty-five minutes in rush hour traffic but it probably wouldn't take too long. She hated letting people down.

'Do we know what's wrong with the parrot, Marcus?'

'Marchwood think it's a broken wing. I'm not sure why the owner couldn't take him to the surgery, but she can't apparently.'

'Right.' Phoebe made a split-second decision. 'Tell her I'm on my way.' There should be plenty of time to get to Lyndhurst and back. She could grab a sandwich for tea and still make it to dog training.

She was just encouraging Roxie to jump into the back of the Lexus when Marcus caught up with her, waving a piece of paper. 'I'm really sorry, boss. I've made a mistake on the address. It's Lymington, not Lyndhurst. Is that still OK?'

Phoebe's heart sank. Lymington was double the distance.

She'd be cutting it really fine, and that was only if it was an in-and-out visit.

'I'm so sorry.' Marcus looked stricken. 'Shall I phone her back and say we can't come? I'll tell her it's my fault.'

'No. It's OK. I'll go. But I need you to do me a favour. Would you mind taking Roxie into the farmhouse and asking Maggie if she can mind her for a bit? Tell her I'll phone from the car and explain.'

'Sure.' Marcus looked puzzled, and Roxie looked disappointed as Phoebe encouraged her to jump back out of the Lexus again and handed her lead to Marcus.

'It's her dog training class tonight. With a bit of luck, I'll be done in time to take her. But if I don't make it back in time, Sam can probably do it. I'd better get going.'

Marcus nodded.

It wasn't like him to make mistakes, Phoebe thought, as she drove out of the five-bar gate from Puddleduck Farm onto the road. In fact, she didn't think she'd ever known him to make a mistake the whole time he'd worked for her. He was meticulous and concise. She hoped nothing was bothering him.

She'd been too preoccupied with the divine Destiny Dolittle today to notice, she berated herself. All that angst, and now it looked as though she wouldn't make it to the class anyway. How frustrating.

The chances of her making it back were growing slimmer by the second. There was a set of four-way traffic lights on the way to Lymington. Where had they sprung from? As far as she could see, despite the rows of cones, there was only one fluorescent jacketed workman in attendance, and he was talking on his phone. She called Sam hands-free from her car and explained what had happened.

'I know it's short notice, but can you take Roxie to class if I don't make it back in time?'

'Of course. I'd love to. I can phone Maggie too if you like. Save you being on the phone while you're driving.'

'Thanks. That would be great. Not that I'm actually driving right now. I'm stuck at the temporary lights on the road to Lymington.'

'Ah, yes, I know the ones you mean. Dad's always complaining about those. He says it doesn't look like they're even doing anything half the time.' He chuckled. 'Hope you're not there too long, sweetheart.'

'You and me both,' Phoebe said, before realising he'd already disconnected. She felt an irrational sense of disappointment. She'd been hoping he'd keep her company while she was waiting. At least he hadn't seemed to mind being asked to take Roxie at the last minute. He'd sounded positively delighted. Phoebe's stomach crunched. She was definitely not going to read anything into that.

The lights finally changed, and Phoebe reached the address on the outskirts of Lymington, with no more hold-ups. The Old Courthouse, number 14, turned out to be one of a row of terraced houses, fronted by double yellow lines. She found a parking space a few streets away, grabbed her vet bag and walked back towards it.

There was a plaque on the wall, proclaiming the building was The Old Courthouse, but apart from that the house didn't look any different to any others on the street. She rang the doorbell and seconds later it was opened a few inches by someone on the other side. A hassled face appeared in the tiny gap.

'Hi, are you the vet?' asked a stressed female voice.

'I am,' Phoebe confirmed.

'I'm Kat. Thanks so much for coming. Can you come in quickly, please. I'm scared Mr Spock will escape.'

Phoebe did as she was told, squeezing through the gap as the door was opened just wide enough for her to enter, before being slammed hastily behind her.

Kat was dressed in black leggings, a pink crop top and white pumps. A wide pink headband held her blonde hair off her face, which was slightly flushed. Phoebe had the impression she'd interrupted a workout session. Kat was pencil slim. Somewhere in the building she could hear the pumping sounds of up-tempo music.

She glanced around, realising she was standing on a mezzanine floor that was the same level as the pavement outside. The place was like a Tardis, much bigger inside than it looked from the street. A flight of stairs led downwards into the main reception area, which was an enormous room with exposed wooden rafters going up to a ceiling that must be more than twenty feet high. At the opposite end of the room, on the same level as they were now, cantilevered witness boxes had been used to create a balcony. Phoebe did a double-take. It was a jaw-dropping space.

'Is Mr Spock your parrot?' she asked apprehensively, because if a parrot was loose in this room the chances of catching it were remote. A bigger aviary would have been hard to find.

'Yes, well... no, not exactly... What I mean is that he's not mine. He belongs to my boyfriend. Darren's a massive Trekkie – that's probably obvious from the name. Although it wasn't to me when we met. But I hadn't met Mr Spock, then.' She gave a loaded sigh. 'If I'd known then what I know now... well, I'd never have agreed to look after him while Darren was on holiday. In fact, I'd probably never have agreed to see Darren again after our first date. But that's another story.'

'Right,' Phoebe said. They were still standing in the raised hallway while Phoebe processed all this information.

'Where exactly is Mr Spock?' she asked anxiously.

'I'll show you. Follow me.'

Kat led her down the stairs into the main area. It was a stunning room with high arched windows, pale green ceilings and wood panelling that looked as though it had come out of the original courthouse.

Three full-sized cream sofas fitted comfortably around a low wooden coffee table that must have been at least five feet square. A dark blue cast-iron wood burner sat on a wide slate hearth and there were blue cast-iron radiators along the walls too. This room must cost a fortune to heat, Phoebe thought, irrelevantly. Despite the February day outside it was snugly warm. But the overall effect of the high ceilings and huge open space was impressive.

'He's up there.' Kat's voice brought her back to the present with a jolt and Phoebe saw her client pointing upwards.

Phoebe craned her neck. She could see a green parrot with a yellow head perched high up on one of the windowsills.

'My receptionist mentioned Mr Spock had an injured wing,' she said. 'But he presumably flew up there.'

'Yes, he did fly up there. That's how he injured his wing. He bashed against the window. I think that's why he hasn't moved. He would normally have come down by now.'

'This is a regular thing, then, is it? Him flying around the courthouse?'

'Yes. Darren told me he does it every night for his evening constitutional, and he always comes back. Mind you, Darren told me a lot of things when we met, not all of which have been true. We met on a fun run, and he said he was training for a half marathon. That definitely wasn't true.'

She shook her head, frowning at the memory. 'Anyway, to be fair, he was right about Mr Spock. This is the first time he hasn't come back. That's why I'm worried he's hurt. I've got his favourite treats as well.'

She picked up a packet of bird seed from the coffee table and shook it. 'Hey, Mr Spock, treat time.'

'Treat time, treat time,' the parrot repeated, and Phoebe smiled.

'Wow, there's no mistaking what he's saying, is there. Does he talk a lot?'

'Unfortunately, yes. He's brilliant at mimicking the doorbell. He always does it when I'm in the middle of cooking clear soup or doing yoga or my Pilates session – I'm forever getting up to answer it and there's no one there. He can also do the sound of a ring pull being pulled off a can. Darren swore blind he didn't drink when we met. Clearly another lie.'

'Soft drinks have ring pulls, though, don't they?' Phoebe ventured.

'Yes, but Darren said he was a fitness fanatic. It was one of the few things I thought we had in common.' She frowned. 'There are no healthy drinks that come out of a can with a ring pull.'

'Right,' Phoebe said. That was her told then. Kat did not seem the kind of person who had much of a sense of humour.

'He also does a perfect imitation of a fry-up being cooked. Darren told me he doesn't even own a frying pan. To be fair, I haven't found any in his kitchen since I've been here looking after Mr Spock. So maybe he was telling the truth about that.' She huffed doubtfully. 'Darren blames Mr Spock's previous owner for it all. Apparently he was a couch potato who lived on pizzas, beer and fry-ups. Can you imagine?' She touched her perfectly flat tummy.

Phoebe had the strong urge to hold hers in. Saying she

couldn't imagine a life where there was no pizza was definitely not the answer Kat was looking for.

She switched the conversation back to the business in hand.

'I'm more than happy to examine him, but we're going to have to entice him down somehow. Any ideas?'

'I thought you might have some suggestions on that front.' Kat looked at her hopefully. 'I assume you've examined lot of birds.'

'Yes, but I don't usually have to catch them first,' Phoebe said, although actually it wasn't that long ago she'd been called out to see to a duck called Quackhead that had managed to get itself wedged into the driver's cabin of a rusting old truck. At least Quackhead had been contained in a small area. A parrot on a windowsill, fifteen feet above her head, in a room with a vaulted ceiling was an entirely different matter.

'I don't suppose you know if Darren's got a stepladder anywhere?'

'There's a ladder he uses to clean the windows. I'll go and get it.'

'Ding dong.' Mr Spock did an almost perfect imitation of a doorbell. 'The witch is dead.'

Phoebe suppressed a grin as Kat rolled her eyes and disappeared.

Phoebe took the opportunity to text Sam and say it was very unlikely she'd be back and could he please take Roxie to class. 'Have fun,' she typed, and added a smiley face for good measure.

'But not too much fun,' she said aloud under her breath.

She didn't have time to think too much about Sam spending another evening with the glamorous Destiny because Kat reappeared with a folded-up ladder and a long net on a pole. The ladder was covered in cobwebs and looked a bit rusty, which Phoebe decided didn't bode well, but Kat reassured her quickly.

'It lives outside in the shed. Darren definitely uses it quite often. I found two frying pans while I was looking for it. They were hidden in the drawer with the secateurs. Would you credit it?'

Phoebe decided it wouldn't be wise to ask Kat why she was looking in drawers for a ladder. It was definitely none of her business. But she felt a fleeting sympathy for the absent Darren.

Kat bent gracefully to unlock the ladder's sections and as each one slid out smoothly, Phoebe began to feel a bit more reassured.

'There,' Kat pronounced triumphantly. 'If you could just give me a hand to get it in position, against the wall.'

Phoebe obliged. The ladder took them in range of the windowsill. That was a relief.

'I got the net so it won't be necessary to go up too high,' Kat said.

'Good move. Shall I hold it, while you go up?' Phoebe wondered if she should be suggesting Kat went up a precarious ladder. This whole situation was beginning to feel like a bizarre dream. She paused. 'Kat, I appreciate you're worried, but maybe you should just give Darren a call? When's he due back?'

'Believe me, I would, but he's in France for another week, climbing mountains. There's not a lot of signal on Mont Blanc. Or at least that's what he told me when he phoned to say he'd arrived. All I could hear in the background was music and clinking glasses. I wouldn't put it past him to have snuck off on a booze cruise.'

'Booze cruise,' repeated Mr Spock gleefully from his perch above them. 'Bye-bye, Darren.'

Kat looked pained. 'To be honest, I'm not keen on heights. That's why I didn't insist on going to France with Darren. I don't suppose you'd be able to go up the ladder, would you...?'

Phoebe was about to point out that her insurance was

unlikely to cover her climbing up ladders to catch her patients, when Kat put her hand on her arm. 'I know it's a big ask, but you won't need to go too high. I hate the thought of him being stuck up there in pain for a week.'

Phoebe hated the thought too. At least they had that in common. 'All right. I'll go up a little way. Maybe see if I can reach him with the net.'

Kat looked massively relieved. 'I'll hold the ladder. If you feel at all unsafe, come down. But at least we'll have tried.'

Phoebe grabbed the pole with the net in her left hand and went slowly up the ladder. With Kat holding it firmly at the base, it did feel quite safe. The floor was carpeted with thick pile cream carpet so it wasn't likely to slide.

As Phoebe got higher, Kat called out encouragement from below, and Mr Spock squawked out random phrases.

'Shiver me timbers! Yo, ho, ho.'

This was definitely the strangest call-out she'd ever had, Phoebe thought, pausing when she got within range of her patient. She wasn't much more than ceiling height in your average room, but hopefully with the aid of the long pole she'd be able to reach.

'I'm going to try and net him,' she called down. 'Please hold the ladder steady.'

'I've got it. Don't worry.'

Suddenly there was a piercing whistling sound. A smoke alarm going off. Phoebe jumped violently. So did Kat, judging by the movement of the ladder.

Then several things happened simultaneously.

Mr Spock squawked and took off from the window ledge in a flurry of green wings, Phoebe dropped the net, and the ladder began to slide to the left. Phoebe felt herself falling with it.

'One, two, three, weeeeeeee,' was the last thing Phoebe heard from Mr Spock before she landed on the carpet with a thump.

For a few seconds she lay on her back, dazed and winded. At least the smoke alarm had stopped blaring, was the last coherent thought she had.

7

She must have shut her eyes because when she opened them again, Kat was bending over her, looking stricken.

'Oh my God, are you OK? Are you hurt? Say something, please. Should I call an ambulance?'

'I'm not sure.' Phoebe tested her limbs one at a time. As far as she could make out, there was no pain. She was more breathless than anything else. She was probably winded. Or maybe it was the shock of sliding off a ladder. Thank goodness for shag pile carpet. She sat up gingerly.

'I don't think I've done any major damage.' Nothing a stiff drink wouldn't cure, she was tempted to say. But she couldn't imagine Kat approving of stiff drinks in any circumstances. Anyway, she was driving.

'I'll make you a nice cup of chamomile tea.' Kat leapt nimbly to her feet.

'Oh, deep joy!' She hadn't meant to say that out loud, but by the look on Kat's face she had.

'Don't you like tea?'

'Tea will be fine. No sugar,' Phoebe called after Kat's retreating back. Still sitting on the carpet alongside the ladder, she rubbed her forehead. Jeez. This was her own fault. She should never have agreed to climb up that flaming ladder. She hadn't got off completely unscathed either. Her left shoulder was a bit sore. But other than that, she'd been amazingly lucky.

She got up slowly and looked around for Mr Spock, who'd gone very quiet. He was no longer on the windowsill. She couldn't see him at all. Had he fallen? She scanned the carpet but there wasn't so much as a green feather on the white shagpile.

Kat reappeared with two mugs. She set them down on the coffee table on coasters. 'Are you all right?' She really did sound concerned.

'I'm OK, thank you. Just a bit shocked. Why did the smoke alarm go off anyway? Was something burning somewhere?'

'I've checked. It never was going off. Another of Mr Spock's tricks.' She held Phoebe's gaze. 'I didn't know he could do that. I really didn't. I'm so sorry.'

'It can't be helped. Did you see where he went?'

'Yes, he's up in the dock.'

'The dock?'

Kat gestured towards the balcony. 'It's opposite the witness boxes.'

Phoebe squinted. She could see a flash of green high up on what looked like a wooden ledge above what was presumably the dock.

'We could probably reach it with the ladder...' Kat began.

'Don't even think about it,' Phoebe interrupted. 'If he can fly up there and do smoke detector impressions, I really don't think there's much wrong with him. In fact, I'd say the dock's a pretty good place for him. As far as I'm concerned, he can stay up there until the jury reaches a verdict and let's hope it's a guilty one.' She rubbed her shoulder and winced. 'He needs to be locked up.'

Kat snorted and Phoebe realised she may have gone a bit far. But then she saw the younger woman was laughing. It was so infectious that she joined in and before long the two of them were in fits of giggles.

It was Kat who broke off first. 'How much do I owe you for the call-out?'

Phoebe told her and she produced a wad of cash from the bum bag around her middle and counted out some £20 notes. 'Darren left me some cash for eventualities,' she said, 'so I'm giving you a bit extra.'

'There's no need,' Phoebe said, but Kat pressed them into her hand. 'Darren wouldn't mind, honestly. And I know I shouldn't have asked you to go up that ladder. Consider it danger money, or hush money. Both if you like!'

They both laughed again and Phoebe decided she needed to revise her opinion about Kat not having a sense of humour.

'How will you get Mr Spock down from the, er, dock?' she asked when Kat finally walked her back to the front door once more.

'I might take your advice and leave him there. He knows where his food is if he's hungry. Thanks again,' she said, as she opened the door a crack and they did the same routine as they'd done on the way in, which involved Phoebe squeezing through the gap and Kat shutting it swiftly.

The last impression Phoebe had of the Old Courthouse was of a muffled sound like tyres squealing when a car is going too fast. At least, as there were no cars in sight, she assumed it was coming from the Old Courthouse – no doubt from the beak of an unrepentant parrot perched high up on his seat in the dock.

She walked quickly back to where she'd left her car, still smiling. One of the things she loved about her job was that you never knew quite what was going to happen next.

* * *

Much later, she recounted the evening's events to Sam, and having checked that she was definitely OK, they both laughed some more, although Sam did also tell her off for going up the ladder in the first place.

'You were really lucky by the sound of it. That could have been a disaster.'

'Yes, I know, but it wasn't. Thank goodness for shagpile carpets, I say. Anyway, enough of me. How was your evening? Was Roxie good? Did you see Destiny again?'

'Roxie was angelic, and yes, we did. She's a really good trainer. Shall I show you what we learned?'

'Yes, please.'

He spent the next few minutes showing Phoebe a command called 'Peekaboo', which involved Sam standing with his legs spread apart while Roxie came up from behind him, walked through his legs and ended in a sitting position between them, looking up at him.

Both Roxie and Sam seemed to find this very entertaining, and Phoebe decided that if she didn't mind the fact that Destiny had been playing Peekaboo with her boyfriend for an entire evening she must be over her irrational jealousy. Hurrah!

* * *

When Phoebe told her staff what had happened on Friday morning, they laughed too.

'Not that I'd advise climbing ladders to examine patients,' Phoebe added thoughtfully.

'That was definitely above and beyond,' Max agreed. 'You

wouldn't get me up a ladder, even if there was a shagpile carpet to land on.'

'Shiver me timbers,' Marcus said, doing a very good pirate impression. 'Me neither. There's a poem there somewhere,' he added, putting his head on one side. 'Mr Spock is in the dock because of an injury to his... Hmmm, what rhymes with dock?'

'Don't even go there,' Phoebe warned. 'At least not while you're sitting behind reception.'

'Aye, aye, captain, I mean boss.'

'She'll make you walk the plank if you're not careful,' Jenna ribbed him.

Everyone laughed some more. Marcus had obviously got over whatever was stressing him, Phoebe thought. He was on fine form today. 'Enough of all this frivolity,' Phoebe said. 'We've got an interviewee coming in just after lunch, so I'll need all hands on deck. Oh, jeez, you've got me at it now.'

More laughter.

'I thought we were interviewing next week – Tuesday and Wednesday,' Max said.

'Yes, we are, but I just got a message on my mobile. Leonora Miles – she's the one who had family in the area – has asked if she can switch to this afternoon. Apparently she's here for the weekend, seeing them. I said it was OK. I've only got one appointment this afternoon anyway. And Maggie and I can interview.'

'Cool,' Max said.

'There's a message from Marchwood too,' Marcus said, looking at his notepad. 'Seth phoned. He wants you to call him. He said it wasn't urgent.'

'Thanks. I'll give him a shout in between appointments.'

Phoebe wondered what her ex-employer and mentor wanted. She hoped he was OK. Seth had become a good friend across the time she'd known him.

The day began and Phoebe was soon immersed in consultations. Her shoulder was aching a bit, not that she'd mentioned that to anyone. She still felt a little embarrassed she'd even climbed up that ladder. It had been foolish. If she'd put herself out of action they'd have been in trouble. They might be employing another vet but that didn't mean she could take things any easier. They had more than enough work for three vets.

She caught up with Seth as soon as she got the chance and it was great to hear her mentor's measured voice. Although the two practices did each other's emergency out-of-hours cover, it was ages since they'd spoken about much but cases they were working on. Seth had years of experience. He'd been working as a vet for twenty-five years and before that he'd been a jockey, so horses were a bit of a speciality for him.

'How are you, Phoebe? Have you brought any animals back from the dead lately?'

That joke never got old, and she giggled.

'I haven't brought a single animal back from the dead recently. But I did do something a bit stupid yesterday.'

'That doesn't sound like you, lass.'

She told him about falling off the ladder and after checking she was OK, he laughed. 'So you learned you couldn't fly as well as an injured parrot.'

'The most annoying thing was that it wasn't even injured.'

'Ah, well, we live and learn. And I imagine you can dine out on that one for a good long while.' She could still hear the smile in his voice.

'So, why were you phoning me? Did you want to change the cover arrangements?'

'No, no, I'd have done that with your Marcus. No, I thought you should be the first to know I've decided to retire. I know I've been threatening to retire for years, but this time it's really happening. I've just sold the practice.'

'Oh my goodness. Congratulations. I'm so pleased for you.'

'Thanks, Phoebe. And don't worry about the reciprocal cover we do. The chap who's bought it says he's more than happy to continue with that.'

'That's good news. Thanks.'

'My pleasure. I'll drop you an email with his details.' There was a small pause. Then he sighed. 'Her indoors is pleased I'm packing it in, too. She reckons I can polish up my golf clubs.'

'But you're not so pleased?' she queried, detecting a thread of sadness in his voice.

'I'm a bit torn, to be honest. Don't get me wrong. I'm happy about the sale and it's high time I took things a bit easier, but playing golf's a bit different than having my arm up a cow, isn't it? Besides, I don't want to play golf 24/7. I don't even want to play it in the winter if I'm truthful.'

'No, but maybe it's time you took things a bit easier. You can spend more time with Myra.'

'Hmm, I don't think she'll be too keen on that. She's got a full schedule, what with WI, book club, and her charity lunches. She won't want me under her feet all the time.'

'I'm sure it'll work out better than you think. One of Maggie's friends retired recently and she was telling us she doesn't know how she ever found the time to work.'

'Yeah, you're probably right. Ignore me and my moaning. How is Maggie anyway? Is she loving married life?'

'She definitely is.' They chatted about Maggie for a while and then Phoebe said, 'I'm sorry, I've got to go. I'm not sure if I told you but we're finally taking on an extra vet, and I'm interviewing our first candidate in about ten minutes.'

'OK, I'll love you and leave you. Good luck with the interview. Keep me posted.'

'Of course I will.'

Phoebe disconnected the call.

It was true that she was happy for Seth. He'd been muttering about retiring ever since she'd known him, but she also felt suddenly unsettled. As if one of the stanchions that held her comfortable world firmly in place had suddenly been uprooted.

It was great knowing Seth was always on the end of the phone. He was a brilliant vet. Intuitive, gentle and calm. Loved by owners as well as the animals. She would dearly miss him.

8

Leonora Miles turned up twenty minutes late, which was annoying as Maggie had moved an arrangement she had with Eddie in order to accommodate the new interview time.

Phoebe and Maggie were talking to Marcus in reception when the practice doors burst open. Phoebe's first impression of her prospective employee was of a petite woman with a red scarf and a scowl.

'Bastard traffic,' she said, hurrying towards the reception desk. 'Although I'd have got here a lot quicker without the crazy speed limits. Forty miles an hour when you can see for miles is ridiculous.'

'It helps to keep the forest animals safe,' Maggie said brusquely. 'I'd have thought you'd know that, being a local girl.'

'Of course.' Leonora glanced at her. 'But it's still maddening. Are you Phoebe?'

'No.' Phoebe could tell her grandmother's feathers were ruffled despite the fact that her tone was perfectly calm. She wasn't surprised. Leonora hadn't even bothered with an apology.

'This is Phoebe Dashwood,' Maggie went on in that same

deceptively calm voice. 'I'm Maggie Crowther, her glamorous assistant.'

'I see.' Leonora didn't smile. She looked slightly nonplussed.

Phoebe stepped forward. 'Leonora Miles, I presume. Please come through. We're out the back. Can I offer you a coffee or tea?'

'Coffee would be good. As long as it's not from a machine. I can't abide those machines. Filter coffee would work. Otherwise I'll leave it, thanks.'

Entitled as well as unapologetic, Phoebe thought. It was not a good start.

She bit her lip and crossed her fingers. Leonora Miles did have a great CV. On paper she was perfect. She'd been one of the most talented vets to pass through the London Vet School, according to a reference from one of her tutors. And since then, she'd gained lots of valuable experience at one of the top practices in London.

Phoebe decided to give her the benefit of the doubt. Maybe her brusque manner was down to nerves.

'Tell me about your current practice,' she encouraged.

Leonora linked her hands in front of her and leaned forward. 'OK. Well, essentially it's a lot bigger than this place. Sargant's is a group incorporating twenty-seven practices and three twenty-four-hour hospitals. Even the one I worked at was huge compared to this. We had nine vets, ten veterinary nurses and twelve job-sharing receptionists, so – essentially – we could ensure the best possible standard of cover at all times.' She glanced around the small consulting room with a slightly disparaging air, and Phoebe wished suddenly that they'd gone into the Puddleduck Farm kitchen instead and sat at the over-sized kitchen table, with Leonora one side and her and Maggie – and perhaps Max too, there was safety in numbers – lined up on the other.

'Essentially, it keeps things fresh. Not that I'm averse to working in a smaller, more provincial practice. Or I wouldn't be here. Essentially.'

'Lucky us,' Maggie said under her breath.

Leonora either didn't hear her or chose to ignore this. She swept on. 'A Central London vet wouldn't usually do a lot on the larger animal side, but the practice where I was based had the benefit of being close to London Zoo, so I've had some experience with larger animals too. Actually, my biggest claim to fame is delivering a giraffe.'

'Wow,' Phoebe said, as Leonora sat back in her chair, beaming proudly. It was the first time she'd smiled since she'd arrived.

'What do you do in your spare time?' Maggie asked her.

'I volunteer for The Feminist Library. I do their accounts essentially. I got a first in applied maths. That was my second-choice career.'

'Being a feminist?' Maggie asked sweetly.

'Accountancy,' Leonora snapped, shooting her a slightly rattled look this time.

'So, tell me why you'd like to come and work at Puddleduck Vets,' Phoebe said quickly. 'What could you offer us, Leonora? Why should I employ you?' She was tempted to add the word 'essentially' but stopped herself just in time.

'Honestly?' Leonora's eyebrows shot up in astonishment, as if this was such an obvious question she was surprised anyone was even asking it.

'Yes. I'd really like to know your thoughts.'

'Well, as I said on my CV, I have family in the area. Essentially I'm planning to move back to Lyndhurst. And as to why you should employ me, well, that one's simple: I'm the best calibre of candidate you're likely to have applying for the job. Unless you're looking abroad, of course. Both Denmark and the US offer high-quality vets. Essentially, their training is equal to or better than ours.' She puffed up her chest in smug superiority. 'Sargant's did actually offer me a placement in Denmark not long after I started there. I turned it down. It was a little too soon for me to leave London at that stage. Essentially it wasn't in my best interests, even though I'm sure I could have offered Denmark a great deal.'

'Right.' It was hard to answer that one. Phoebe closed her file with a snap, and brought the interview to a close too, with her final stock question.

'And if we were to offer you the position, when would you be able to start?'

'If I did accept the position, I'd have to let you know.' Leonora waved a careless hand. 'I know Sargant's would be sorry to see me go. It's not often they get the opportunity to work with a vet of my calibre. But I'm sure we could negotiate some kind of severance package.'

Phoebe saw her out and returned to the back consulting room. Maggie hadn't moved from her position at the desk. She glanced up into her granddaughter's eyes.

'Oh, my days, please tell me I imagined that interview. She wasn't real, was she?'

'You didn't imagine it.' Phoebe blew out a long breath. 'I think that Leonora Miles is one of the most self-important people I've ever interviewed. Or met, come to that!'

'Essentially,' Maggie added, and they both giggled. 'Lucky old Sargant's, having that calibre of vet deigning to work for them.'

'And Denmark definitely missed out.'

'I bet Sargant's got the measure of her straight away and were devastated when their plan to ship her off to Denmark backfired.'

'She did deliver a giraffe, though,' Phoebe said.

'Essentially,' Maggie murmured, and they burst into more laughter.

There was a knock on the door and Phoebe glanced up in alarm. It would be awful if Leonora had popped back because she'd forgotten something. Just because she'd been a nightmare interviewee, it didn't mean *they* had to be unprofessional with such blatant mickey-taking.

To her relief, Max popped his head around it.

'There's an awful lot of frivolity going on in here. Was she any good?'

'Erm – essentially not,' Phoebe told him with a wink at Maggie. 'She might be a good vet, but I definitely couldn't work with her.'

'That's a shame.' He frowned. 'I just got a call from one of the other candidates. He's been offered another job and so he won't be attending his interview next week, after all.'

Phoebe nodded. 'Thanks, Max. Fingers crossed for the next one.' She frowned. 'Otherwise it will be back to the drawing board next week.'

'Also, I wanted to let you know I've got a call-out to see a goat. Another new customer.' He glanced at a yellow Post-it note in his hand. 'A couple called Fliss and Neville Anstey. They're quite local. They have a business near Burley called Acting the Goat.'

'Better not over charge them then,' Maggie said, laughing at her own joke and then jumping in to explain when no one laughed. 'Goats charge at people. Well, I thought it was funny. How do you stop a goat from charging?' she said, before adding gleefully, 'You confiscate his credit card.'

'No kidding.' Max came back quick as a flash. 'I've goat to go.' He winked at Phoebe, as both she and Maggie groaned loudly.

'I got lucky when I employed Max,' Phoebe said as he disappeared again. 'I've been really lucky so far with all of my staff. I guess I just thought it would continue.'

'They've all come from recommendations, though, haven't they – or they were people you already knew and liked.'

'I guess they were.' Phoebe thought back. Jenna had once worked for Seth, but she'd taken maternity leave years before and had never gone back.

Max had been someone she'd met at the New Forest Show, and she'd liked him on sight. He'd been looking for his first job, so it had been a match made in heaven.

'Marcus came through the normal channels, though,' she mused.

'Yes, but didn't Seth vouch for him?' Maggie screwed up her face, trying to remember. 'I liked him as soon as I met him, I know that. He's an all-round nice chap. And that was obvious from the off. Don't worry.' Her eyes glinted with humour. 'Not everyone's as perfect as us. Your next chap will probably be ideal for the job.'

'He will,' Phoebe said. 'Think positive.'

* * *

Phoebe had high hopes when Oliver Petworth came for his interview the following Tuesday morning. He arrived early, was chatty and personable and seemed perfect for the job. She could see Maggie liked him too. Her grandmother was as relaxed around him as she was when she liked a prospective owner for one of the sanctuary animals.

The interview had gone really well and Phoebe had just asked him the million-dollar question. 'So if we were to offer you the position, when would you be able to start?'

Oliver leaned forward, his face earnest. 'I'm not currently working so I'd be able to start as soon as you like, but in the interests of being up front and honest, there is something I need to tell you.' He cleared his throat. 'OK, full disclosure. I've been offered a job at a practice in Denmark, but my contract with them doesn't begin until August, so I'd only be available until then.'

Phoebe felt her heart sink. 'I see.'

Maggie looked despondent.

'I'm sorry if I've wasted your time,' Oliver added. 'I should maybe have told you that in advance. If it's any help, I could do something on a temporary basis. Until you find someone else.'

'I'll have to let you know,' Phoebe told him. 'That might work but really we're looking for someone permanent.'

'Of course.'

The interview was over. They all stood up, shook hands again and Phoebe showed him out. When she came back again, Maggie was standing up, reading a poster on the wall about neutering. She turned as Phoebe opened the door.

'That was a bit of a bugger,' she said, her face crinkled up in consternation. 'I liked him.'

'Yes, me too. What is it with Denmark – taking all our vets?'

'Would it work to take him on temporarily?'

'I suppose it might. We are pretty desperate for help. But then we're going to have to go through the whole thing again minus a vet when we're a few months down the line and probably even busier.' She sighed. 'I'll ask Seth if he's got any ideas. Did I tell you he's retiring in March? He's just sold the practice.'

'No, you didn't. Good for him.' She paused. 'You'll miss him though, love.'

'I will. Even though I didn't work for him for all that long. He's always been there in the background. He was amazingly supportive when I set up on my own. He even cut the tape on my opening day and then he gave that speech about me setting up in competition to him, and how thrilled he was that it was me. He's always been so brilliant. I can't imagine him not being on the end of the phone.'

'I expect he still will be.' Maggie's eyes softened. 'Even if he is on the golf course. Everything changes.' She hesitated and Phoebe sensed she wanted to say something else.

'What?' she prompted.

'I had a visit from Rufus Holt yesterday.'

'Really?' Phoebe felt a little jolt that could have been shock. She looked at Maggie keenly but her grandmother didn't seem unduly perturbed. 'What did he want? Was he dropping off your invite to his wedding?'

'No.' Maggie smiled. 'Do you really think we'll get an invite to that? I didn't invite him to mine.'

'Tori thinks it's a dead cert. Mind you, it is for her because Harrison will be his best man.'

'Rufus came round for a completely different reason. To be honest, love, I'm still trying to get my head around it. Shall we sit down again for a minute?'

'Blimey. Now you're worrying me. What on earth did he want?'

They sat down and Maggie took a deep breath. 'He came in his capacity as landlord. You remember how we sold all the grazing land back to him when we closed the dairy farm, and then I ended up having to rent it all back again when the place ended up as an animal sanctuary?'

'Of course I do.'

'Well, Rufus's opening gambit was that he can no longer rent the land to me.'

'What! He can't do that!' Outrage burst up from Phoebe's heart and out of her mouth before she had a chance to think. 'He knows you need it for the animals. How dare he!'

Maggie put her hand over Phoebe's. 'No, no, let me finish. He can't rent it to me any more because he's giving it to me. He was absolutely adamant about it. He doesn't want any money for it. He'd already got the paperwork drawn up. He said it was what he wanted, and he insisted he wasn't taking no for an answer.'

'Wow!' Phoebe looked at her grandmother in amazement. 'I don't know what to say.'

'Neither did we. Eddie was there too.' Maggie shook her head. 'To be honest, we've been reeling a bit all night. I wanted to tell you earlier, but I thought we'd be able to focus on that interview better if I didn't.' She blinked a few times and Phoebe knew she was close to tears.

'It's amazingly generous of Rufus,' Maggie continued softly. 'And it means I'll never have to worry about the future of Puddleduck Pets again. Not paying that rent will make quite a difference. I feel as though the land finally really and truly belongs to the Crowthers. After all of those years of disquiet.'

Phoebe swallowed. Disquiet was an understatement. Way back in the mists of time, Puddleduck Farm and all of the surrounding land had been owned by the Holt family. Then in 1905, Maggie's grandfather, Henry, had won it fair and square in a drunken poker match from Walter Holt, the gambling and womanising son of Lord William Holt, who'd been the lord in residence at Beechbrook House at that time. Lord William had honoured the bet his son had made, but he hadn't been happy and there had been bad blood between the two families ever since.

'Wow,' Phoebe said again. 'That's such an amazingly generous thing to do. Did Rufus say what had prompted him?'

'He said something about his father's will specifying there should be a charitable donation to a local worthy cause, and Rufus thought of us. He said he felt there had been enough dissent between the Crowthers and the Holts across the years and that this would resolve things once and for all. He also said his father dying had made him realise that a lot of things needed to change in his life, and that this was one of the changes that was top of his list.'

'Gosh.' Phoebe felt humbled. 'He actually said all that.' In the time they'd been close, Rufus had been a tortured soul, repressed and closed down by his past, but she'd always known that underneath it all he had a good heart. 'That's truly amazing.'

'Yes, my sentiments exactly. I think your Rufus has changed quite a lot in the last few months. I think he's finally beginning to make peace with his past. Not just make peace with it but alter things to change some of its consequences. That shows great strength of character.'

'It's not just the death of his father that's changed him,' Phoebe said thoughtfully. 'It was falling in love with Emilia, wasn't it? You always say that love can work miracles.'

'Do I?' Maggie chuckled, and then they hugged each other tightly in the little consulting-cum-interview room.

'It's nice to be right occasionally,' Maggie said, when they finally drew apart.

9

Rufus Holt had at that moment just been summoned to the snug by Emilia, his fiancée. She was sitting on one of the Chesterfields by the little coffee table with her hands tucked tightly together in her lap. Even her fair hair, tied back in its customary ponytail, looked like it was drooping a little. She had none of her usual bounciness and her face was very serious. He was sure she'd been fine first thing this morning.

There was something different about the room too. Although he couldn't put his finger on exactly what it was. He sniffed the air, which smelled stale. Did they usually have the window open in this room? He was slowly replacing the old curtains with new blinds.

He opened a small window and pulled a cord to open the blinds more fully, before crossing to the Chesterfield.

'You look very serious,' he said to Emilia. 'What's up? Have the caterers upped the quote for the wedding breakfast again?'

She shook her head and something in her eyes halted him in his tracks. She was a little pale too, Rufus observed now there was more light in the room. Suddenly he was on full alert.

'What? It's not Archie, is it?' Alarm ricocheted through him. Archie, his son, was coming up twelve and away at boarding school, but he thought he'd heard the phone go a few minutes ago.

'No, don't worry. Archie is fine. As far as I know.' Emilia patted the leather cushion to the left of her with her hand. 'Rufus, will you sit down a minute. I need to talk. Ja.'

'Of course.' A little niggle of foreboding sneaked into him. He sat next to her, on full alert. 'Talk away. I'm listening.'

In answer, Emilia uncurled the fingers of her right hand and he saw that she'd been holding something which she now handed over to him. 'I'm so sorry,' she said.

It took him a moment to register what it was he was looking at. An oblong shape made of white plastic. Some kind of test kit by the look of it. Oh, good lord. Was it a pregnancy test kit? He didn't think he'd ever seen one before, but suddenly he was sure that was what it was.

'Emilia, is this what I think it is? Are you telling me you're pregnant?'

'Ja.' She huffed. 'For such a clever man, Rufus, I do sometimes think that—'

He cut her off mid-sentence by grabbing her in his arms and pulling her close. 'Oh my God. That's wonderful. That's the most amazing news. You really are pregnant.'

She hugged him back, briefly, then pulled out of his arms and looked at him. And he saw relief and also uncertainty in her blue eyes. 'Yes. I'm pregnant. I did the test twice. I thought you'd be cross.'

'Cross – no. Um, why did you do it twice?'

'Because it did not seem possible. It was a very great shock.'

'It's wonderful. Why on earth would I be cross?'

She relaxed for the first time since he'd come into the room and she laid her head against his shoulder.

'Because we are planning a wedding – not a baby. We didn't plan this at all. Pfff.' She glanced at the pregnancy tester which he'd put back on the table. 'I have been taking pill. I do not understand how this can happen.'

'I know but it's amazing. A miracle. I can't believe it. When did you find out?'

'Today. When I did the test. And then the second test. I suspected maybe something was wrong last week. I've felt sick for a few mornings and today I find that I cannot drink coffee.'

He realised suddenly what was different about the room. The rich scent of coffee was absent. There was no cafetiere on the table. Coffee and Emilia were inseparable in the mornings.

'But really, darling, you do not mind this?' There were tears in her eyes now and Rufus was horrified.

'No, my love. I can't think of anything better. A little brother or sister for Archie. It's wonderful. Are you happy about it?'

'I am very happy,' she said. 'But the wedding. I don't think that it can go ahead in August. I will be too big. You cannot have a fat bride. It is disaster – ja?'

'I don't give a stuff about the wedding. We can reschedule that. We'll have it next year – or the year after – whatever.'

'Really?' There was hope in her eyes. 'But I thought that you wanted for us to get married first, and have children later, because of the title – because all of the legal things – this is important to you, ja. And now I have ruined it all.'

He remembered a discussion they'd had, just after she'd agreed to marry him. They'd talked about titles – it was a big thing in Emilia's family too – she had a title herself, and while she may have renounced her family, and she did not wish it to be general knowledge that she was a titled princess, they had spoken about the legal implications of having children out of wedlock.

'Maybe we can bring the wedding forward then.' Rufus waved a hand. 'Or better still, we can scrap the society wedding idea altogether. We can get married quietly with no one there apart from you, me and Archie. I never wanted a big society wedding anyway.'

'You didn't?' Emilia stared at him in amazement. 'But I thought you did. I thought you wanted all this – how do you say? The pump and ceremonial.'

'Pomp and ceremony,' he corrected with a smile. 'Well, I don't.' He caught hold of her hands. 'Although I can see why you thought I did. When we started planning, it got out of hand so quickly, and then I thought it doesn't matter – it's what my father would have wanted. But my father isn't here, Emilia. And I've been learning that I don't need to hold on to the past, the old ideas. This is a time for change. We can get married next week if you like?'

'Next week!' She looked aghast.

'I'm joking.' He let go of her fingers and ran a hand through his hair. His head was spinning with excitement. 'Next week might be pushing it, we'd need to find a date at a venue, and we'd need to arrange for Archie to be off school. Perhaps we could do it on Valentine's Day, although that only gives us ten days. How about half-term? That would give us longer.'

'You are really serious about this, aren't you?'

'I have never been more serious about anything in my life.'

He leapt up and then he bent and drew Emilia gently to her feet so that they were standing in a pool of sunlight that came through the slatted open blinds. It was the exact spot where he'd asked her to marry him, Rufus realised. Another of the happiest moments of his life. Or at least it had been when she'd said yes.

'So what do you think, my love? Of the idea that we sneak away and get married, just you and me and Archie?'

'I think this is a very good idea.' She had some colour back in her cheeks and her eyes were sparkling, and Rufus felt a huge rush of tenderness. He hated the fact that she'd been scared to tell him. That she'd actually thought he might be cross. Clearly he needed to do more work on the new and improved Rufus. The way he felt inside could not have translated properly to his outside. He must still be portraying austerity when he wanted to exude warmth.

Now, he linked his arms around Emilia and drew her close. The tenderness he felt for her was overwhelming. For a moment, his throat ached so much he thought he might weep. He laid his cheek against her hair, breathing her in.

'I love you so much,' he whispered into her hair.

'And I you.' Her voice matched his in its softness. 'I am so glad you do not wish for the pump and ceremonial.'

'Oh, me too. Me too.' Rufus felt as if a huge weight had been lifted from him. It was very similar to how he'd felt the previous day when he'd gone to see Maggie Crowther at Puddleduck Farm.

Doing the right thing – even if it was a million miles away from what he'd known his father would have wanted – was beginning to feel bloody fantastic. And each time he did it, another little drop of guilt slipped away, and the dictatorial voices in his head quietened a little more. It was as though a lifetime of oppression, conformity and pressing things down was being chipped away at, bit by bit.

Why on earth had he ever bothered with the years of therapy? All he had needed to do was to break some rules, to carve out his own path, to allow himself to be the person he'd always wanted to be. It was a revelation.

* * *

Sam was as blown away as Phoebe had been by the news that
Rufus had signed over the Puddleduck farmland to Maggie.

They were at Woodcutter's and had been discussing it over
supper. A mud-splattered Roxie was curled in her basket in the
kitchen and the room smelled of wet dog and garlic bread.
They'd just polished off the remains of a spag bol that Sam had
made the day before.

'That was a really decent thing to do,' Sam said, feeling a new
respect for the current Lord Holt. 'He's changed his tune a bit,
hasn't he? Compared to what he used to be like, I mean.' Sam still
had memories of Rufus scooting around the country lanes in a
black Mercedes with slightly darkened windows at a speed no
sensible local would drive.

'He's changed since his dad died,' Phoebe said. 'At least that's
what Tori says. Harrison's been encouraging him to move into the
twenty-first century. To throw off the shackles of the past, as she
puts it. But I think he's a lot happier.'

'That's good news,' Sam said. He'd never really warmed to
Rufus but he certainly wouldn't have wished him harm.

'It's great news for Maggie,' Phoebe murmured. 'She'll have all
the space she needs for the foreseeable future and she won't have
the outlay of the rent. She can retire, knowing that the future of
Puddleduck Pets is guaranteed and she doesn't have to worry
about money – well, apart from the cost of keeping the animals,
of course.'

'How's that going?'

'It's more sustainable than it used to be. They do well on the
adoptions now for the animals that are permanent residents.
Eddie's quite a good salesman on the quiet. They had a website
built and he and Natasha regularly upload pictures of animals

who need adopting. They send out newsletters to the adoptees – I think Eddie enjoys doing all that stuff. It gives him a focus.' Her face was thoughtful. 'He's never been one to sit around on his backside, has he?'

'No, I know. Life as a farmhand couldn't have been easy.'

'Eddie had the rentals as well, don't forget,' Phoebe added. 'I think he sold one but he's still got two of them. They're managed through an agency, but they give them an income, other than their pensions, I mean.'

'Do you think they'll ever properly retire?'

'If you mean will they stop working completely and sit around playing Scrabble all day, no, I don't think so. Although they do play Scrabble in the evenings occasionally. Eddie told me the other day that Maggie cheats,' she added with amused affection.

'How can you cheat at Scrabble?'

'She makes up words that aren't in the dictionary and then she finds them online in all sorts of questionable contexts. I think Eddie's rueing the day he taught her to be an "expert on-liner".' Phoebe mimed the inverted commas around the words with her fingers in the air and they both laughed.

She caught his gaze. 'I'm so glad Maggie ended up with Eddie. It's a real happy ever after, isn't it?' Suddenly she looked wistful and Sam sensed her change of mood. He cleared the plates from the table and took them to the sink. Then came back to where she sat.

'Hey, you. You've gone all quiet on me. What are you thinking?'

'I'm thinking that this house is too small for a nearly full-grown dalmatian. Especially a wet, muddy one.' She sniffed the air and wrinkled up her nose. 'We definitely need a bigger place. Where we can all live. Snowball too. It's hard work living in two places, isn't it? Not to mention time consuming going backwards and forwards.'

'Yes, it is.' He caught her hand. 'I've finished most of the painting now and Dad knows a carpet fitter who's going to replace the bedroom carpet next week. So I can get my place on the market as soon as he's done. Let's make a plan. Why don't we book an appointment with a mortgage broker? If we find out how much we can borrow, we can start looking for our own place. How does that sound?'

'That sounds great.' She brightened. 'I'm on call for the rest of this week, but next week I'm free, so we could book an appointment towards the weekend. Although I am going to be back to the drawing board on finding a new vet. We can fit in an appointment with a mortgage broker as well, though, I'm sure we can.'

On the table her phone buzzed and Sam waited patiently while she answered it.

'I shouldn't have mentioned being on call,' she said, grimacing when she finally put the phone down. 'I need to nip out.'

'Nothing too serious, I hope?'

'No, it's a new customer, actually. They've got a smallholding and they keep goats. Max went out to one of them last week, but now they've got another one they're worried about. He's cut his foot and they think it needs a stitch or two. Hopefully I shouldn't be too long. They're only in West Wellow.' She blew him a kiss across the room.

Suppressing a sigh, Sam blew one back. 'OK. Keep me posted, I'll run you a bath for when you get back.'

'I knew there was a reason I loved you, Sam Hendrie.'

She was gone a few moments later and Sam washed up and gave Roxie her dinner. Phoebe was right. It was hard work living in two places. Although his flat was only a twenty-minute drive away, he invariably left things there that he needed here, and vice versa. Timewise it was getting worse. He felt as though they barely had time to blink these days. Their weeks flashed by in a rush of work, and him seeing Ninja and Phoebe doing overtime. He knew it wasn't sustainable. Unless they had some time off – which would be difficult for Phoebe until she found another vet – he couldn't see how they'd have time to look for a house as well.

And as for planning their dream wedding... Sam sighed. Neither of them had mentioned that lately either. So much for living the dream.

10

The smallholding in West Wellow was owned by Felicity and Neville Anstey and it was easy to find even on this pitch-black February night. Max had mentioned that it was behind a modern bungalow, which had no neighbours, and Phoebe's satnav took her straight there. She grabbed her vet bag from the back, locked up her Lexus and went and rang the bell.

It was answered almost immediately by a tall, thin, grey-haired woman in a mustard-coloured boiler suit liberally dotted with what looked like splotches of blood. There was even a spot of red on her cheek.

Phoebe looked at her in alarm. A couple of stitches in a cut foot was beginning to seem like an understatement.

'Hi, I'm the vet.' She rearranged her face into what she hoped was a less shocked expression. 'This looks pretty serious. Er...'

For a moment the woman looked puzzled, then she caught on. 'Oh, don't worry, this isn't blood. It's red paint. I've been painting with Eliza, my great-niece, I haven't got changed.' She chuckled. 'I'm Felicity, but everyone calls me Fliss. Do come through.'

Phoebe followed her along a beige hallway towards a warm, brightly coloured kitchen where a table was still covered in newspaper and pots of paint and an array of artist's paper splodged with red swirls. Phoebe felt slightly embarrassed that she'd mistaken paint for blood. Hopefully Felicity, everyone calls me Fliss, wouldn't hold that against her.

They went through the kitchen and out into a floodlit yard towards a stable block.

'It's Arthur who's cut himself,' Fliss explained as they reached the closest stable, which had both its top and bottom doors bolted. Fliss paused to unbolt the top door.

'He did it on the way out of his field. We should have called him Houdini. That would have made more sense. He's forever escaping from wherever we put him. He gets out of fields, stables, you name it. We haven't had him long but I'm beginning to think that's why his previous owner was so anxious to get rid of him. It's a shame. He's a handsome fellow.'

Phoebe peered in gingerly. She was half expecting to be charged at by a goat, but the snowy white goat in situ merely turned his head to look at his visitors and blinked his sleepy amber eyes. He looked like butter wouldn't melt in his mouth.

'Don't let that innocent expression fool you,' Fliss said, unbolting the bottom half of the stable door and ushering Phoebe quickly inside. 'Arthur is a master criminal disguised as a goat.'

There was huge affection in her voice and Phoebe found herself liking her immediately. The nature of her job meant that she mainly saw people who really cared about their animals, but some definitely cared more than others. Fliss was obviously in the latter category.

She was now stroking the goat's nose and he nuzzled into her hand affectionately.

'I've put a collar on him, but he'll probably keep pretty still. Do you need him to be on the floor?'

'Let's have a look, shall we?' Phoebe put down her vet bag on the straw that covered the concrete and hunkered down beside the goat. Her shoulder was still a bit sore from falling off the ladder so she was hoping that Arthur wasn't going to be too difficult a patient and she was glad of Fliss's help.

At least it was obvious which leg it was. A trickle of blood ran down the goat's right foreleg and although blood always looked more startling on white animals, Phoebe could see why she'd been called out. The cut was a ragged tear rather than a neat slice and it was still oozing.

'What did he cut himself on?' she asked as she cleaned the wound. To her relief, Arthur barely flinched, although the cut was quite deep too. They'd been right that it needed stitching.

'Barbed wire. He got out of his own field without too much trouble, that's stock fenced, but he went through a barbed wire fence as well, which was closer to the house. I'm not too sure how we're going to keep him in, to be honest. Nothing much seems to stop him.'

'It's not mating season, is it?' Phoebe queried. 'Was he trying to get to a female?'

'No – well, he may have been, but it wouldn't have done him any good. We're past mating season. Most of our nannies are already in kid.'

'I'm going to give him a local anaesthetic, so he'll be more comfortable when I close the wound. And also a shot of antibiotic.'

'Thank you.'

To her surprise, Arthur suffered this patiently. He closed his eyes and leaned against Fliss, who was stroking him while

Phoebe worked. He seemed almost hypnotised beneath his owner's touch.

'He's the sweetest soul,' Fliss said. 'They're not all as good natured as him. Billies can be antisocial beggars.'

'Have you thought of stabling him when there's temptation around?' Phoebe asked as she finished up. 'Would that stop him escaping?'

'We're not keen on it, to be honest. Knowing Arthur, he'd probably do himself a serious mischief, trying to climb out, and we can't keep him locked up permanently. We've only had him a couple of months.' She sighed. 'Neville thinks he's a pain in the neck, but I'm really fond of him.'

It was clear that this was reciprocal. Phoebe had never seen such a display of affection from a goat.

When Phoebe had finished with Arthur, Fliss took her back into the farmhouse so she could wash her hands and offered her a mug of coffee and a fat slice of Madeira cake, which apparently Neville had made, although Fliss's husband was nowhere to be seen.

'Neville was a pâtissier at the Ritz before we retired,' Fliss confided.

Phoebe, who found it almost impossible to say no to cake, told Fliss truthfully that it was best she'd ever tasted. Even Maggie's cake wasn't this good.

'We started small with goats,' Fliss told her. 'At first, we just had a couple of rescues. British Saanens. They're very good milking goats. But then last year we bred for the first time, and we started selling the milk. Neville deals with that side. He loves it. His father was a dairy farmer. To be honest, it's not really about the money. We're both retired. We do it for fun.' She hesitated. 'I was a headmistress back in the day,' she confided. 'I've always loved kids but I have to say that goat kids are on the whole a lot better behaved than human ones.'

Phoebe laughed. 'I bet. And I bet you were a brilliant headmistress. Were you local? My mum's a teacher.'

'No. North London.' Fliss's eyes sparkled. 'I was at a private school. Not that we didn't have our share of awkward entitled pupils, but I'm of the old-fashioned opinion that you can usually trace an awkward, entitled pupil to an awkward, entitled parent. Have some more cake.'

'I'd better not,' Phoebe said, mindful of Sam waiting patiently at home. 'But thank you. It's delicious. Please thank Neville too.'

Phoebe felt warmed as she left the smallholding, despite the fact that it had been cold sitting in the stable and it was getting colder by the second. Frost sparkled on the wooden buildings and the bungalow roof glittered in the reflected glow of a nearby streetlight. The weatherman had forecast a cold snap – she'd passed a gritter on the way here – and they were obviously right to be gritting the roads.

She drove home carefully with her heated seat turned fully up and warm air blasting into the car. And she dreamed about hot baths and thought how lucky she was to have a partner like Sam.

* * *

The rest of the week passed in a blur of work. Phoebe had been looking forward to taking Roxie to dog training on Thursday and meeting the miracle worker, Destiny Dolittle, but once again her plans were thwarted when she ended up working late and Sam had to take her instead.

On Friday she had a phone call from Fliss to say that Arthur was recovering well and they'd decided to keep him stabled just until his foot was fully healed.

'I do take him out for gentle walks around the lanes, though,' Fliss had added. 'Eliza and Benjamin, her brother, love it and Arthur's very amenable. I just wanted to check that was OK. I know you said it was important that he got some exercise.'

'It's fine as long as you don't overdo it,' Phoebe said with a smile in her voice.

She visualised the tall, skinny Fliss in her boiler suit and a couple of children, who in her imagination looked like mini-Flisses, strolling along the country lanes, with the snowy white goat trotting beside them, and she liked her newest client even more.

'I did have another thought about Arthur's habit of escaping,' she told Fliss thoughtfully. 'This is a bit of a long shot but my grandmother has an animal sanctuary and she had a similar experience with Diablo, one of her donkeys. Diablo used to escape on a regular basis and no one really knew why, but it turned out that he just wanted to be closer to my grandmother. When they shifted him into a field nearer the farmhouse, he stopped escaping because he could see her wandering around. He still occasionally turns up at the kitchen door but he doesn't do it so much.'

'Really?' Fliss laughed delightedly. 'Thank you. I'll see what we can do.'

* * *

On Saturday Phoebe had an unexpected visitor in the shape of Seth, who turned up just after morning surgery. She heard laughter when she came out into reception and there he was, leaning against the reception, in his tweed jacket and flat cap, chatting to Marcus and Max.

She wasn't expecting to see her old boss and mentor, although she had phoned him and asked if he knew anyone who might be looking for a job. She'd ended up leaving a message on his voice-mail and then he'd ended up leaving a message on hers.

'Hello, Phoebe,' his cheery voice greeted her. 'I thought I'd come in person. Save playing voicemail tag. I hope I've timed it right.'

'You've timed it perfectly.' Phoebe couldn't believe how pleased she was to see him. As always, he looked the epitome of a country gent. Seth wasn't that tall, but he had a big presence. His ruddy face, bushy eyebrows and beaming smile gave him the look of an avuncular uncle. Phoebe wasn't exactly sure how old he was, but like Maggie, he always seemed ageless.

'I thought I might take my favourite vet for a spot of lunch,' he continued, 'or just a coffee if you're in a hurry. I have a proposition for you.'

'Lunch would be brilliant. What kind of proposition is it?'

Phoebe's gaze flicked between Marcus and Max, both of whom were grinning, but neither of them enlightened her.

Max shook his head and Marcus shrugged enigmatically. 'We don't know any more than you do, boss.'

'I thought I might speak to you first,' Seth said mysteriously. 'Shall we go in my car? Are you done for today?'

'I can finish up here,' Max told her.

'And I'll help,' Marcus added.

Seth held out his elbow. 'In that case – if she's willing, of course – I shall steal your boss away.'

Half an hour later, they were at the Brace of Pheasants, a country pub, near Godshill in the New Forest, famous for its pies. It was Phoebe and Sam's local and one of the barmaids greeted her cheerily when she came in with Seth and then did a double-take when she saw Phoebe wasn't with Sam.

Phoebe introduced them and Seth had soon charmed her, as he charmed everyone he came into contact with.

She was really going to miss Seth, Phoebe thought, as he took two menus to a table by the pub's inglenook fireplace, having been assured by the barmaid that she'd bring their drinks over. Even though they didn't see a lot of each other these days, it was lovely knowing he was always on the end of the phone.

'So...' they both said simultaneously, as they sat in range of the big old log burner, which chucked out so much heat that everyone in the vicinity had abandoned their jackets.

'You go first,' Seth gestured.

'I was just going to say that it's so lovely to see you, and that I can't imagine you not being around,' Phoebe said, leaning her elbows on the table and cupping her chin in her hands.

'And I was just going to ask you if you'd found a new vet yet.' Seth's eyes were twinkling. 'Although to be fair that was just a polite opening gambit because Max and Marcus did already tell me they didn't think you had.'

'They were right. You don't know anyone, do you?' Phoebe leaned forward eagerly. Seth obviously had something to say on the subject. He looked far too animated to be making polite conversation.

'Possibly. But there is a condition.' He paused to thank the barmaid who'd just arrived with their drinks.

'Are you ready to order or shall I come back?' she asked.

They both ordered chicken and mushroom pie, which was that day's special, and the barmaid smiled at Seth again and disappeared.

'What's the condition?' Phoebe asked Seth.

'The chap I have in mind doesn't want to do full-time.'

Phoebe felt her heart sink. 'I'm not sure part-time will be enough, though, Seth. It's going to take us a while to get him into the swing of things. I'm really looking for someone who's relatively new to the profession, you see. That's mainly because of the salary we're offering – and if they're part time as well, I'm not sure how much that will help us.'

'What if I was to tell you they're quite experienced but only want to do thirty hours a week for personal reasons?'

'If that was the case, I don't think I'd be able to afford them.'

'Oh, I think you can. Max told me the salary you were offering.' He sipped his shandy. Seth wasn't a big drinker. Half a shandy was about the most she'd ever seen him drink.

Phoebe picked up her Diet Coke. 'Well, in that case, tell me all about him. Is he someone you know? Why does he only want part time? Is he trying to fit his hours around his family or something?'

'He's winding down. And yes, I do know him. So do you as it happens.' He was grinning from ear to ear and suddenly the penny dropped.

'Are you talking about yourself?' Phoebe gasped. 'Or have I got completely the wrong end of the stick here?' She broke off because he was nodding emphatically.

'That's exactly what I'm talking about. What do you think? Could you work with me, lass?'

'Well, of course I could work with you. I'd love to have you at Puddleduck. But you're supposed to be retiring. You've just sold your practice.'

'And I'm regretting it already.' Seth's face sobered. 'I can't give up veterinary practise, Phoebe, not entirely. I don't know how I ever thought I could. I've been depressed ever since we signed on the dotted line. At first, I thought that was a temporary reaction – you know, change, moving on, getting old – all of those things, but it's just got worse and worse.' He waved a hand. 'And then I thought, I know what I'll do, I'll do locum work. That'll fill the gap.'

'That's a good idea,' Phoebe said slowly. 'And it's good money. I can see that working out well.'

'I can't. Going to different practices all the time, working with different people, there'd be no continuity. No follow-ups, no getting to know anyone. It would all be very unsatisfactory.' He paused for a sip of shandy. 'Myra worked for the NHS for years and years and then she went across to agency nursing so she didn't have to do full-time, and she hated it. For precisely the reasons I just mentioned.'

Their pies arrived. Phoebe dished out their cutlery, which was wrapped in green serviettes and stood in a pot on the centre of the table. The scents of meat and pastry were making her mouth water.

'Think about it while you eat your lunch,' Seth said. 'But I'm serious, Phoebe. Even if it's only a stopgap for a year or so. You'd be doing me a huge favour if you said yes.'

He'd be doing her a huge favour too, Phoebe thought as she dived into her pie. Seth was hugely experienced and worth double the amount he'd just offered to work for. That was her main reservation. She couldn't let him work for so little. It wasn't fair.

She told him this between mouthfuls.

'I can't afford to pay you enough, Seth. And I can't let you work for peanuts. It wouldn't be right.'

For the first time since they'd arrived, he looked serious. He swallowed the mouthful of pie he was eating and abandoned his knife and fork.

'OK. Cards on the table. It's not about the money. I have enough money in the bank for Myra and I to kick back our heels and never do another day's work – even if we both live until we're ninety-five. Which I sincerely hope we do. I just know that I can't do nothing – not while I've still got my health. Myra agrees with me.' He paused. 'I also understand if you think it wouldn't work. You might not want an old codger kicking about at Puddleduck. You might think I don't fit in with all you young things.'

'Oh, blimey, Seth, no. It's not that.' She felt mortified he might think she didn't want him. 'It would be fantastic to have you at Puddleduck. I can't think of anything better. Are you really sure? Do you want to try it for a while first?'

'Happy to do a trial.' The smile had come back into his eyes.

'In that case, you're hired.'

'Shall we shake on it?' He held out his hand.

'I think this calls for more than a handshake, don't you?' She leapt to her feet and in the next moment they were hugging.

They were both laughing as they drew apart, and Phoebe became aware of people at the surrounding tables looking over with interest.

'Welcome to the team, Seth,' she said quietly. 'You've made my day. You really have.'

'It works both ways, lass.'

11

By the time Seth had dropped Phoebe back at Puddleduck Vets, the rest of her staff had gone home. Currently the surgery only opened on Saturday mornings. Although that might possibly change at some point in the future.

Phoebe couldn't wait to tell everyone the exciting news. Everyone liked Seth. He was going to be a wonderful asset. Because Puddleduck and Marchwood practices had done each other's out-of-hours cover for the last couple of years, he already knew many of her clients too, just as she knew some of Marchwood's clients.

As Seth had said previously, the two practices would still cover out-of-hours for each other, but having Seth giving them thirty hours a week as well would be amazing.

They did the paperwork while they were at Puddleduck. Phoebe ushered Seth through to the back, printed off a contract and handed him a pen. 'I want to get you signed up before you change your mind.'

'I'm not going to change my mind, but as we said, we'll stick to the three-month trial. So you've got a get-out clause, if you need it.'

They celebrated with a mug of coffee and then Seth said he'd better get back and tell Myra.

'She'll be relieved I'll be out from under her feet. She was dreading me hanging around like a lost soul.'

Phoebe waved him off as he edged his old Mercedes out of the car park. No wonder he had plenty of money, she thought wryly. He'd had that car for about twenty years – Jenna had told her that – and he lived in the same few outfits too. Seth never seemed to buy anything new. He was the total opposite to flash.

She went to find Maggie and Eddie. They'd be pleased he was joining the team. But annoyingly they weren't about.

'They've gone to pick up some hay,' Natasha said. 'They won't be long. Can I help?'

'No, it's fine.' Phoebe was tempted to tell her the news, but Natasha was with a couple who'd come to choose a dog to rehome and she didn't want to hold her up. Besides, she should probably tell Marcus before she told his girlfriend. And Max, come to that. They were the people who'd be most affected.

Still bursting with excitement and frustrated that she couldn't share it with anyone, Phoebe decided she'd go and tell Sam, who was at the stables with Roxie. He'd said he had lessons between two and four, and then he was heading home to feed Snowball, but if she left now, she'd catch him. She couldn't wait until tonight.

He was just finishing a riding lesson when she arrived. Brook Riding School's layout meant that you had to drive past a paddock and one of the outdoor schools before getting to their main gates that led into the yard.

Phoebe could see Sam in the outdoor school abutting the road, with a youngster, whose mother was watching from the post and rail fence that surrounded the arena. The mother, who was fair-haired, had her back to Phoebe. But as Phoebe parked her car, the lesson came to an end. The rider, a girl by the look of it, dismounted from the pony, and waved at her mother, who hurried across to her and Sam. The little trio stood in a huddle, presumably discussing the lesson, their breath puffing out in the freezing air, and Phoebe could hear the buzz of their chatter as she got out of her car.

It had been another cold day. Despite the brilliant blue sky, the grass in the shady areas of the paddock was still white-tipped where the sun hadn't melted the frost. Phoebe pulled her coat a bit tighter around her as she made her way along the pavement to the five-bar gate entrance of Brook Stables.

She hadn't seen Roxie at the outdoor school. She assumed their dog would be safely shut up in Ninja's stable. Roxie wouldn't be allowed to run around unsupervised while Sam was teaching.

Phoebe reached the yard from the front at the same time as Sam, and his pupil and her mother arrived from the back. The pony's hooves clip-clopped across the concrete yard. The rider, who still wore her black hat, was leading the pony now and Sam was chatting to her mother. She and Sam were laughing at something, both oblivious to Phoebe's presence. The woman touched Sam's arm in a gesture that was over-familiar and rang warning bells in Phoebe's subconscious. Then, for the first time, Phoebe got a proper glimpse of the woman's face and her heart stopped.

Those sculpted cheekbones and amber eyes were unmistakable. It was Destiny Dolittle. What on earth was she doing here? Phoebe blinked several times, trying to clear her head. She must be wrong. It must be someone who looked like her. Surely Sam would have mentioned it if he was giving her child riding lessons?

Clearing her throat loudly to alert them to her presence, she walked across.

'Hi, Sam.'

The look of shock on his face as he saw her was unmistakable.

'Phoebe. What are you doing here? I thought we were meeting up later.' He managed to get some composure back in his voice. 'Is everything OK?'

'Everything's fine,' she said tightly, although everything felt far from fine. 'I just wanted to catch you to tell you something.'

'Great.' He looked flustered and he was definitely flushing now. 'I don't think you've met Destiny, have you? Destiny, this is Phoebe, my other half. And that's Laila. We've been having a riding lesson,' he added unnecessarily, as he gestured towards the youngster, who'd already tied up the pony to a ring by a stable and was busy taking off the small saddle. Clouds of steam rose up from the sweaty patch beneath it on the pony's back and Phoebe caught the strong scent of horse on the air. All of her senses felt heightened. She wasn't sure whether that was the shock of seeing Destiny or the fact that this was Sam's domain.

Destiny gave her a polite nod and Phoebe felt like an outsider. This was enhanced by the fact that everyone in the vicinity wore jodhpurs and Barbour jackets apart from her. The uniform of horse, Sam sometimes called it. Phoebe was in her old jeans, and she hadn't renewed her make-up since lunch with Seth. Destiny's lipstick looked perfect – and she looked just as stunning in jodhpurs as she had in the sequin dress she'd been wearing at the New Year's Eve party where Phoebe had first seen her.

From somewhere close by there was a bark and Phoebe realised that Roxie must be in a stable as she'd thought and that the dog had recognised her voice.

Sam moved away from Destiny and went across to a nearby stable. He unbolted it and emerged holding the lead of an ecstatic Roxie.

'Hello, gorgeous girl,' Destiny said.

'Hello, darling.' Phoebe realised she and Destiny had spoken at the same time and Roxie, strained on her lead, seeing both of them, and then hesitating, clearly not sure who to greet first.

To Phoebe's chagrin and hurt, Roxie chose Destiny, wagging her tail madly, her claws slipping on the cold concrete as she tugged on her lead to get closer to the trainer.

Phoebe bit her lip. It was crazy to feel so humiliated. Of course Roxie would be more excited to see Destiny, she only saw her once a week. Or maybe more, Phoebe reminded herself, as she was here. Whereas she saw Phoebe and Sam every day.

The woman was now stroking Roxie's head. 'Hey, poppet, your mumma's here.' She glanced apologetically at Phoebe. So did Sam. 'Go say hello.'

Sam was hauling Roxie back towards Phoebe.

'It's OK,' Phoebe said. 'She sees me all the time.'

At the sound of Phoebe's voice, Roxie looked at her, and then came over, wagging her tail uncertainly as if aware she'd done something wrong. Sam handed her the lead. 'I'm just going to sort Laila out,' he murmured, striding away to the pony and leaving her and Destiny alone.

Phoebe bent her head over the dalmatian. She could feel the sharp sting of tears in her throat. She fought for composure as she stroked Roxie's soft head. She was aware of the hustle bustle of other people in the yard as the clatter of hooves heralded the sound of a returning hack.

Finally, she felt composed enough to look up again. Destiny was fiddling with her phone, but she stopped and met Phoebe's eyes.

'Good to meet you at last,' she said. 'Sam has mentioned Roxie's co-owner.'

Roxie's co-owner. Was that how he'd described her? Phoebe wanted to blurt out that actually she was a bit more than Roxie's co-owner. She was his fiancée, and they were planning their wedding, but that would have seemed ridiculously childish, so she managed to keep her reply coolly polite.

'My name's Phoebe. It's good to meet you too. Unfortunately, I haven't managed to get to class yet, but I'm definitely planning to be at next week's one.'

'I'll look forward to that.' Destiny's voice was cool too. But those amazing amber eyes certainly seemed genuine enough.

Sam and Laila arrived back again, minus the pony. The little girl was now carrying her riding hat and both she and Sam were smiling. Some of the tension had gone. Phoebe was beginning to wonder if she'd imagined the shock on Sam's face when he'd seen her. He seemed perfectly fine now.

Laila slipped her hand into Destiny's. She was the image of her mother, Phoebe thought. And at least that meant there was a father around somewhere. Not that Destiny was any threat to her and Sam, she berated herself inwardly.

'See you next week, Sam,' Laila called.

'Thanks, Sam,' Destiny mouthed. 'Bye, Phoebe. I'll look forward to seeing you in class sometime.'

And then it was just Phoebe and Sam once more.

'I'll just finish up in the office,' Sam said. 'What was it you wanted to tell me?'

'Just that Seth's coming to work with us.'

'Wow. That's exciting. How come?'

Phoebe glanced around the yard, which was now full of horses and riders. She felt in the way.

'I'll explain properly later. Shall I take Roxie back with me?'

'That would be helpful. Thanks. I'll nip by and feed Snowball and have a shower, then see you back at Woodcutter's – yeah?'

'Perfect.'

He blew her a kiss. She blew him one back.

It was only when she was in her car that she wondered why he hadn't just kissed her. They'd only been two paces apart.

Sam disliked public displays of affection, she reminded herself. It was the way he'd been brought up. His whole family were far more stiff-upper-lipped than hers was. That was the only reason.

Back at Woodcutter's, she took Roxie for a quick walk up the woodland track at the side of the house before it got too dark, and phoned Tori.

'Have you got five minutes? I need someone sensible to tell me I'm being ridiculous,' she said.

'You're being ridiculous.'

'I haven't told you what I'm talking about yet.'

'No, that's true. Go on then.'

Phoebe filled her in and at the end of it, she said, 'I am being ridiculous, aren't I?'

'I'm not sure, but then I'm not feeling very sensible. I didn't get much sleep last night.'

'I'm sorry, Tori. I'm so full of my own stuff, I didn't even ask. How's Vanessa Rose? How's Harrison?'

'She's beautiful. We're all tickety-boo.'

Phoebe listened to her expounding on the frustrations and delights of having a new baby in the house for a few minutes, which was actually quite calming. The sound of her friend's voice, the rhythm of walking through the trees, the rustle of the forest and its damp woody smells, these were all soothing things.

'You may be overreacting,' Tori said. 'But to be sure, you need to talk to Sam. Have a really honest conversation, I mean. It's odd he didn't tell you he was giving Destiny's daughter riding lessons. Although on the plus side the fact she has a daughter does probably mean there's a man in the picture, and so therefore there is nothing to worry about anyway. Not that there'd be anything to worry about even if there wasn't a man. If you know what I mean?'

'I do,' Phoebe said, feeling vindicated. She could hear noises in the background. A clattering sound.

'Are you cooking supper?'

'Harrison's cooking us lasagne from scratch. It's his signature dish. He has a lot of signature dishes. Have you got any further with finding a place for you and Sam or...?'

There was a yell that drowned out the last part of her sentence.

'I'd better go,' Tori said when the ear-splitting screaming had quietened a bit. 'Sorry, honey. I don't think you're being ridiculous. Talk to Sam.'

They said goodbye and Phoebe disconnected.

She felt better. Sometimes all it took was a listening ear, she decided. She would make Sam a lasagne too. It wasn't often she cooked a meal from scratch either.

Sam arrived earlier than she'd expected for supper. He'd showered and shaved too, she thought with satisfaction, as he came into the kitchen and kissed her.

'Something smells good.' He sniffed the scents of herbs and garlic that filled the small space.

'You can thank Harrison for that.' She explained what she was talking about, and he nodded, before producing a bunch of service station flowers from behind his back.

'What are you feeling guilty about?' Phoebe quipped, before realising she was only half joking.

'Do I have to feel guilty about something to bring my sweetheart flowers?' He met her eyes steadily. 'And it is nearly Valentine's Day.'

'I know. Of course not. Sorry. I think I'm feeling a bit insecure.' She turned back to the stove and Sam put his arms around her from behind and nuzzled her neck.

'Is that why you came to talk to me at the stables?'

'No. Gosh, no. That was about Seth coming to work with us, like I said. He's going to do thirty hours a week, which means I won't have to find another vet. It's brilliant news. I couldn't imagine a better person to work with. It's good for us too. We'll have some more time to look for our own place.'

'That all sounds great. The perfect solution. So why the insecurity?'

Phoebe turned into his arms and took a deep breath. 'Why didn't you tell me that Destiny's daughter was having riding lessons with you?'

He looked startled. 'Seriously?'

'Er, yes, seriously.' She felt wrong-footed now.

'OK.' He took a step back from her and rubbed a hand across his forehead. 'Well, for one thing I don't usually tell you details about people I teach – I didn't realise you were that interested – and for another thing, today was her first lesson. I wasn't even sure she was coming until I saw it in the diary.'

'Oh.' Phoebe felt even more wrong-footed. 'I see.'

'I once mentioned to Destiny that I taught riding,' he continued quietly. 'She said Laila was thinking of having riding lessons and she'd offered to take her. Laila's not her daughter, by the way, I think she's the daughter of one of her friends.'

'Right. They – er – look very similar, don't they? I just assumed...'

'They do look similar, yes.'

Despite the heat of the cooker, the atmosphere in the room

had gone very cold. Phoebe felt close to tears again. Now she was convinced she was being ridiculous. Her jealousy was definitely unwarranted, and the expression on Sam's face told her he was completely taken aback by her questions.

'The lasagne's almost ready.' Phoebe tried to retrieve the situation. 'Do you fancy opening a bottle of wine?' They often had a glass of wine on a Saturday night if she wasn't on call.

For the first part of the meal, they ate in silence. Phoebe knew Sam well enough to know he was trying to find the words for a difficult conversation.

In the end, he just came straight out with it. 'So this insecurity you're feeling then – has that been going on for a while? Or is it a new thing? Where's it coming from, Pheebs? Have I done something wrong?'

'No, you haven't. It's me.' Phoebe put down her fork. She sighed. Be honest, Tori had said. But she couldn't tell Sam she was ragingly jealous of a woman she'd only just met. She didn't want to sound like an over-possessive girlfriend. Especially when Sam had given her absolutely no reason to doubt him. Ever.

But both of her exes had. She'd been with Hugh for six years when he'd had an affair with their mutual boss. It had started with them growing closer through work and then culminated in a public smooch at their work Christmas party, and Phoebe hadn't noticed what was going on right under her nose until she'd witnessed them kissing beneath the mistletoe. Then there'd been Rufus – he hadn't actually two-timed her – but he'd been very quick to start something with Emilia as soon as he'd thought she was out of the picture. Emilia wasn't dissimilar in looks to Destiny. They were both blonde and beautiful and younger than Phoebe.

She blinked, trying to swallow down her feelings. She couldn't tell Sam all this. Her past had nothing to do with him.

'I think I'm probably ultra-sensitive because I'm hormonal,' she improvised. 'I expect it's PMT. I've had it quite badly lately.' It was a white lie, but Sam looked instantly concerned.

'Oh, Pheebs, you should have said. Can I do anything? Is your shoulder fully healed now or is that still playing you up?'

'My shoulder's fine.' Phoebe felt guiltier than ever. 'Let's talk about something nicer. Have you organised an estate agent to come round to value your flat yet and how did you get on with booking an appointment with the mortgage broker?'

'The estate agents are coming on Monday after work. I asked two. One of the nationals is coming and I've also asked the local one from Bridgeford. And yes to the mortgage broker. I got us an appointment for six thirty on Wednesday. That should give you enough time to get to Bridgeford, shouldn't it?'

'Plenty of time. Hang on a minute, isn't that Valentine's Day? That's not very romantic.'

'You're right, it is Valentine's Day. I think that's why they had a free appointment.' He smiled and added, 'Discussing our future is pretty romantic, I thought. But I've also booked a table at the Turkish place you said you fancied in Bridgeford. We can go straight there afterwards.'

'Thank you.' She leaned across the table. 'I'm sorry about earlier.'

'Nothing to apologise for.' He kissed her, then filled up her glass. 'Here's to us, Phoebe. Here's to a very exciting future. Onwards and upwards.'

They touched glasses. Phoebe was glad she hadn't told him the real reason for her insecurity. 'Onwards and upwards,' she echoed.

12

On Valentine's Day, Rufus and Emilia had an appointment with a celebrant Harrison had recommended.

'His name's Denzel Mansfield. He's a bit eccentric,' Harrison had told him. 'And he can talk the hind legs off a donkey, but underneath all the bluster he's a good guy. The sort of person who'd be utterly discreet if you asked him to be. He works from home. You could visit him incognito if you wanted to check him out first.'

So Rufus had done what he'd suggested and booked an appointment for 2 p.m. on 14 February, and he and Emilia had just arrived outside a smart semi-detached house in Bridgeford. Archie, who was on half-term, had gone with them on the condition they go to the dessert shop in Bridgeford afterwards.

Rufus rang the doorbell and it was answered by a man with long hair in faded jeans, a shirt and a red and white spotted cravat.

'Good afternoon, come in, come in. I work from my garage. Do come through. Please, this way. Mind the cats.'

'After you,' Rufus gestured Emilia and Archie ahead of him.

He couldn't see any cats but there was a faint smell of them in the hallway, which quickly opened out into a kitchen, in which he spotted a tabby lounging on a radiator cat bed and another black cat curled up in a basket. This was enough to distract his son, who stroked the tabby on the way past before being reminded by Emilia to be careful.

'Not all cats are friendly,' she murmured.

'That one's OK,' Denzel said reassuringly before he crossed to a door that presumably led out into the integral garage.

Rufus had a brief impression of cluttered worktops and the smell of curry before they were all ushered through.

He observed that this space couldn't have been more different to the kitchen. Neat and streamlined, its cream walls were dotted with pictures of weddings and wedding venues and the floor was wood-panelled and covered with beige herringbone jute rugs. The air smelled of something sweet, possibly vanilla, but it was hard to tell if it came from the tall vases filled with flowers that stood in the corners of the room or from a more artificial air freshener. Either way, it was classy and clearly designed to put people at ease.

Denzel indicated they should all sit on the plush, pale-pink corner sofa and he took the matching chair opposite them.

'May I offer you coffee? Or wine? Or a J20?' He gestured to a small fridge beside him.

Rufus glanced at Emilia, who shook her head. Then at Archie, who said, 'Apple and Mango J20 for me, please.'

Denzel jumped up, handed Archie what he'd requested, then got himself a bottle of sparkling water from the fridge, and proceeded to chop up cucumber slices, which he put in a glass before pouring the water on top and adding a squirt of liquid from a bottle of what looked like Angostura bitters close by.

Finally seated again, he looked at them. 'How can I help you?'

'Maybe you could start by telling us about weddings where you've officiated,' Rufus said.

'I certainly can give you a general overview. Without being too specific about the details because of privacy and data protection laws, you understand. Yah?' He spent the next ten minutes telling them about some of the places he'd taken weddings in the previous year. They ranged from a Scottish castle where the entire family had worn kilts to a beach in Dorset where the bride and groom and all their guests had worn nothing at all. They'd been naturists, Denzel explained.

'Lovely couple they were, and not worried about enforcing the rules where I was concerned. What I'm saying, of course, is that they let me keep my clothes on for the ceremony.' Denzel mimed mopping his brow. 'That was a relief, I can tell you. I'd have had to take them off if I'd wanted to attend the reception, but as it happened, I had other unmissable plans for the evening.'

Emilia let out a guffaw of amusement and Denzel grinned at her. Archie was also sniggering. The ice, if there'd ever been any, was well and truly broken.

'I've not let you get a word in edgeways, have I? That's not like me. Yes, it is. I talk far too much. I'll shut up.' He made zipping motions across his lips. 'Tell me what you good people want. That's why we're here.'

'We'd just like to get married in a beautiful place,' Rufus said. 'Is it true we can get married anywhere we like if we use a celebrant? Will it still be legally binding?'

'You'll need to do the legal paperwork separately from the actual ceremony. Most couples do that a few days earlier. But once you've done that bit then yes, you can get married anywhere you like. Indoors, outdoors. On a plane. Underwater if you like – some people do that. Did you have a venue in mind?'

Rufus and Emilia exchanged glances. 'We're thinking of

getting married at home,' Rufus told him. 'We have quite a large garden.'

That was an understatement. There was at least an acre of lawn at the back of Beechbrook House and at the front a quarter-mile drive ran through lavender fields up to the house itself.

'There is also woodland,' Emilia offered. 'Can a couple marry in woodland?'

'And lavender fields,' Archie said helpfully. 'Tons of lavender fields.'

Denzel looked puzzled. 'You've got a big place then. That's a bonus.'

'We live at Beechbrook House,' Rufus told him. 'I'm Rufus Holt and this is my fiancée, Emilia, and my son, Archie.'

Denzel's eyes widened a little. 'My apologies, Lord Holt. I would have used the appropriate address straight away if I'd known who you were.'

'No need to apologise. I don't bother with the title very much. Rufus is fine.'

'OK. Er, Rufus. Yes, I can see exactly why you would want to get married in your own home. Privacy, beauty, space for plenty of guests.'

'Privacy is what we're most concerned about,' Rufus said. 'How are you with heights?'

'Heights!' Denzel echoed. 'OK, I think. Er, why?'

'We thought we may like to get married in a tree house,' Emilia told him. 'It's a place that is special to us. Ja?'

Archie clapped his hands in excitement and Denzel said, 'Er, ja, I mean yah. But you won't be able to fit very many guests into a tree house.'

'We won't be having many guests,' Rufus told him. 'Maybe two or three. Just close family and friends.'

'I see. Right. Yes, well then, a tree house would probably fit the bill very well.' He paused. 'You are wanting a very private wedding. Now I understand.'

'My friend Harrison recommended you,' Rufus told him. 'He said you were the soul of discretion, and I can see that you are.'

Denzel nodded. His eyes were serious now. 'If it is your wish that no one knows you are to be married, then it certainly will not come from me. Either before or after the event. Do you have a date in mind? As the venue availability isn't going to be an issue, then we're pretty free to choose – subject to my availability. That's if you would indeed like to employ me.'

'We'd like to employ you,' Rufus said. 'And as for the date, the sooner the better. We'd get married tomorrow if we could, but what are the legal restrictions?'

'Legally, you will need to register your intent to marry with the registry office and book your appointment to sign the legal documents. So you'll need to see what appointment you can get. That will very likely mean the soonest date would be more than a month away. At a guess, I'd say six weeks. And as for my time,' he stood up, 'I will get my diary.'

Half an hour later, Rufus, Emilia and Archie left Denzel's house with big smiles on their faces. They'd tentatively picked three possible dates in April.

'One of them should work,' Denzel had told them. 'But let me know as soon as you've spoken to the registry office and we can firm up.'

They'd shaken hands on the deal.

Ten minutes later, they were in the dessert shop. When Archie nipped off to the loo, having already put in his order for the biggest chocolate sundae on the menu, Emilia whispered to Rufus, 'My tummy shouldn't be too big by then. I will be still only around four months pregnant.'

'It doesn't matter if your tummy's as big as a balloon. There will be no one to see it except Archie, and Harrison and Tori, and Sofia if she is flying out for the occasion.'

'She is coming,' Emilia confirmed. 'She is my best friend. She does not want to miss my wedding.'

'I don't think we should be marrying inside the actual tree house, though, my love. You can't risk falling.'

'Pfff, I will not fall. I am not idiot.'

'We can argue about that later,' Rufus said. There was absolutely no way he was letting Emilia climb up any ladders, no matter what she said. But he also knew there was absolutely no way he'd talk her out of getting married wherever she 'damn well pleased'. Her words, not his. So for now, he'd agreed to the tree house. Fortunately, he had a back-up plan. But he'd decided to keep that to himself for a while.

They hadn't told Archie about the baby yet, they'd decided to wait until after the wedding, but Rufus didn't envisage his son would mind too much. He loved Emilia and as for himself, Rufus couldn't remember a time he'd been happier. If someone had told him this time last year that he'd be feeling like this, he wouldn't have believed them.

* * *

Sam and Phoebe's Valentine's Day appointment at the mortgage brokers was not going anywhere near as smoothly as Lord Holt and the future Lady Holt's had gone.

They were currently sitting in the office of Andrews and Family behind a wooden desk in an open-plan office in front of a plate-glass shop window. The mortgage broker they'd been allocated, a young lad, who in Sam's opinion, didn't look old enough to have left school more than a few months earlier, had just given them some bad news relating to the amount they could borrow.

'That's barely enough for a bedsit,' Sam said. 'That's crazy. We're both working and we've got a big deposit.'

'Banks and building societies are very cautious these days,' said Liam Bartlett, who had a plaque on his desk pronouncing him as 'independent senior mortgage broker'. 'They don't like lending people more than they can afford.'

'We can afford a lot more than these monthly repayments,' Sam said. 'Phoebe's a vet with her own practice.'

'That's part of the problem, sir. Banks don't like self-employed people much either. Not unless they've got at least three years' accounts showing a healthy profit.'

Which Phoebe didn't have because Puddleduck was a new business and in its first year they'd barely made a profit.

'But we can't afford to buy anything with the amount you're proposing we can borrow,' Phoebe said. 'Even – possibly – a bedsit.'

Liam was shaking his head. 'What you've also got to bear in mind is that this is a very expensive area. The New Forest National Park is one of the most desirable places to live in the south of England.' He steepled his hands and studied them. 'Perhaps you'd consider living in one of the outlying areas. Southampton, maybe. There are cheaper properties there.'

Sam exchanged glances with Phoebe, who looked stricken.

'I didn't realise being self-employed would be such a problem,' she murmured. 'Is there any way round it?'

'A guarantor, maybe.' Liam raised his eyebrows hopefully. 'Do you have anyone who'd step in and guarantee the payments if you couldn't make them? A parent would work.'

'I know what a guarantor is,' Phoebe snapped. 'And no. We're not kids. We're both thirty-seven.'

Sam took her hand beneath the desk and squeezed it. He wanted to tell her that this youngster was talking nonsense and that of course they could borrow more money than he was suggesting, but he had a horrible suspicion that Liam was right and they couldn't. Everything he'd said so far had made perfect sense. Even if it wasn't what they'd wanted to hear.

'There must be some way around it,' Sam said, thinking back to when he'd arranged his last mortgage. 'What about if we pick a longer term? Could we borrow a bigger amount over a longer period?'

'You'd still need three years of accounts. But yeah – I can run those figures.' He tapped away at his keyboard, and quoted an amount that may have stretched to a flat if they picked a cheaper area. 'You could maybe consider buying a smaller property and renting it out until you've got your three-year accounts,' Liam suggested. 'That way you'd have got your foot on the property ladder too.'

'Thanks,' Sam said. 'Maybe we should go home and have a think about it and get back to you.'

Phoebe was nodding. She looked utterly resigned. Sam hated seeing that expression on her face. So much for his brilliant idea of a trip to the mortgage brokers being a romantic thing to do. He felt as though he'd ruined Valentine's Day.

Five minutes later, they were outside once more and walking along Bridgeford High Street.

'I can't believe that just happened,' Phoebe said. 'Do you think he's right? Maybe we should get a second opinion.'

'We will definitely get a second opinion. But he might be right. It wouldn't surprise me. Try not to worry, there's always a way around things.'

She nodded again, but she didn't look much happier. Sam swallowed down his own worries. He'd always known he was punching above his weight with Phoebe. It was he, after all, who had the lowly shop worker's job, and she was the high-flyer, but when it came down to getting their own mortgage, the fact she owned her own business had counted against them. The irony wasn't lost on him.

The way she'd been on Saturday had worried him too – that insecurity she'd mentioned, the one she'd passed off as being hormonal. He had a feeling there was more to it than that. Something she hadn't told him. What if she was having second thoughts about marrying him? They still hadn't set a date. Sam pressed that thought down as hard as he could. He couldn't deal with that right now.

13

The Turkish restaurant Sam had booked in Bridgeford was set up for Valentine's night. A red rose in a stem vase sat in the centre of every white-clothed table for two. Heart-shaped red Valentine's Day helium balloons bobbed above every table, and mood lighting gave the restaurant a romantic feel. A pretty guitarist was just setting up an amplifier to one side of the bar.

It turned out that their table was almost adjacent to the guitarist. Phoebe hoped she wasn't going to be too loud, but she needn't have worried. She started a few moments later. She had a beautiful voice and the volume was only a little louder than the background music that had been playing previously. Not at all intrusive.

When the waiter came to take their order, he poured something into a dish in the centre of the table that turned out to be dry ice and it swirled between them briefly before dissipating into the air. He beamed at them both, happy with his magic trick, and Phoebe and Sam smiled back. The restaurant was certainly making an effort to add romance to the evening.

They ordered flatbreads and a selection of creamy and roasted red pepper dips from the Valentine's menu for starters and then chicken kebabs, zucchini fritters and rice to follow.

One of the dishes on the menu included veal, but Phoebe could never bring herself to eat veal, despite the fact that Puddleduck Farm had been a dairy farm for so many years and she'd been brought up knowing the facts of life. Or maybe it was because of this. The dairy farm was the reason Maggie had gone vegetarian when she'd retired. It was also one of the reasons her grandmother had opened Puddleduck Pets.

She'd once told Phoebe she was trying in a very small way to give something back to the animal kingdom, after all that she had taken.

'Are you OK?' Sam's voice interrupted her thoughts. 'You've been really quiet since we got here.'

'I'm OK, thanks, Sam.' She caught his hand across the table. 'I've just had my mouth full. The food is really delicious.'

'It is.' His eyes were still concerned. 'I hope I haven't ruined Valentine's Day. That meeting was disappointing.'

'It was a reality check, though, wasn't it? I hadn't thought being self-employed would be such a disadvantage.'

'It won't be forever.' He looked strained. 'I wish I earned more. I wish it didn't matter what you did.'

'Oh, Sam. It's not your fault. It's just how things are these days. Like the guy said, it doesn't help that we're looking to buy a place in one of the most expensive areas of the south. Maybe we should be looking further afield. There are some nice parts of Southampton. And if we looked outside of the National Park, that would help a lot.'

'But that isn't the dream. You don't want a forty-five-minute commute to work every day.' He looked despondent. 'And that would be on a good day.'

'It would be worse for you,' she pointed out. 'Although I suppose Brook is kind of on the way from Southampton to work. The trouble is, we've been spoilt, haven't we? What with me living practically next door to Puddleduck at Woodcutter's and you living practically next door to Hendrie's.'

'We could have a look for a place in the Salisbury area,' he suggested.

'Yes, that would work for me and you for work, but it's not exactly convenient for you to go to Brook.'

'Maybe it's time I gave up Ninja. Then I wouldn't need to go to Brook so often.'

Even in the romantic mood lighting, Phoebe saw his eyes dull a little.

'No, Sam. You love that horse. We want to enhance each other's lives, not make them worse. That's what we've always said.'

'Yes, I know, but things change. I...'

'No buts. Ninja's a big part of your life. I'd never ask you to give him up.'

'In an ideal world, I wouldn't offer. But in an ideal world we'd be able to buy our own place and it would have a few acres of land, and we'd keep him there. There would be plenty of space for Roxie and Snowball...'

'And our kids would grow up in the same fantastic setting we did,' Phoebe finished for him. 'That's what I've always imagined happening, but I've been living in fantasy world, haven't I? We can't afford that kind of life. Not in the New Forest, anyway. Maybe if we were to pick somewhere up north we could do it.'

'Miles from all our friends and family.' Sam shook his head.

There was a little pause as the waiter who'd dry iced their table came to collect their plates and offered them the dessert menus.

They both chose chocolate mousse and he disappeared again.

On their right, the singer-guitarist, who'd gone for a break, resumed once more, and Phoebe heard the opening bars of Whitney Houston's classic, 'I Have Nothing'.

For a few moments, she and Sam didn't speak as they listened to the beautiful words.

Then Phoebe was struck by a thought. 'Hang on a minute. We've been missing something really obvious. Why don't you keep Ninja at Puddleduck? Then you wouldn't need to travel to Brook every day. Maggie wouldn't mind, I'm sure she wouldn't. She's got the space and she owns all the land now. Ever since Rufus made that lovely gesture.'

'*Maggie* owns it,' Sam said with the emphasis on the word Maggie. 'That's the whole point, Phoebe. I'd need to pay her rent if I was to keep Ninja there. The reason I work at Brook – or at least one of the reasons – is so that I don't have to pay for his keep. If I had to pay the commercial rates, well, I couldn't afford to. So I don't think that would help.' He shrugged. 'Besides, you know she's not properly set up for horses, so she might not want to set a precedent. I thought there was only one stable anyway. Isn't Casey's Girl in that?'

'No, she's mostly out these days. She doesn't need to be stabled. Anyway, Maggie's doing her best to find her a home. She won't be there forever. I'm sure she wouldn't mind if Ninja had that stable. She'd be pleased to help us out.'

'No,' Sam said.

'I can afford to pay the rent for his keep for a few months. It's not as though it would be forever.'

'No,' Sam said again, and she saw that his mouth was set in a stubborn line. Phoebe knew there was no way she was going to convince him to let her help subsidise his horse's keep. Sam was way too proud for that.

The waiter arrived back with their chocolate mousses, which were served in heart-shaped glass dishes with a mini chocolate heart on top. Each one was sprinkled with edible gold glitter and presented on a plate sprinkled with rose petals.

'Ahh,' Phoebe gasped. 'How beautiful. It almost seems a shame to eat them.'

'I'll eat yours if you like,' Sam offered, winking at the waiter, who was clearly pleased they were impressed.

'Not a chance.' Phoebe cupped her hands protectively around her plate. 'Don't worry. I'll make a supreme effort.'

The waiter laughed now and Phoebe thought, to him we must seem like a normal couple having a wonderful romantic night out. He has no idea that we're discussing our future and realising it's not quite as rosy as we thought.

Suddenly she envied Tori and Harrison, who were also planning their future. They were getting married this year, but had the advantage of already owning a property in the New Forest. Tori's grandparents had given her Woodcutter's a few years ago when they'd gone off to travel the world. It might not be big enough for them to want to live in with Vanessa Rose but as Tori owned it outright, the money from the sale would enable them to put a substantial deposit on something bigger.

Another thought struck Phoebe and she swallowed. What if that was one of the reasons they hadn't sold it? What if Tori had been worried about making her homeless? Oh, blimey, she should ask her friend. Last year Tori had told her they'd decided to rent a place just while the interest rates settled. What if she'd only said that to help Phoebe out?

'What is it?' Sam asked, tuned in, as always, to her thoughts.

She told him and he shook his head. 'I'm sure Tori was telling you the truth. She knows you can move out at the drop of a hat because you can move in with me. I know it's not ideal, but we can live at mine at a push. No direct access to the garden for Roxie isn't the end of the world. We'd manage if we had to.'

'Yes, I know.' Phoebe's heart was hammering with stress. It was beginning to dawn on her that she really had been living in an idealistic dream these last three years. Setting up her vet practice at Puddleduck, getting a dalmatian puppy with Sam, planning a wedding – not that they'd actually planned any of that yet, as they hadn't even set a date – it had all seemed to be part of a perfect life that was unfolding. A great bubble of positivity had surrounded it all. Just like one of the helium Valentine's Day heart balloons that were tied to every table in the restaurant.

Right now, Phoebe felt as if someone had come along with a great big pin and stuck it in the middle of their balloon. The bang had been deafening.

She was determined not to let Sam see how she felt. It wasn't fair. He'd done his absolute best to make this a romantic day. And none of this was his fault. It was hers, if anything. Getting a big mortgage was key to it all and she'd just assumed it wouldn't be a problem.

Sam paid the bill and they went out into the cold February evening, hand in hand. He hadn't drunk this evening – so that she could indulge – but the two glasses of wine she'd had weren't taking the edge off her sadness.

Sam squeezed her hand as they walked back to the car park. Their breath puffed out into the frosty night air and Sam cleared his throat.

'There was one thing that struck me that the mortgage broker said. We could rent out my flat and then rent a bigger house for us to live in. Just until you have three years' accounts.'

'I might need more than three years. I need to have profitable accounts. But yes, it's definitely worth considering. Would you mind renting it out?'

'Not if it would help, no.'

Phoebe felt cheered. She squeezed his hand back.

'There's always a solution,' Sam said. 'Sometimes it just takes a little time to work out what it is.'

14

After the disappointment of their meeting with the mortgage broker, Phoebe was determined to take inspiration from Sam's positive attitude and look on the bright side. They would find a way to live together more easily than flitting between their two homes. It wasn't the end of the world if they didn't buy their own place straightaway. Other things were more important.

At least she wouldn't have to worry about finding another vet for the practice. Knowing Seth was coming to join them was a huge weight off her mind. The rest of her staff had been thrilled with the news too. They all liked and respected him.

Seth was starting the following week – technically he'd do an induction on Monday to get up to speed on the practice routines, but Phoebe knew he wouldn't need much of an induction. Seth was already familiar with the way they worked, and he'd said he was happy to go on the on-call rota as part of his thirty hours so if they knew they had a quiet week of appointments coming up, he'd happily do the on-call cover that week.

Phoebe was also determined to take Roxie to dog training this

Thursday. She was sure that if she got to know Destiny Dolittle better she would stop feeling so threatened by her.

However, it was Destiny herself who cancelled the fifth week of dog training. Sam forwarded Phoebe a text he'd got from the trainer on Thursday afternoon.

> Apologies all. Tonight's dog training is cancelled. The hall has a problem with the electrics, and it's too late to find an alternative venue. You won't lose out. This class will be added onto the end of the course.

So much for that then. Phoebe felt deflated when she read it. Having decided to take positive action, it was annoying to be thwarted.

'Come and have supper with me instead,' said Maggie, who happened to be in reception picking up some medication for one of the Puddleduck cats, when Phoebe found out. 'You can pop in after you finish up here.'

'What about Sam? That'll be too early for him. He's got to sort out Ninja.'

'I wasn't inviting Sam. I was inviting you. Can't he cook his own supper for once?'

'He often cooks his own supper.'

'Yes, I'm sure he does. Very capable chap, your Sam. What I really mean is that it would be nice if it were just the two of us. Eddie's out with some of his mates.'

'Why didn't you say that in the first place?' Phoebe chided but Maggie just smiled.

'I was trying to be tactful and diplomatic. Not my forte, I know!' She frowned and added, 'I just had a phone call from Seth about taking in a horse from a Wiltshire rescue. Did he mention anything to you about it?'

'No.'

'I don't suppose he saw the need. I said I'd help. The place is called Duck Pond Rescue – if we were towns, we'd be twinned with each other, wouldn't we? How could I possibly refuse a request from a spiritual twin?'

'Fair enough. How does Seth know them? Were they a client of Marchwood?'

'No, apparently they're a client of his nephew, Aiden, who's a vet in Salisbury.'

'I didn't even know Seth had a nephew, let alone one who was a vet in Salisbury.'

'Maybe he said godson – I forget, but the point is they have a mare in season and they also have a gelding who's getting frisky with her.'

'Awkward! Are they sure it's a gelding?'

'Yes, but apparently sometimes the op, so to speak, doesn't quite work. I think they're going to do some tests on Mr Frisky to check. But in the meantime, they're desperate to place this mare somewhere else. I said I'd help out. It's only for a month or so. She can keep Casey's Girl company.'

Phoebe nodded. All animal rescues helped each other out if it was at all possible. It was how it worked, although it was a shame her grandmother was getting landed with another horse when Puddleduck Pets weren't really set up for horses. The neddies were different – Maggie didn't mind neddies – but horses were much more specialist.

'Are you sure you can cope with another horse?'

'What sort of a silly question is that?' Maggie said with a grin. 'Jade, the girl with Duck Pond Rescue, is quite young by the sound of it. I'm more than happy to help her if I can.'

Of course she was. Maggie would help any animal in trouble or any person who was looking out for an animal. Phoebe just hoped this Jade person wouldn't take advantage of her good nature.

As soon as Phoebe had finished surgery – there were no hold-ups for once – she walked up to the farm, where she discovered Maggie making soup. The kitchen was steamy and filled with the scent of cinnamon, garlic and simmering vegetables. Maggie's soups were amazing. There was also the glorious smell of home-baked bread wafting around the kitchen, which must mean it was out of the Aga already because cooking smells from Agas went up a flue outside rather than into the kitchen itself. It was the one thing Phoebe didn't like about Agas – you couldn't smell what was cooking inside their ovens.

Buster and Tiny were sitting as close as they could to Maggie without getting trodden on, hoping she would drop something tasty, and Roxie, who'd very quickly worked out that Maggie's cooking meant there'd be food in the offing, was clearly eager to join them. She gave a small whine as Phoebe shouted out a greeting from the stable-style back door. The top half of which had been open to let out the steam.

'Come in, come in.' Maggie turned from the pan she was stir-ring. She was wearing an apron over her boiler suit. It was black and had the words 'real cooks don't use recipes' printed on it in white. Her face was flushed with the heat of the room and she had something white on her nose.

'Leave the top half of the door open. I'm surprised I haven't set off the smoke alarm with all this steam.'

'I'm surprised you've got a smoke alarm.'

'It was Eddie's idea. He's turned into a proper health and safety nerd lately. Watches too many scaremongering videos on the worldwide webby. We've got a carbon monoxide alarm too.' She gave a disparaging snort. 'It's in the cupboard.'

'In the cupboard. What good's it going to do there?'

'It was on the wall, but it fell off so I put it away. I don't like clutter.'

'It's not clutter. It's an alarm and it needs to be able to do its job. Eddie's right. Which cupboard's it in? I'll get it out again.' Phoebe started opening cupboards. That line about clutter wasn't true. Maggie loved clutter. The amount of it on the huge dining table was testament to that. She didn't like being told what to do, though. Even by Eddie, it seemed. The honeymoon period must be wearing off.

She found the carbon monoxide detector and set it up on a high shelf, which she knew Maggie wouldn't be able to reach. Maggie was the only person in the family who'd missed out on the height gene. Both Phoebe and her mother, Louella, were tall.

'Don't think I don't know what you're doing,' Maggie called. 'I can always climb on a chair and get it down again.'

'You won't, though, because you love me, and you know I've only got your best interests at heart.' Phoebe went across to kiss her grandmother.

'Hmmm. OK. You've made your point.'

'Just as you made yours.'

Maggie picked up a bread roll from a cooling rack. 'Try one of these. They're not those part-baked ones from the supermarket. I made them from scratch with the bread-maker Eddie got me for Christmas.'

Phoebe took a bite. 'Jeez, they're amazing. I need to get a bread-maker. I bet they're even more gorgeous with butter.'

'They are. It's on the table. Can you clear a space please, love?'

Phoebe did as she was told and a few moments later she was sitting opposite her grandmother. They both had steaming bowls of soup in front of them and there was a basket of bread rolls and a yellow pat of butter between them.

'I must get into proper cooking. This tastes amazing.'

'I don't suppose you really have time, do you, love?' Maggie's hazel eyes, so like her granddaughter's, were soft. 'You and Sam have pretty full-on lives.'

'Yes, but it's not like you and Eddie don't. All those animals out there to look after. When's the new horse coming over?'

'At the weekend, I think. It's fine. Natasha and the paid part-timers do most of the work, and we have numerous volunteers, as you know. I do a lot less than I used to and it's different when you're in and out of your house. You can do bits and pieces that you can't do if you're stuck in an office – or indeed a vet practice. I think that's one of the reasons people like working from home so much.'

'Yes,' Phoebe sighed, and Maggie tuned straight in.

'How's it going with you and Sam commuting between two houses? Any news on getting a place of your own together?'

Phoebe hadn't been planning to tell her what the mortgage broker had said, it was too depressing, but suddenly it all came pouring out.

'I know it's only temporary. But it was quite a reality check to find out we can barely borrow enough for a garden shed if we want to stay in the same area we live in now.'

'Yes. I bet it was.' Maggie put her head on one side and looked thoughtful. 'What about a guarantor? Did your financial chap mention that? Eddie and I could do that for you. It's not as though you're not good for the money.'

'Thanks, but no. I wouldn't be happy with that. Sam wouldn't go for it either. Besides which, you've already helped me enough financially when I set up Puddleduck Pets.'

'That helped me too. Knowing I had you around a lot of the time to keep an eye out for me helps me a lot.'

'You've got Eddie for that now.'

'Pride is not an attribute if it gets in the way of letting people help you when you need help,' Maggie said gently. 'Then it can become a defect.'

'I wonder where I get that from.' Phoebe put down her spoon. 'You hate accepting help from anyone.'

'I've changed.' Maggie pursed her lips and a stubborn glint appeared in her eyes. 'I accepted the land from Rufus. That was a gift, you know. I didn't pay him anything for it.'

'That's totally different.'

'You're right. It *is* totally different. Rufus wasn't even family.'

There was a loaded pause.

'I'm really grateful for your offer to be guarantor,' Phoebe said, choosing her words carefully. 'Don't think I'm not. But we're going to sort it. We've got a plan.'

'Maybe Eddie and I can be your back-up plan then. As long as you know you can always ask.'

'Thank you. Don't think we don't appreciate it.' And she did appreciate it, but she knew Sam was never going to accept financial help from her family when it came to their future. Deep down, Phoebe really respected him for that.

There was a scuffle over by the Aga. A growl and a woof, followed by something rolling across the flagstone floor.

'I think Roxie's just stolen Buster's tennis ball,' Phoebe said. 'Hey, Roxie, you naughty girl.'

'He probably let her have it. He's not up to chasing balls too much, these days.'

'Even so. She can't just pinch whatever she likes.' Phoebe got up and liberated the tatty old tennis ball from an unrepentant Roxie. 'That's not yours, darling.' She gave it back to Buster while Roxie wagged her tail sadly.

'It's my fault, I don't do any training with her. Sam does it all when he takes her to the stables.'

Within five minutes of Phoebe sitting back down, Roxie had the ball back again and was knocking it around the kitchen.

'I think Buster gave it to her that time,' Maggie observed from her seat. 'You see, love. The old ones give their stuff to the young ones to help them out. It's the natural order of things.'

It was Phoebe's turn to say, 'Hmmm.'

Maggie knew better than to push the point. She chuckled and changed the subject. 'And talking of Rufus. Well, we were earlier, have you had your invitation to the society wedding of the year yet?'

'No. Why? Have you?' Phoebe asked.

'No. It's gone very quiet on that front. Maybe we won't get invited after all.'

'I'll ask Tori. She'll know what's going on. Or Harrison will anyway. He's best man.'

'You and Sam haven't set a date yet, I take it?'

'Not yet.'

'Well, I do hope someone's getting married this year.' Maggie got up stiffly from the table. 'I do like a good wedding. Now would you like some more soup before you head back to your intended?'

* * *

Neither of them said anything else about finances or weddings, but Phoebe realised she felt a lot better just for talking about things with her grandmother. As she drove back to Woodcutter's, she felt lighter than she had for a while.

Sam wasn't there when she got in. He'd no doubt gone straight from sorting out Ninja at Brook to feed Snowball at his place in Bridgeford.

She decided to phone Tori for an update on weddings and all the other things they had to catch up on.

'I'd literally just picked up the phone to call you,' Tori said, when she answered within one ring.

'Oh, brilliant. Was it christening news? Have you finalised the date?'

'You read my mind. We've okayed it with the other godparent, who as you know is Rufus, and it'll be on 15 June. That's a Saturday. Hope that's OK for you?'

'It's perfect,' Phoebe said. 'I can't wait to be a godmother.'

Tori hesitated.

'What?' Phoebe prompted, sensing she wanted to say something else.

'There was one other thing I wanted to run past you that also affects you. We'd also like to buy our own place this year if possible, which means I'm going to need to put Woodcutter's on the market. There's no massive rush or anything. I don't think we'll have a problem getting a buyer. The market's pretty buoyant at the moment.' Tori's breathless voice came to a halt and Phoebe guessed she'd been building up the courage to tell her.

'Say something,' Tori said. 'Is that OK? I don't want you to feel I'm pushing you out. I'm assuming you and Sam will be wanting to buy your own place anyway.'

'You're right. We are. We're working on it now. We went to talk to a mortgage broker this week in fact. We should be able to borrow a decent amount.' Phoebe was surprised how effortlessly the lie came to her lips.

It was worth it when she heard her friend let out a relieved sigh. 'That's great news.' Tori sounded massively reassured. 'Will you sell Sam's place and then look? Or will you try to coordinate the sales?'

'We thought we might rent somewhere together while we look.' Phoebe realised she was digging herself even deeper in.

One lie leading to another, although it was true they were going to look for a place to rent.

'Yes, that's a good idea. You're in a much stronger position when you go in as first-time buyers. Then there's no chain. That's another reason we need to sell Woodcutter's first. We're going to do the same thing.'

'We're hoping we can find a landlord who's happy to take a dog and a cat,' Phoebe added.

'Ours does, I think. Hey, it's a pity we can't sublet this house to you. It's got a great garden for a dog. We could definitely put in a good word for you with the landlord if the timings work out.'

'That isn't a bad idea. Thanks. I'll have a word with Sam.'

'And I'm so glad you're going to be buying your own place too,' Tori added happily. 'Get us – being all grown up and getting mortgages.'

'I know! Who'd have thunk it?' Phoebe gave a little laugh, and they said their goodbyes.

Maggie hadn't been joking when she'd said that pride could become a defect. Phoebe couldn't remember the last time she'd lied to her best friend.

15

'It's not the end of the world,' Sam said when he and Phoebe were discussing it all. 'Maybe it's just fate giving us a nudge to get on with things.'

'I didn't know you believed in fate,' she teased. 'You always say everything's down to careful planning and hard work.'

'That's true as well. But I reckon fate has a hand in things when it comes to timing. After all, the timing was perfect with Seth. He sold his practice at exactly the same time you needed a new vet.'

'I can't argue with that.'

'Did Tori give you three months' notice?'

'No, she said I can move out whenever I'm ready. But I don't want to hold her up, Sam. They need to sell Woodcutter's before they can buy anything. I said I'd leave ASAP. I can't see the point in waiting. I'm assuming it's OK to move over to yours.'

'Yes, of course it is.'

'It would be easier to move all our stuff from one place to a rental than from two places to a rental anyway.'

'It would.' Sam kissed her nose. 'We can spend the weekend

looking at rentals. Maybe arrange to go and see a few. Bridgeford isn't as expensive as I thought. And I've got the new carpet in the bedroom so there's no reason not to put mine on the market.'

'We'll also need a landlord who'll take pets. Tori said theirs does. She said she'd put in a good word for us if we wanted. It's a really nice place. Big garden, nice kitchen. We were half joking, but actually it's not a bad idea. If we moved in when they move into their forever home, it would be perfect timing.'

'If we did that, we wouldn't even need to go looking,' Sam said thoughtfully. 'It would mean being at mine for a few months, though, while they sell Woodcutter's. Can you cope with that?'

'Of course I can, Sam. And if we were only paying one lot of rent and bills, we could save up some more towards our deposit.'

'You don't need to contribute to bills at mine.'

'Yes, I do, if I'm living there full-time.'

'I've got it covered.' The stubborn look in Sam's eyes reminded Phoebe of her grandmother.

'We can argue about that later.' She decided now wasn't the time to remind him she earned far more than he did. She knew he felt bad enough that his earnings alone wouldn't raise enough for a mortgage to buy anywhere in the New Forest.

Mind you, not many of the locals could afford to buy a house in the most expensive national park in England.

Maybe Sam was right about fate giving things a nudge along. As he'd said, it had certainly worked in their favour with Seth.

'I'll have a word with Tori about speaking to the landlord then. Do you want to come and have a look first? You might not like the place.'

In the end, they did that at the weekend instead of looking at anything else and Sam really liked the house too.

'I'll speak to the landlord,' Tori promised. 'I can't imagine he'd say no. He's a nice guy and it would be far easier for him to get someone who comes with a recommendation rather than have to go through the rigmarole of advertising. That's if you're sure you don't mind waiting until we've sold Woodcutter's and bought somewhere. You might find your own place to buy before we do.'

'We're in no hurry at all,' Sam had said quickly. 'We want to take our time looking around and plan our wedding before we get too involved in house buying, don't we, Pheebs.'

'Of course you do.' Tori had smiled delightedly. 'My sensible friends. You're doing things in the right order, aren't you? Getting your ducks in a row. Wedding first, house next, babies later. Not like us. Total chaos.' She made funny faces at Vanessa Rose and the baby giggled. So did everyone else.

And Phoebe thought, *if only*. She would have to tell Tori the truth some time. That they had no idea when they'd be able to afford a mortgage on their own place. But not today. At least they had the maisonette. It might not be ideal. But it wasn't as though they were homeless.

Phoebe also had to pop into Puddleduck Vets at the weekend to give a client some test results she'd promised them. She was chatting to Maggie in the yard on her way in to make the phone call when a horsebox drew up.

'Ah, this must be Jade and Aiden,' Maggie said, glancing across. 'The people from Duck Pond Rescue.'

A guy in a Barbour coat with short cropped brown hair jumped down from the cab. But before Maggie or Phoebe could introduce themselves, he ran round to open the door on the other side of the horsebox and a young woman emerged with some difficulty as she was carrying two large bags. The faded black jeans, well-worn hoodie and lack of make-up didn't detract from her very natural girl-next-door prettiness, Phoebe thought, as the guy leaped to her aid and took the bags.

If this was Jade, she was young to have set up an animal

rescue. She couldn't have been more than mid-twenties. Fleetingly, Phoebe wondered about their relationship. The guy was fussing over her, solicitous, but a little unsure of his welcome. Not quite natural enough to be her partner.

He looked around, spotted them watching and came across. 'Hi, which one of you young ladies would be Maggie?' He smiled and blushed and his words, which could have come across as smarmy, just felt slightly awkward, as if he was more used to dealing with animals than people. Lots of vets were, Phoebe thought, warming to him, as Maggie made the introductions.

The girl arrived beside him. 'I'm Jade from Duck Pond Rescue, and this is Aiden. I'm so grateful to you.' She looked straight at Maggie. 'This is such a massive help. I've brought over a bag of Rosanna's food and there's some hay in the horsebox, and there are also some other things in this bag.' She held it out. 'Chocolate cookies from the farm shop near us, and a bottle of wine. They're for you, not Rosanna. A little thank you. I hope that's OK?'

She was lovely, Phoebe decided. She looked vulnerable but was clearly in charge.

They chatted briefly about Seth and their mutual connections with him – Aiden was his nephew, it turned out. He'd done some work experience at Marchwood but as he actually lived north of Salisbury, it had been easier to get a full-time job in the city when he was fully qualified.

Phoebe, having made sure Maggie didn't need her help, left them all chattering about animal rescue and went to phone her client. When she came out again, Aiden and Jade were just unloading the horse, a gentle-looking bay mare. Phoebe guessed Maggie was right. In some ways it would be good for Casey's Girl to have some company that wasn't a neddie.

* * *

Sam's maisonette in Bridgeford actually had quite a bit going for it. It was bigger than Woodcutter's and very comfortable. Location wise it was perfect. Sam could walk to Hendrie's for work on the days when he didn't go in to see Ninja first. Phoebe had a fifteen-minute drive as opposed to a five-minute one, but that was hardly a dealbreaker.

The living together bit was great. They slotted really well together, they always had, and it was a lot easier being in one place and not finding you'd left your charger or your toothbrush in the wrong house on a regular basis.

It was also handy being around for Snowball. The fluffy black cat had always got on well with Roxie. The only downside was the maisonette being on the first floor. A flat with no direct access to the garden wasn't an ideal place to keep a dog. Especially when it came to Roxie's last outing of the evening, which meant a traipse downstairs with Roxie on the lead, into the cold darkness and around the side of the house to the garden. Sam usually did the last thing at night sessions, but Phoebe missed the freedom of just being able to just open their own back door and let their dog roam freely in the garden.

'It'll make getting our own place so much more precious,' Sam had pointed out. 'And it won't be forever. It's only until Tori and Harrison sell Woodcutter's and find their own place.'

In the meantime, Sam put up a gate at the side of the house which led into the garden. This meant they didn't have to worry about Roxie running back up the drive and possibly out into the road. Roxie's recall was pretty good, that was the only thing that Phoebe had made sure they did, but no dog was guaranteed.

Unfortunately, they'd missed the last couple of dog training classes too, which had been a mixed blessing. There'd been so much going on that neither of them had time to take her and they hadn't signed up for any more classes.

'We can get back into it when Paula starts again,' Sam had said, and Phoebe knew he was trying to reassure her without directly saying it that he wouldn't be bumping into Destiny Dolittle again any time soon.

He'd also mentioned in passing that Laila, Destiny's friend's child, had decided riding wasn't for her, which meant that Phoebe's glamorous rival was totally off the scene.

Not that she'd really ever been a glamorous rival, Phoebe reminded herself. There had never been anything going on between Sam and Destiny. It had all been in her head. Even so, it was nice to know the stunning blonde wasn't meeting up with Sam on a regular basis.

* * *

Seth fitted into the Puddleduck Pets team perfectly. As winter gave way to spring, and the New Forest burst into life with new growth, Seth proved his worth over and over. It was perfect timing in another way too. Lambing season was at its peak during March and he was in his element. Seth's speciality was large animal practice, with a nod towards horses, which he'd brought with him from his jockey days. This meant Phoebe could pass much of the farm animal work to Seth and be at Puddleduck doing routine appointments and small animal work with Max. She still kept her hand in on the farm side, which she loved, but it meant she didn't have to do quite as much.

The mare, Rosanna, had gone back to Duck Pond Rescue less than a month after she'd arrived in the end and, to Maggie's delight, Jade also took a cat with eight kittens that had landed on her doorstep the previous week.

'That Jade is a diamond, if that's not a contradiction in terms,' Maggie told Phoebe cheerfully. 'The cattery's bursting at the seams at the moment. We could have kept the kittens in the barn, but it's tricky for Natasha with Saddam wandering around too.'

Phoebe smiled, pleased her concerns about Jade taking advantage were completely unfounded. Aiden, who she'd never got the chance to exchange more than a few words with, was clearly as lovely as his Uncle Seth.

16

Maggie offered to host everyone for dinner on Easter Sunday, which fell early in April, so the Dashwood family were all getting together at Puddleduck Farm.

Louella and James, Phoebe's parents, had insisted they bring a cooked ham to save Maggie cooking everything and Frazier and Alexa were bringing desserts. Alexa was a dab hand at making desserts, and still created fabulous ones every time the family met up, despite the fact she now had twins under five and was expecting another baby in July.

'Alexa makes me feel inadequate when it comes to food,' Phoebe confided in Maggie the week before the dinner. 'What can I bring?'

'How do you think I feel? I'm throwing this party and I won't have a thing to do,' Maggie grumbled. 'You don't need to bring anything. You can just bring yourself.'

'What about vegetables? We've got to have something with this ham.'

'I thought I might do creamy leeks and scallop potatoes. And maybe some of my bread.'

'You'll have loads to do then – I need to bring something. How about drinks? Cider goes with ham, does Eddie like cider?'

'Eddie loves cider. But bring some soft drinks too. Most people will be driving.'

'Sorted,' Phoebe said happily.

It was lovely to catch up at Puddleduck Farm with her family. Phoebe hadn't seen them en masse since Christmas. She hadn't even been to her parents' much since then. It was difficult to find a time when they were all free.

Louella was a teacher and always snowed under with work and James worked for a family law firm, as did Phoebe's brother Frazier. This meant Frazier and their father saw a lot of each other, and Alexa, her sister-in-law, probably saw more of Louella than Phoebe did because of the grandchildren.

'At least we'll have loads to talk about,' Phoebe told Sam as they drove over with Roxie in the back of the car.

And so they did. The volume was so loud over dinner, Phoebe was sure no one would have heard any conversation but their immediate neighbour's as ten people crowded around the huge farmhouse table in Maggie's kitchen.

After they'd eaten, during a lull in conversation, Maggie said in a voice ostensibly to the children but in reality to everyone, 'There's something very exciting outside in the yard. Who wants to come and see it?'

'Me, me, me,' Flo shouted at the top of her voice.

'Yes, me.' Bertie, her twin brother, was slower but only by a millisecond.

'We'll need to shut the dogs up for a bit,' Maggie warned. 'Or at least any dogs that can't be relied on not to chase things.'

This definitely included Roxie, but Eddie volunteered to keep an eye on her while everyone else trooped out into the yard.

Maggie led them out of the first gate and into the walkway

that led to the kennels and the cattery and then they walked in a big straggle on to the neddies' field.

'Is it a new neddie?' Alexa asked.

'Neddie, neddie, neddie,' Flo shouted. It was clearly a thing to say words in threes.

'Shush,' Maggie hushed her, 'or you'll frighten them off.' She turned back to her great-granddaughter. 'Now you'll need to start looking any time now. And we'd better keep an eye out for Bruce Goose too. I think he's in the field but we don't want him chasing us with his sharp beak, do we?'

'Naughty Bruce Goose,' Flo said, but she did as she was told. Her eyes were wide as she scanned the surrounding paths and bushes, but it was Bertie who spotted the chicks first. 'Baby ducks,' he called in a voice full of breathless wonder.

And then they all saw them. A troupe of bright yellow ducklings followed their mother, a white Puddleduck, in a straight line along the edge of the path.

'Is that Jemima?' Phoebe asked.

'It is indeed. She had a clutch of eggs hidden away that no one found. More mouths to feed,' Maggie grumbled, but it was obvious she found the babies as endearing as everyone else did.

For a few moments they all oohed and ahhed over the ducklings' antics as they scratched around in the grass with their mother, who Maggie was distracting with fresh peas, one of Jemima's favourite things. The babies really were gorgeous.

'A perfect little Easter family,' Alexa said, clapping her hands. 'Will you keep them all, Maggie?'

'Not if I can help it. Natasha's trying to find them good homes.'

'Can we have one?' Flo asked.

'Pleeeeze, Mummy,' Bertie backed up his sister.

'We haven't got room for a duck in our garden,' Frazier told them. 'Ducks need lots of space.'

'But they're only tiny,' Flo implored.

'They're not tiny for long. Your father's right. They need a pond to splash in and lots of room for running around. And besides, we're having a baby, aren't we?' Alexa patted her stomach. 'You've got a new brother or sister in here.'

'Baby says he wants one too,' Flo pouted.

Alexa turned towards Phoebe, who was standing closest. 'She's been calling this baby a "he" ever since she knew it was coming. We wanted a surprise, so even we don't know the sex. It will be interesting to see if she's right.'

After they'd finished watching the ducks and had walked down and patted the neddies, then said hello to the kennel dogs and waved at Saddam, who was strolling around on the cattery roof winding up the cats that were waiting to be rehomed, they went back inside for coffee.

The chat turned towards Frazier and Alexa's imminent arrival.

'You're going to need a bigger house, aren't you?' Maggie said to Alexa. 'With your expanding brood.'

'We might be able to convert our loft,' Alexa said. 'Frazier's looking into it, aren't you, love?'

'It's certainly a project for the future,' he said thoughtfully. 'The cost wouldn't be much different to moving. If we do that, we'll be phoning Sam's dad for some advice on the refurb.'

'He'd be happy to help,' Sam said.

'Thanks.' Frazier glanced at him. 'So how are you two getting on with finding your own place?'

Sam explained they were planning to take over the tenancy of Tori and Harrison's house once their friends had found somewhere to buy.

'We're not planning to buy our own place for a couple of years,' Phoebe added. 'We want to get married first. And we've decided to move that to next year. Planning a wedding's enough to do what with us both working all hours.'

'Very sensible,' Frazier said. Both her parents were nodding happily.

Phoebe avoided Maggie's eyes. She was the only one who knew the truth about their financial circumstances.

17

Saturday 13 April was Rufus and Emilia's wedding day. They were getting married, just as they'd wanted to, in the bluebell woods at the back of Beechbrook House.

As Rufus walked down to their chosen spot, he thought that he couldn't remember ever doing anything as crazy and as romantic as this in his entire life. It was one of those beautiful spring days when the sky was the palest of blues, there was more than a hint of warmth in the air, and his woods were awash with bluebells. A sea of them wound in and out of the dozens of silver birches. As he'd once told Archie, it looked as though the sky had fallen down and had been scattered in handfuls amongst the trees. The sweet scent of their fragrance mingled with the mulchy dampness of the forest floor. Rufus breathed it in and smiled. He and Emilia weren't having the kind of wedding where they needed to pick a colour theme, but if they had, the colour would have been bluebell.

Last night he'd lain awake, and he'd thought about Rowena, his late wife, and he'd wondered what she would have made of today's plans. Not just the fact he was marrying again, she'd definitely have wanted that for him, but the kind of day he'd planned. He had a feeling that Rowena would have approved of that too. At heart, Rowena had been as unorthodox as he was. She and Emilia would have got on well.

A soundtrack of birdsong was all around him. In that moment of reflection, as he stood alone in his woodland, Rufus mused that a single bluebell was a delicate and fragile bloom but when blue-bells thronged together in their thousands, they were monumentally powerful. A little like people, he thought, vulnerable alone, but invincible when they were connected to each other.

He never had thoughts like these. Maybe he should pinch himself to make sure he was awake and not in the middle of some surreal, beautiful dream.

Ouch! He was definitely awake, he thought, having tried it. Get a grip, Rufus, he told himself as a few moments later he came out into the small clearing where their wedding would take place.

The tree house wasn't built in one tree, but between several. It was positioned in a spot where the tall, skinny-trunked silver birches were clustered close together so it spanned more than one tree. A cleverly designed spiral staircase wound up between the trunks, linking two wooden platforms, one above the other. Each platform held a small house made of slatted wood: the first was just under three metres up and the second was a few metres above it. Both of the houses had pointy wooden roofs and an open-plan viewing window. They were artfully designed to blend in with their surroundings and looked as though they had been fashioned by some master craftsman. Which indeed they had. Rufus's father had commissioned the structure from a Swedish company that specialised in building fantastic tree houses which would become one with the landscape where they were placed.

But today Rufus's tree houses were not blending in with their surroundings. They were separate from it, proudly lit up and entwined with thousands of fairy lights that sparkled and shone as the midday sunlight caught them through the dappled leaf canopy of the trees. Inside the tree houses themselves were more fairy lights, and red rose petals were scattered on the wooden floor.

Rufus had recommissioned the Swedish company to come across and increase the size of the lower tree house so that there was an extra platform alongside the original, and the two spaces could comfortably and safely hold him, Emilia, Denzel, the celebrant, and Archie, of course.

It had cost a fortune, but it had been worth every penny. The company had also made sure the ladders were safe. Rufus had no intention of letting his bride-to-be climb a ladder but there was himself and the others to consider. It would be handy to make sure that they could get to the wedding venue in one piece.

* * *

A snapping of twigs and a scrunching of footsteps on the forest floor heralded the arrival of Harrison and Archie, both dressed in grey morning suits, and close behind them, Denzel, who'd skipped formal and was wearing a red embroidered vintage jacket, more steampunk gothic than formal. But his long hair was tied back in a neat ponytail.

Rufus turned to greet them with a smile on his lips.

'Good morning, good morning, good morning,' Denzel said. 'What a fabulous spot this is – I can totally see why you'd want to tie the knot here. Stunning place. Absolutely stunning. Yah.'

'I like it,' Rufus said.

'Morning,' Harrison murmured. 'You all set then? No second thoughts?'

'Absolutely not. Marrying Emilia is the best thing I've ever done.'

'I was thinking more about the venue.' Harrison's eyes glimmered with humour. 'There's still time to change your mind, you know. We can have the ceremony down here on solid ground. No need to go clambering around in trees.'

Archie's face fell. 'But we want to go climbing around in trees, don't we, Dad? This is the coolest idea ever.'

'Of course we do, son. And we will, don't worry.'

'Great,' Denzel said, rubbing his hands together. 'Another original setting to add to my portfolio. You will not be identifiable in any photos,' he added quickly. 'Don't worry about that.'

'I suppose I should thank my lucky stars that you're not having the reception up a tree,' Harrison said wryly.

'You should,' Rufus said. 'It did cross our minds.' He winked at his best friend.

There wouldn't be very many people at the reception. Emilia and Rufus had agreed on closest friends only. None of Emilia's family were coming – she hadn't invited them – but her best friend, Sofia, would be there with her partner. Tori would be there with Vanessa Rose. Jack, Archie's best friend from school, would be there. And there were a few friends of Rufus and Emilia's, people that they both knew and trusted not to take photos and leak them to the media.

They were having a barbecue on the back lawn of Beechbrook House. An outside caterer Rufus and Emilia trusted to be discreet would be serving up the hog roast. There would be champagne and wedding cake, but there would be no speeches. This was Rufus and Emilia's idea of a perfect wedding.

It might not be traditional, Rufus thought, and he knew that his father wouldn't have approved one bit. Although he also thought his father would very probably have enjoyed it if he had managed to put aside his fixed ideas. At heart, Lord Alfred had liked the simple pleasures. Golf, his shooting days, drinks at his club with his cronies.

In some ways, Rufus wished his father could have been here to see him get married. But if his father had still been alive, Rufus was pretty sure none of this would have been happening.

The sound of Harrison clearing his throat brought Rufus back to the present.

'Right then, is it about time I went and collected the bride, would you say, m'lord?' Harrison winked.

'Yes, please, and drive carefully.'

'Do not fret. I will drive your precious cargo with infinite care.' Harrison took a step closer to Rufus and slapped him gently on the back. 'Good on ya, mate,' he said in a voice only Rufus could hear. 'This is the best thing you've ever done. I couldn't agree more.'

Rufus had to swallow an ache in his throat at the emotion in his oldest friend's voice.

'I know,' he said softly.

'Now then…' Denzel turned towards Rufus and Archie. 'It's about time we made our ascent, is it not?' He tipped his head back and looked upwards. 'How high actually is it?'

'Around three metres to the first one,' Rufus told him. 'It's not that high. And the spiral ladders are very easy. It's quite hard to fall off them.'

But not impossible, which was why he had a back-up plan for Emilia. 'Archie will show you,' he added to Denzel. 'Do you want to go up first, son?'

Archie didn't need telling twice. Seconds later, he was on the ladder and climbing swiftly up. Denzel, clutching his clipboard, followed more slowly. He was wearing trainers, Rufus observed. Sensible chap.

He let them get up to the tree house and inside before following them up the ladder. His stomach was crunching with excitement. He couldn't believe this was really happening. For a moment he had the same surreal, dreamlike feeling he'd had earlier. But it dissipated once he was on the ladder. He'd spent a lot of time up here as a child, watching the birds and woodland creatures unobserved. Feeling a part of nature, feeling like a normal kid. It was the perfect place to get married.

There was a great view from the lower tree house. Not quite as good a view as there was from the topmost one, but practicalities had meant that it had been much easier to enlarge and reinforce the bottom one than the top one, where the trees were thinner, so that's what they'd done.

Rufus stood by the viewing window staring out across the trees. He could see the narrow path along which Harrison would drive Emilia. He wished he could have been there to see her face when she first laid eyes on her wedding transport. But that was one of the few traditions they'd decided to observe.

They'd agreed not to see each other on the night before their wedding day. That wasn't too difficult to arrange when they lived in a place the size of Beechbrook House. Last night, Rufus had slept in their bed and Emilia had slept in the bed she'd used when she'd been Archie's nanny. It was the last time she would ever sleep there, they'd both agreed, so it was symbolic as well as practical.

He didn't have any idea what she was wearing today either. She knew that he, Archie and Harrison were in morning suits – she'd had a hand in choosing them – but she'd given Rufus no clues as to what outfit she would choose.

'I may turn up in jeans and boots – this is suitable attire for the woods, ja?' she had quipped.

'You can turn up in whatever you wish,' Rufus had told her. 'As long as you turn up.'

He'd just caught a glimpse of yellow through the trees. He turned towards Archie and Denzel. 'They're on their way. Look. Quick.' He pointed.

'Where? Where?' Archie craned his neck to see.

So did Denzel. The celebrant had been a brilliant choice. He was as enthusiastic as a child about everything. It was wonderful.

Harrison was driving slowly. Partly because the unmade track was rutted and difficult to traverse and partly because the yellow cherry picker wasn't made for speed.

It looked great, though. Yesterday Rufus and Harrison had jet washed it while Emilia was out, buying what she called last-minute wedding stuff. Then they'd valeted it so the inside was spotless. Rufus could have paid someone to do these things, but it had been fun doing it with Harrison. A male bonding thing to do. They'd laughed a lot.

When they'd finished, it had been Harrison who'd stepped back a few paces and studied the gleaming vehicle. 'It's still missing something, though, isn't it? What do you reckon – white ribbon or blue?'

'I haven't got any of either.'

'Lucky I was a boy scout then, isn't it.'

Harrison had tapped his nose before producing a large roll of white ribbon from his pocket. 'White's traditional. Let's use this. Now are you sure that Emilia's going to be happy? She's not secretly expecting some white Rolls Royce with a chauffeur to drive her through the woods, is she?'

'Definitely not.'

'She is a princess, after all.' Harrison was the only person who knew that Emilia was related to the Prince of Liechtenstein.

'She'll like it,' Rufus had said confidently and had hoped he was right.

Emilia had got in it anyway, Rufus thought now, as he looked back at the cherry picker, adorned with white ribbons and with two jaunty white bows attached to its wing mirrors. That was a very good start.

Its lifting platform was currently folded up. Harrison and Emilia were in the cab so he couldn't see what she'd decided to wear. He felt a fizz of expectation. He decided that he wouldn't look until she was actually here in the tree house beside him.

The cherry picker had disappeared again behind the screen of trees. As it got closer, it disappeared completely. But a few minutes later they could all hear the low thrum of its diesel engine beneath them.

Rufus heard voices. Emilia and Harrison were talking in snatched sentences a few metres below them.

'What are they doing?' Rufus asked, unable to contain his impatience. 'He's not letting Emilia climb the ladder, is he?'

'No, don't worry, Dad. He's in the cab pressing buttons. Oh, wow. He's operating the long arm thingie. Is she coming up in that?'

'They're both coming up in that,' Rufus told him.

'Heavens to Betsy. Good lord!' Denzel exclaimed. 'Are they really coming up in that? You don't do anything by halves, do you?'

Rufus wanted to laugh. But he thought if he did, he would never stop. Archie was now giving him a running commentary on what was going on.

'Harrison's helping her to get in. Has it always had that wire netting stuff around the cage? I don't remember that?'

'It's new,' Rufus said. 'I don't want to risk them falling out.'

'I think it's making it harder for them to get in,' Archie said. 'But that's because of her dress.'

'Don't tell me about her dress. I want it to be a surprise.'

'OK, I won't tell you. It's OK, she's in.' He paused. 'Now Harrison's getting in too. And he's in.'

'And they're off,' Denzel added. 'They're off. They're on their way. Don't worry, Lord Holt. No chance of them falling out. Harrison's got an arm around her shoulders too.'

'Does she look OK? Not too, er, surprised?' Rufus finished. He didn't want to say 'cross'.

'She's smiling, I think.'

'She's laughing,' Archie said. 'She's happy, Dad. Why wouldn't she be happy? She's marrying us.'

18

Archie's excited words, 'She's marrying us,' were one of the many lovely highlights that Rufus would remember from his wedding day.

Another was the moment that the cherry picker's crate with Harrison and Emilia in it arrived beside the tree house.

He and Harrison had rehearsed this bit several times during the last few weeks. The positioning of the cherry picker's cage alongside the tree house's new entrance was a delicate operation. The transference from cherry picker to tree house was another.

To make it entirely safe, they'd attached chains to the cherry picker platform that would link it together with the tree trunk itself.

During the initial trials, Rufus had worried that his plan B to keep Emilia safe was actually far riskier than if she had just climbed carefully up the ladder, but by the end of the trials, he and Harrison had got it down to a fine art.

As long as the cherry picker's cage was in the right place and the chains were locked in, there was no chance at all of a disaster.

Rufus knew he couldn't risk leaving that to anyone else. As the cherry picker settled against the tree house, he turned and caught his first glimpse of his bride.

His breath caught in his throat. She had gone for tradition after all. She looked absolutely stunning in a simple cream bridal gown that skimmed her slenderness and was artfully cut over her tummy so there was only the merest curve. The bodice was sewn with tiny pearls. She wore a pearl-studded headdress with a tiny veil, but now she lifted it up and smiled at him.

'Have I ever told you that you are a crazy man?'

Rufus couldn't speak – his throat was too full of emotion. So he contented himself with nodding, and for that long, long second there was no one else on the entire planet but for the two of them.

'You look so beautiful.' He managed finally to find his voice. 'The most beautiful I have ever seen you look.'

'This is good thing for our wedding day – ja?'

'It is very good thing.' He found himself slipping into her Swiss German rhythms. That had happened a lot lately and Rufus loved it. It was as though their two worlds, their two languages were merging. He had even started learning high German, which was also Archie's chosen language at school, so he could speak her language, although he didn't think he'd ever be as fluent in it as she was in English.

They sorted out the practicalities of locking the two platforms together and finally, Rufus and Emilia were facing the celebrant together.

They'd opted to keep the actual ceremony short. Both had written and memorised their especially chosen words and they said them, in turn, up amongst the trees with the sun slanting its rays down into the wooden house and lighting the oak floor with leafy patterns of gold.

'By the power vested in me, I now pronounce you husband and wife.' Denzel smiled at them but Rufus and Emilia only had eyes for each other as he leaned forward, lifted her veil once more and they kissed gently.

Archie and Harrison cheered and then Archie said with his customary candidness, 'I'm starving. Can we go and get something to eat now that's over and done with?'

Everyone laughed.

'I just need a couple more photos for the album,' Rufus said. 'No one's getting down until I've got them.'

Archie sighed good naturedly and put on his best photograph smile.

Twenty minutes later, they were all back on the lawns of Beechbrook House, where a mini marquee had been set up just in case any April showers had cropped up to spoil the day. It contained a table that held the wedding cake, which was modest by anyone's standards, two tiers of white icing, the corners decorated with icing sugar bluebells and simple beading. On top were a sugar paste couple, the bride in white, and the groom in morning suit-grey, but the most notable thing about them was that both figures were smiling. Which was a perfect reflection of reality. Neither Rufus nor Emilia could stop smiling.

A few people had already put presents beneath the wedding cake table, although there had been no wedding list, the happy couple having agreed that they already had everything they wanted.

There were no April showers. The sky was still a pastel blue and Harrison and Archie had gone ahead of the newly married Holts to warn the guests of their arrival and so when Rufus and Emilia arrived, they were met by a small cheer and showered with clouds of eco-friendly confetti that would be eaten by the birds before the day was out. Emilia's best friend, Sofia, and her partner, Rudi, were the first to congratulate them.

There were more photographs taken and then Rufus declared that everyone should eat and drink and get on with enjoying themselves. Several wooden picnic tables had been put out for the occasion and a sound system played music which was just loud enough not to be intrusive.

Sometime around mid-afternoon, at a prearranged signal from Rufus, Harrison stood up, tinged a spoon on the side of a champagne glass and announced that Mr and Mrs Holt were going to dance their first dance. The music changed. Tori was in charge of music and the opening bars of a waltz thrummed across the warm spring air.

As Rufus and Emilia waltzed across the bowling green lawn, totally at home in each other's arms, Rufus realised he had never been so happy as he was in this moment. He didn't think it had been possible to be any happier when they'd exchanged rings and vows, but this was even better. A dream wedding with his dream woman.

They had asked Denzel to join them for the reception and he'd said he wouldn't miss it for the world.

'That was one of the smallest, and one of the most beautiful weddings I've ever had the privilege to officiate at,' he told Rufus and Emilia much later when the hog roast was starting to cool and the wedding cake had been cut. 'It was an honour to be a part of it, Lord Holt.'

'Rufus, please,' Rufus had told him as they shook hands. 'Thank you so much for being so accommodating.'

'I'd love a photo of the tree house venue, if that's possible?'

'I'll ask Harrison to send you one. And thank you again.'

Rufus and Emilia finally waved off their last guest around 9 p.m. They were spending their first night as a married couple in their own bed, which was what they'd both wanted, and when Archie was back at school they were off to Saint Lucia for their honeymoon.

They'd invited Archie to go with them, but he'd declined.

'No, thanks. Honeymoons are for lovey-dovey couples; I'd rather go and stay with Jack if it's out of term time. Then we can go riding every day.'

'That's fine with me, son.' Rufus had ruffled his hair. 'You can let us know if you change your mind.'

'I won't.' Archie had grinned. 'Thanks for the offer, though, Dad.'

Rufus had felt so proud of Archie, who, at just shy of twelve years old, already knew his own mind, and felt secure enough to know his father would support whatever he wanted to do.

True riches were not about wealth and privilege, Rufus thought, both of which he'd been lucky enough to have all his life. True riches were about having the freedom to be yourself. This was something he had never truly had until he'd decided to marry Emilia and to dispense with tradition and formality.

Rufus also knew that as far as freedom went, today was only the beginning. He had put his stake in the ground. From this day forward, he had a whole new approach to life.

* * *

While Rufus and Emilia were entertaining their guests on the bowling green lawns of Beechbrook House, Phoebe and Sam were out riding in the New Forest.

Sam was riding Ninja and they'd borrowed a grey mare called Storm from one of the other livery owners for Phoebe to ride.

Riding out together was something they'd talked about often but hadn't ever done because the timing never seemed to work out. But on this particular Saturday, Sam's last lesson of the afternoon had been cancelled because his student had gone down with a stomach bug and Phoebe was not on call.

Roxie was with them. She was good around horses. She stayed beside them, but a couple of horse lengths away so she was out of kicking range. Right now, she was running in an easy lope beside them on a wide forest track while they trotted briskly.

The sun was shining through the leaf canopy of trees, casting patches of dappled shade on the path. The horses were blowing, they'd been trotting for a while. It was still warm, and Phoebe's thighs were beginning to ache from using unaccustomed muscles.

'Let's walk for a bit,' she called to Sam, reining in her horse, and seeing Ninja's impatient head toss as Sam did the same.

Ninja was always in a hurry. For a few moments, the big bay horse jogged at walking pace while Sam sat easily on his back, totally still in the saddle. Sam was so at one with a horse. Slowly Ninja calmed back down into a walk.

'Isn't this beautiful?' Phoebe gestured to a swathe of bluebells through the trees, their luminous violet colour lighting up the shady spots. She took a deep breath of the spring-scented air. The fragrance of bluebells and damp earth and the scent of horse filled her nostrils.

'It's glorious,' Sam said. 'I can't think of anywhere I'd rather be. Or anyone I'd rather be with.'

'Same,' Phoebe said. 'Just us and the horses and Roxie. We're so lucky.'

There was a little silence filled with birdsong and the muted thud of the horses' hooves on the path and the occasional creak of the saddles.

'We've even got our own birdsong orchestra,' Phoebe added. 'It's perfect, Sam.'

'Almost perfect.' He turned in the saddle towards her. 'You're not too disappointed that we can't buy our own house yet, are you?'

'No, I'm not.' She smiled at him. 'Seriously, I've got my dream man and my dream job. What more could I want?'

'Your dream house, maybe?' His voice was light, but his eyes were serious.

'I don't mind waiting for that. We can move into Tori's old place as soon as it's available.' Tori's landlord had just agreed he was more than happy for them to do that. 'Then having our own place later will be all the more precious when we get it.'

Sam searched her face and then gave a little nod, as if he'd seen what he wanted there and was at least partially reassured.

'I'd live with you and Roxie and Snowball in a bedsit, Sam, if that was the only place we could afford. And your place isn't a bedsit.'

'I'd live with you in a tent,' he said, 'although I'm not sure about Roxie and Snowball.'

'I'd live with you in a cardboard box in a shop doorway,' she countered.

'I'd live with you in just a shop doorway.' He laughed, getting into the swing of the game, and she was relieved to see the worry had gone out of his eyes and the optimistic Sam she knew and loved was back.

The track they were on had just opened out into a clearing with a five-bar gate that led onto a track, beyond which was a long path that sloped gently upwards towards a distant hill. Without dismounting, Sam opened the gate and pushed it wide with his knee to allow Phoebe and Roxie through it. Then he shut it again with a clank.

The path up to the hill was wide and sandy. Vibrant pink heather stretched away on either side of it.

'I usually canter up here,' Sam said, gathering his reins and causing an eager Ninja to bunch up his hindquarters and canter on the spot.

Phoebe gathered Storm's reins too, and the mare responded instantly. Phoebe closed her heels against the mare's grey sides and she sprang into a canter. 'Race you to the top, Sam,' she called back over her shoulder as they accelerated from a standing start to a full-on gallop up the hill.

Sam was gentlemanly enough to give her a head start, but as she crouched low over Storm's withers, urging the horse to give it all she'd got, she could hear the thundering of Ninja's hooves not far behind her.

For a few moments, there was nothing but the rush of the wind, the fresh air on her face, and the pure frantic adrenaline of the feeling of being on a powerful horse going flat out. Storm's muscles bunched beneath her. The elemental feeling of human and horse as one.

Phoebe reached the crest of the hill maybe a couple of lengths before Sam and as Storm slowed to a breathless halt, she turned in triumph in her saddle.

'We won, we won,' she shouted, laughter flooding her voice.

'Well, I'm definitely second,' Sam yelled back, gesturing at Roxie, who was still only three quarters of the way up the slope. They both waited breathlessly, the horses thoroughly excited and sweating profusely, for the young dalmatian to catch up.

'We should do this more often,' Sam said, and Phoebe thought, yes, we should. We both work too hard. We don't relax.

'Look, we're on top of the world.' Sam held out an arm as he and Ninja circled slowly around, gesturing at the panoramic view of pink heathland and the distant forest all around them.

And he was right. They were on top of the world in every sense of the word. Just for a moment, Phoebe thought she heard the sound of music and distant laughter – someone must be having a party somewhere, sound travelled miles in the forest – but she soon dismissed it. She couldn't remember the last time she'd felt so at one with nature and so totally and utterly exhilarated. Who needed a dream house when she had such a dream life?

19

May was one of Phoebe's favourite months of the year. Brown New Forest foals, with their dark manes and tails and gangly pale legs, skittered around behind their mothers. Tourists making the most of the lovely late-spring weather descended in their droves and ice cream vans set up in laybys.

Vibrant pink heather covered the stretches of heathland between the trees. The bluebells had been amazing this year. Walking along forest paths between vast carpets of blue was magical. It was impossible not to feel uplifted as Mother Nature got out her brightest palette of colours and painted the country-side in shades of pink, yellow and blue and a thousand shades of green, so that everywhere you looked there was colour.

Trees and flowers burst into bud. There were new beginnings everywhere.

Nowhere more so than at Acting the Goat in West Wellow, Phoebe thought, as she went to do a call-out one Saturday afternoon.

The patient wasn't Arthur this time, but a pregnant female called Dora. Apparently Arthur had been behaving himself lately.

When she'd called, Fliss had told her he hadn't escaped from anywhere since she'd moved him into a paddock closest to the bungalow.

'I think you were right,' she'd told Phoebe happily. 'That daft goat just wanted to be nearer to me. Between you and me, I don't bother about putting him in a field until night-time. He just follows me around the farm like a little dog. Now he can see me he doesn't seem to want to go anywhere. It's such a relief. It means we can keep him without worrying that he's going to do himself an injury.'

Phoebe loved a happy ending. She hoped her current visit would have one too. When Fliss had phoned, she'd said that Dora was struggling to give birth and she thought it was time for medical intervention. Phoebe didn't think Fliss was the overcautious type, but Phoebe had never delivered a kid. Goats weren't known for having multiple births, it was rare they had more than one or two, particularly first-time mothers, and this was Dora's first kid.

To her surprise, Fliss greeted her with a beaming smile on her face.

'I've got you out here under false pretences, Phoebe. The babies have arrived. There were triplets. Not the two we'd thought. Lord knows how we managed to miss one. They've all been scanned. No wonder Dora was struggling, bless her.'

'It's absolutely no problem. And I may as well just check her over while I'm here. I was in the vicinity anyway. And it's a lovely drive.'

'This time of year is so beautiful,' Fliss agreed happily. 'There are new beginnings literally everywhere you look.' Her face sobered a little. 'And actually, now you're here, I do have another nanny I wouldn't mind you taking a look at. I probably wouldn't have called you out especially to her, but I am a little puzzled.'

'Oh? Is she another pregnant one?'

'Er, no, although... saying that. It's probably easier if I show you.'

Phoebe followed Fliss out to the stables. Acting the Goat was an idyllic place at this time of year. The smallholding might not be very big, but it was truly beautiful. The neat patchwork of fields looked lush and there were goats and their adorable kids everywhere you looked. It was impossible not to ooh and ah over them as they went past the fields.

Once Phoebe had checked Dora and found her and the kids to be doing well, Fliss led her into one of the smaller paddocks, where she whistled, and several goats came gambolling across. There were no kids here, but a few of the goats still looked pregnant.

'It's that one there.' Fliss pointed out a small white goat not far from them. 'Her name's Mary, which is actually a very apt name for her at the moment.'

She didn't say why, just unlatched the five-bar gate to give them access into the field. Seconds later, they were beside Mary, and Fliss had caught her and was leading her back towards the gate. Phoebe could see the goat's stomach was swollen, although she wasn't as big as some of the other nannies.

'She's not very big. Is that what you're worried about? When is she due?'

'Well, yes, that is what I'm worried about. But not for the reasons you're thinking.' Fliss fondled the goat's chin and like the rest, Mary seemed to love the attention and closed her eyes dreamily. 'You see, Mary's not actually pregnant.'

'Really?' Phoebe had one of those vet moments when the world slips sideways because the owner is telling you something that clearly can't be correct. 'She, er, looks pregnant.'

'Yes, I know, but she can't be. Not unless it's an immaculate conception. Which is why I said her name's rather apt.'

'Are you sure she couldn't somehow have escaped?'

'I'm as sure as I can be. She hasn't been near a billy goat this year. When the others were being mated, she was inside. I didn't want her having kids this season. She's getting on a bit, you see. I felt she needed a break.'

Phoebe crouched down and gently examined the goat's abdomen. It was certainly swollen, although she wasn't as big as some of her contemporaries. 'How long has she been swollen up like this? When did you first notice it?'

Fliss frowned. 'Maybe three or four weeks ago. At first, I didn't think too much of it. Then I thought I might be imagining things. To be honest, it's been so hectic around here, it was easy to overlook.'

Phoebe nodded. She could imagine how hectic it was.

'I think the best thing I can do is to give her an ultrasound,' she murmured. 'Just so we can make absolutely sure there's no kid in there.'

'That would be great. Can we do that now?'

'Yes, technically we can. Although I haven't got the portable ultrasound with me, I'm afraid. It's not a problem, though. I can bring it back later.'

'Thank you.' Fliss looked worried. 'But if we find out that she's not pregnant – bearing in mind the size of her – what else could it be?'

Phoebe racked her brains. 'To be honest, I'm not exactly sure. But why don't we do the ultrasound first and rule out pregnancy?'

Phoebe phoned Seth from her car and told him about Mary.

'I'm over at the Barkers' farm in Lyndhurst,' he said. 'So I'm not a million miles away. I think I'll be finished up here in about half an hour. Would you like me to come and meet you? I've got the ultrasound scanner in my car.'

'I was hoping you might have. I was also hoping you'd be able to shed some light on what might be going on with Mary the goat. Fliss, my client, thinks we have an immaculate conception on our hands.'

'And she might be right,' Seth said with a chuckle.

'Er – what did you say?'

'I'll explain when I get there,' he said mysteriously. 'Shall we say I'll meet you back at Acting the Goat about 3 p.m.?'

'Perfect. I'll let Fliss know what's happening.'

At just after three, Phoebe and Seth met in the agreed spot. Seth locked up his car and came towards Phoebe, carrying the portable ultrasound.

'I should invest in another one of these,' Phoebe commented, 'but we only need one of them most of the time.'

'Baby season will be over soon.' Seth arched an eyebrow. 'I do like this time of year, though.'

'Me too.' They smiled at each other. 'Thanks for coming over. Fliss said she'd meet us round the back, so no need to go to the bungalow. I know which paddock Mary's in.' She paused. 'Tell me more about immaculate conceptions before we get there.'

Seth chuckled. 'More commonly known as pseudopregnancy in goats. And it is surprisingly common, especially in older nannies. The primary clinical sign is hydrometra. Build-up of fluid within the uterus. It quite often happens to mated animals but it can happen to unmated ones, too. It causes all sorts of speculation amongst the uninitiated. I'm surprised the owners haven't come across it before.'

'They've only been breeding for a couple of years. By the sound of it they had a few more kids this year than they'd planned.'

'Ah! Well, that makes sense.'

They'd been walking as they talked and had just arrived via a side gate at the rear of the bungalow.

'What a beautiful place.' Seth shielded his eyes against the afternoon sun and looked out across the paddocks. Beyond the cultured fields, the land gave way to the scrubland of the forest. A line of pylons stretched across the forest in the far distance, and on into the horizon, but there wasn't another house in sight.

'Yes, isn't it? This is the Ansteys' retirement project apparently.'

'They must have had flaming good jobs to buy a smallholding like this as their retirement project. I dread to think how much a place like this would set you back. What do you think? Two million?'

'At least.' Phoebe gave a wistful sigh. The Ansteys' smallholding was the kind of place that she and Sam dreamed about owning whilst knowing the chances of ending up with it were as remote as the stars. 'How the other half live. Mind you, they've worked hard all their lives by the sound of it. Fliss was a headmistress in North London and Neville was a master cake baker, apparently. Although I've never met Neville. I'm actually beginning to wonder if he even exists!'

'And then they ended up in the New Forest with a bunch of goats.' Seth blew out a breath. 'Isn't it amazing what people do?'

There wasn't time to say more. Fliss had spotted them and was heading across. She was accompanied by an equally tall man – the elusive Neville, Phoebe presumed – who looked younger than she'd expected. He had a ginger goatee beard, that was appropriate, she thought, and twinkly eyes.

Introductions were made.

'Neville's as curious as I am to discover why we seem to have a goat with an immaculate conception,' Fliss told them.

'Well, let's go and find out,' Phoebe said.

Ten minutes later, having given Mary, who wasn't quite as obliging as Arthur had been about being examined, an ultrasound, they'd established that she definitely wasn't pregnant.

'So what is going on?' Neville, who'd been crouched down observing the examination closely while Fliss held Mary, rocked back on his heels.

Phoebe looked at Seth. 'Would you like to tell them?'

'OK. Well, I'd say it's very likely a phantom pregnancy,' Seth said. 'Believe it or not, they're actually quite common in older nannies.'

'Oh, bless her,' Fliss exclaimed. 'So she thinks she's pregnant. Even though she's not.'

'Her body certainly does,' Phoebe agreed.

'We had a bitch who had a phantom pregnancy once,' Neville mused. 'She made a bed and she carried a toy around with her for weeks.'

'It was heartbreaking,' Fliss murmured, her eyes misting over. 'You should have seen her little face.' She and Neville exchanged glances and there was a little pause, and Phoebe sensed a changing of the mood, which up until that point had been one of curiosity and hope.

For the first time since she'd met her, the light had completely gone from Fliss's eyes and Neville's face sobered too.

Then Neville cleared his throat. 'What can we do about Mary?'

'We can give her a shot of a hormone that should sort her out,' Seth said. 'That should hopefully result in her getting rid of the excess fluid that's built up inside her. Sometimes we need to give a second injection, but usually one's enough. It should then naturally disperse.'

'Can you do that now?'

'We can,' Seth said. 'I brought the medicine with me, just in case.'

Phoebe watched him administer the shot. We live and learn, she thought. That was another thing she loved about her job. The fact that she was forever learning. Seth had told her once that he was still learning after twenty-five years and expected that to continue until the day he put down his vet bag.

'The phantom pregnancy shouldn't affect Mary's ability to breed in future,' Seth told the Ansteys and they both thanked him and Phoebe profusely.

They were ushered back to the bungalow for coffee and cake. This time it was fruit cake, gloriously moist. Seth closed his eyes in bliss as he ate it.

And then, because neither of them had any more calls, they spent a happy half hour chatting to Fliss and Neville.

They finally left just after four.

'What a lovely couple,' Seth said, as they hesitated outside their respective cars.

'Yes, aren't they?'

'Did you notice that odd moment when they were talking about their dog's phantom pregnancy?' Seth paused as he opened his car door. 'They both seemed terribly sad.'

'I did notice it, yes.'

'Maybe today triggered something for them, pressed a few buttons. Maybe they couldn't have kids of their own. The human variety, I'm talking about. There were no photos of kids in the house, were there?'

'No, but they have got grandchildren,' Phoebe said, thinking, not for the first time, how observant Seth was. 'The first time I ever met Fliss, she was painting with a grandchild.' A memory flickered at the back of her mind. 'No, actually she wasn't. She said she was painting with a great-niece.'

'That'd be her sister's grandchild, I think.'

'You might be right then,' Phoebe exclaimed. 'Gosh, that's sad. Imagine being surrounded by other people's children all your working life, but not being able to have any of your own.'

Seth was silent for a moment and Phoebe realised suddenly that he wasn't just talking about Fliss and Neville as she'd assumed, but his own life too. She'd always known Seth didn't have kids, but she'd never given much thought to the reason. She supposed she'd assumed that maybe he and Myra just hadn't wanted any. That Myra had been too tied up with her nursing career and Seth had been too tied up with being a vet for them to have time for a family.

For a second, as they stood by their cars less than a few metres apart, she didn't know what to say. Should she be offering words of comfort? She'd never felt awkward around Seth before. Before she could formulate a coherent thought, Seth broke the silence.

'I know it's just speculation…' He gestured back towards the bungalow. 'But it does put things into perspective, doesn't it? What I'm trying to say is that however good it looks on the outside, there aren't many people who have everything their hearts desire, Phoebe. Not when you take a closer look.'

20

Phoebe thought about Seth's words a lot over the next few days. It was true. Not many people had exactly what they wanted. Not having children when you'd wanted them was a biggie. If all that she and Sam were lacking was their own house, they were pretty darn lucky. And it wasn't that they couldn't *ever* buy somewhere lovely. They just had to wait a little longer than they'd planned.

Sam's maisonette was very comfortable. They had much to be grateful for.

'I couldn't agree more,' Sam said, when she voiced this to him one supper time. 'We should focus on all the good things in our lives. All the things that we are grateful for.' He reached out a hand to touch her cheek. 'People we love. Dogs, cats, great friends and families.'

'I know. And talking of families, how's your mum doing now?'

'Really good, thanks. She and Dad went out for a meal the other night. Just to their local in Bridgeford, but that's a massive step for her. And it must be good for Dad too. Getting out socially, I mean. It's been ages since they've really done very much of it.'

'That's really brilliant. I'm guessing it's easier if things are more low-key. Is that right? Is it the distance or the amount of people that makes a difference?'

'I think it's a mixture of both. We've talked about it a few times. It's hard to quantify it exactly but I think it's down to how much pressure she feels under. The more high-pressure something is, the more likely she is to have an attack.'

Phoebe thought back to Maggie's wedding, which Sam's whole family had missed, because of Jan's agoraphobia, and she nodded.

'I'm not sure agoraphobia is something you cure and that's the end of it,' Sam said. 'Like a lot of mental health issues, it's more something you learn to manage.'

'Do you think she'll be OK for *our* wedding?' It was a question she'd wanted to ask Sam for ages, but she hadn't dared to voice. In case the answer was no.

'I hope so.' He met her eyes and his were serious. 'It's really hard to call that one, isn't it? I guess it depends on so many things. When we have it. How she feels at the time. How many people there are there. Obviously I really want her to be there, but I'm not thinking about it too much at the moment.'

'It's one of the reasons we haven't set a date, isn't it?' Phoebe said softly. 'It's not just the time factor and the money factor, is it?'

'Yeah, I know.' Sam stroked Snowball, who had just leapt onto his lap for a rare cuddle. Snowball had been much more affectionate since they'd lived at Sam's full-time. 'Are you anxious to set a date?' he continued slowly. 'Has the fact we haven't set a date been bothering you? Is that why you were feeling insecure about Destiny?'

Phoebe considered this for a moment before shaking her head. She hadn't thought about Destiny lately and it jolted her a little that Sam had brought up her name. He paused from stroking Snowball and looked at her.

'I'm not feeling insecure any more. I really think that was just a blip.'

'We could set a date anyway,' Sam suggested. 'We don't have to tell everyone when it is yet.'

'We probably should. For a start, you have to book a church date months ahead. We are getting married in a church, aren't we?' She realised as she spoke that this was another thing they'd never talked about. It wasn't just the 'when', it was the 'where'.

Neither of them went to church. Neither of them was particularly religious. They'd both been brought up loosely as Christians, but their parents didn't go to church either.

'Do you have strong feelings either way about getting married in church?' Sam asked her now.

'No, I guess I don't. I think, well, I just assumed that's what we would do. Tie the knot in a pretty little church – maybe the same one as Maggie got married in – do you have strong feelings then?'

'Not really. But you're right. I hadn't really envisioned us getting hitched in a registry office. Do you think that's hypocritical?' He frowned and she reached for his hand and got a sleepy-eyed glare from Snowball when Sam stopped stroking him to take it. He was being serious, she knew. A man of integrity, Maggie had once called Sam, and it was so true. He did have a lot of integrity.

'Maybe it is hypocritical,' she said. 'I guess, like you, I haven't given it much thought. But it's not as though we're atheists, is it? I was quite happy to be godmother at the twins' christening. It just seemed the natural thing to do. And it's Vanessa Rose's christening coming up, isn't it? Did you remember to get the day off from work?'

'15 June is burned on my brain,' Sam said. 'Well, it's circled on the calendar anyway. Which is much the same thing.'

'After that I shall be godmother for three babies. That's going to be expensive when they're older. One of a godmother's duties is to buy expensive birthday and Christmas presents.'

'Is it? I thought that their main duty was to take over legal guardianship if anything happened to the parents. That would be even more expensive.'

'The role of guardian is separate from a godparent's role,' Phoebe corrected him with a grin. 'Although sometimes they can be the same person. A godparent is supposed to be a spiritual role model, and I'm not exactly sure I'm that. What with us living in sin and all.' She slanted Sam a glance to see how he was taking this conversation.

'Let's set a date for our wedding.' He didn't even miss a beat. 'What season do you fancy? Spring, summer or autumn – or winter even? We could have our wedding in an ice hotel in Lapland?'

'Brrr, no thanks.' Phoebe giggled. 'Summer for me. Tori's got the right idea about wedding dates. You can't go wrong with August.'

'So an August wedding then? Any particular date you'd like?'

Roxie, meanwhile, not wanting to miss out on a stroke while her humans were sitting down for once, had her head on Phoebe's knee.

'I also quite fancy getting married on the longest day,' Phoebe said. '20 June or 21st, whatever it is. That way the best day of our lives could also be the longest day of our lives too.'

'I'm liking that idea. All right. June next year. We'll check what day the summer solstice falls on.'

'But it can stay our secret for now,' Phoebe said. 'So as not to put any pressure on your ma.'

'It's a deal.'

* * *

Phoebe decided Maggie didn't count as far as wedding day secrets went and told her the next time she saw her at Puddleduck Farm.

Maggie clapped her hands. 'That's fantastic news, I will buy a new hat.'

'You don't wear hats.'

'You know what I mean.'

They hugged.

'Have you got a minute?' Maggie said as they drew apart. 'I'd like you to look at a neddie.'

'A neddie. Do you have a problem with one of yours?'

'Not one of mine. He came from Skegness. Do you remember that lovely Jade from Duck Pond Rescue who brought over the horse?'

'The one who came with Seth's nephew and all those yummy cookies. How could I forget?'

'I knew you wouldn't forget those cookies,' Maggie quipped, but then her face shadowed. 'The story is that Jade went to Skegness to rescue this donkey from some woman who had him in her back garden. The woman had actually rescued him herself apparently, it doesn't matter who rescued him – he's ended up here. Jade knew I had others and she phoned me for some advice. The upshot is, I offered to take him. Neddies are better when they're with their own kind. Poor little chap's not in very good condition, though. I was hoping you could help.'

'I'll grab my stethoscope.'

A few minutes later, they were standing beside the stable Maggie had used for Casey's Girl when she'd been in the habit of jumping out of her field. Fortunately, she stayed in her field these days and didn't need to be stabled.

The donkey did look sorry for himself. He was standing with his head down and his ribs stuck out through his pale grey coat.

Phoebe slipped into the stable and examined him and he submitted with a resigned acceptance.

'He's a bit thin,' she told Maggie, a few minutes later, 'but I don't think there's much else wrong with him. By the look of his teeth, he hasn't been eating properly. They need floating. A couple of them are too sharp and must be hurting him. No wonder he's thin. I'll ask Seth if he can sort that out. He's the expert.'

'Thank you. I'll introduce him to the others later. I didn't want to do that before he was checked over. Just in case.'

'How were Aiden and Jade doing?' Phoebe asked as she gave the donkey's ears one last stroke and came out of the stable. 'I liked those two.'

'Aiden didn't come this time. Jade was with another chap, Finn, I think he said his name was. He works for her, although they looked like they were a bit more than workmates to me, if you know what I mean.' Maggie's eyes were speculative. 'Not that it's any of my business, obviously. I just happened to notice that Aiden seemed quite smitten with her when they came before.'

'Yes, I noticed that too. Poor Aiden.'

'Well, Jade's very pretty and she's a sweetheart,' Maggie remarked. 'Very attractive qualities in a woman. She's probably fighting them off.'

* * *

Seth sorted out the new donkey's teeth the following morning, and agreed with Phoebe that there didn't seem to be too much wrong that some TLC and decent grazing wouldn't cure. Then he, Phoebe and Maggie introduced him to his new field mates, and by the time they left, the four donkeys seemed to have settled nicely.

'Give my best to Aiden next time you see him,' Maggie said as they walked back up towards the practice.

'Yes, me too, I hope he's well,' Phoebe added.

'I think he's all right,' Seth said. 'He's a great lad. Although he does seem to have a rather turbulent love life. Don't ask,' he added with a grin. So no one did, but Phoebe and Maggie exchanged glances. Maggie had probably been right then, about Aiden being smitten with Jade.

Phoebe decided that Tori didn't count as far as wedding date secrets went either and decided to tell her the next time they met, which was at the rehearsal for Vanessa Rose's christening, a few days before the actual event.

Tori, Harrison, Phoebe and Rufus, who was the other godparent, were all standing at the font of the small, modern church in Bridgeford where the christening was taking place. The vicar, a young, cheerful chap with a booming voice perfectly suited to sermons, had just run through the order of events.

'Is everyone clear about what's happening?' he asked them.

Everyone nodded. It was a sunny afternoon and light streamed through the big stained-glass windows and touched their faces. Vanessa Rose had barely squawked. She'd been asleep through most of the proceedings. There had been no awkwardness between Rufus and Phoebe. In fact, he'd looked happier than she'd ever seen him, Phoebe thought. Emilia hadn't come to the rehearsal. Phoebe guessed she was taking care of Archie, but Phoebe knew she would see her at the real thing next week. She missed Archie.

The vicar clapped his hands. 'Great, well, if there are no further questions, I will look forward to seeing you all again on the 15th.'

As they trooped out of the church into the sunshine-filled cemetery that encircled it, Phoebe leaned over and whispered in

Tori's ear and then Tori nearly gave the game away by squealing with excitement. 'The longest day! What a brilliant idea. Why didn't I think of that?'

'What's a brilliant idea?' Harrison asked. He was standing on Tori's other side, carrying Vanessa Rose.

'Nothing. It's a secret,' Tori told him. 'Only a temporary secret,' she added hastily.

Harrison raised his black bushy eyebrows. 'Right.'

'Can I tell him?' Tori asked. 'He's good at keeping secrets, aren't you, babe?'

'I am,' Harrison confirmed, and he and Rufus exchanged glances.

'Sam and I have set a date for our wedding. It's going to be on the longest day in June next year.'

'Cool,' Harrison said. 'Why's it a secret? Aren't you going to invite anyone?'

'Of course we are,' Phoebe said, suddenly feeling guilty she'd just told three more people. 'It's just that Sam's mother suffers with agoraphobia periodically and we're trying not to put any pressure on her. You know, by having a big build-up and all that. So I'd really appreciate it if you could all keep it to yourselves for a bit.'

'I won't be making any announcements in *New Forest Views*, don't worry,' Tori said.

'And my lips are sealed,' Rufus added. He caught her eye and smiled. 'I'm a fan of low-profile weddings, as it happens. Low profile, low pressure.' He held out his left hand and Phoebe realised that a gold ring glinted on his third finger.

'You and Emilia got married?' she gasped. 'When did that happen? And how did I miss it? I don't mean I was expecting an invitation,' she added quickly, feeling flustered. 'I'm just surprised it came and went without me hearing anything about it. Or you?' She glanced at Tori suspiciously.

'I was sworn to secrecy,' Tori said.

'We only had a handful of guests,' Rufus informed her. 'We got married in April but we decided we didn't want a big fuss. It was a good decision.' His eyes lit with warmth and Phoebe thought, wow, Emilia's been so good for him. She couldn't imagine he'd ever have strayed so far from the path of convention if his father had still been alive. There'd have been a society wedding with fanfare and photographers and months of gossip and fuss.

There was a quiet confidence about Rufus that she had never seen before. The kind of confidence people have when they're following their own path and know it's the right one.

'Congratulations, I'm so pleased for you both.'

'Thank you, Phoebe.'

'And thank you for what you did for my grandmother,' she said in a voice only loud enough for Rufus to hear.

'I was glad to be able to help.'

'You do know that Archie's welcome to come to Puddleduck whenever he likes? Just get him to text me. My number's the same as it's always been.'

'Thank you. I'll do that. He's been busy with his pony. But I'm sure he'd love to see you in the summer holidays.'

Harrison and Tori were fussing over Vanessa Rose, who'd clearly had enough of being a model baby and had just started to get more vocal.

'I think we'd better get this little one home,' Tori said, glancing at Phoebe and Rufus. 'But thank you so much for coming. And let's hope the weather stays as good as this for the real thing.'

A few minutes later, they all went their separate ways again.

Just before they separated, Tori leaned close to Phoebe. 'I'm really pleased you two have set a date. Don't worry, I won't mention it to anyone else. Have you told Maggie?'

'Yes. I probably shouldn't have. Maggie's hopeless at keeping secrets. Mind you, by the look of it, so am I. I'm amazed you didn't say a word about Rufus getting married.'

'I couldn't. Harrison would have killed me.'

'They really did want low-key then. Whose idea was that?'

'Both of them, I think.' She lowered her voice further. 'Oh, gosh, I might as well tell you. You're going to find out in a few days anyway. Emilia's pregnant. They wanted to get married before the baby was born for legal reasons. You know – the title and such-like. Apparently you have to be married before the baby's born if they're to inherit the title. Not that it matters too much because Archie's the first-born son and heir. But I suppose it would matter if anything happened to him.'

'Wow,' Phoebe said. 'No wonder Rufus looks so happy. How amazing.'

'It is. Harrison's made up for him. I know it was a terrible time when he lost his father, but it's been the making of Rufus. It really has.'

21

Tori got her wish and the day of the christening dawned bright and beautiful with pale blue skies and the promise of it being another scorcher. The south was on a mini heatwave. They'd had a week of hot weather. Flaming June was living up to her name and according to the scientists had broken even more weather records than the year before.

'I know this is probably down to climate change, but it is beautiful,' Phoebe murmured to Sam as they stood outside the small modern church the following week with the sun on their faces and birds singing everywhere in the surrounding trees.

'Yes, I do know what you mean.' He squeezed her hand. They'd just seen Emilia, who was sporting her bump proudly, with Rufus by her side. Archie was with them, of course, dressed in a smart grey suit like his father's, which made him look very grown up. An impression he ruined when he'd raced over to Phoebe as soon as he'd spotted her.

'Hi, Phoebe. Hi, Sam. Dad said you were going to be here. Did Dad tell you that Enola and I won a clear round rosette at pony club?' That was aimed at Sam. He hopped from foot to foot. Archie had never been one for keeping still much.

'Well done,' Sam said.

'And I'm getting a new brother or sister,' he added as an afterthought. 'That's pretty cool, isn't it?'

'Very cool,' Phoebe smiled at him. 'How's school?'

'Yeah, it's OK, I suppose.' Archie stuffed his hands in his pockets. 'Some lessons are better than others. I might be a vet when I grow up. Did Dad tell you that?'

'I don't think he's mentioned it, no.'

'He said I should ask you about work experience.' Archie looked at her hopefully. 'We're allowed to pick where we want to go. Can I come to Puddleduck Vets and help you?'

'Of course you can, when you're ready. I'd love to have you helping.'

Archie beamed. 'That would be so cool. Can I watch you do operations?'

'We'll have to talk about that nearer the time.'

'Wow.' His eyes were brighter than stars.

Rufus and Emilia arrived alongside Archie, and Emilia greeted Phoebe warmly. Their relationship was so different than it had been when they'd first met, Phoebe thought. They'd gone from frosty to friendship and all because of a talk they'd once had when Emilia had poured out her heart about her feelings for Rufus.

'I hear congratulations are in order,' Phoebe said, gesturing to her ring finger. 'Should we address you as Lady?'

'No,' Emilia said with a glint of amusement in her eyes. 'We don't very much use the titles.' She caught Rufus's hand. 'I'm trying to bring him into the twenty-first century, ja!'

'She's succeeding,' Rufus said. They exchanged a look of huge tenderness, which was heart-warming to see. Phoebe wondered if it was the first social event the newly married couple had been to. Tori had said it was mainly family but there were quite a few people milling about. Tori's parents were there, as were Harrison's family. Clearly a lot of bridges had been built between Harrison and his family, who for years had been estranged from him. Phoebe recognised a few of them from Rufus and Emilia's New Year's Eve party. It was amazing how a baby could reunite people.

Laura, who worked for Tori, as her assistant editor, was there, and a few of Tori's other friends from work. Maggie and Eddie were there too, and Phoebe's parents. Frazier and Alexa had planned to come too but one of the twins was ill so they'd sent their apologies last minute.

Sam's parents had sent their apologies too. Phoebe guessed the prospect of mixing with people had felt too much for Jan and she sympathised. As Sam had said, agoraphobia was an unpredictable illness. But there were enough people here, Phoebe thought, to make it special and memorable without it being overcrowded.

During the rehearsals, Phoebe hadn't felt particularly emotional, but today as the vicar read out the solemn words of the christening promises, his voice filling the church, it hit her more forcibly. Sam was right. Being a godmother meant so much more than just buying expensive gifts on birthdays and Christmases. And although Phoebe still didn't think she was a very good example of a spiritual role model, she felt so moved she had to brush away a tear.

Maybe it was because being a godmother meant that someone had utter faith in her, she thought. Trusted her enough to look after their child if they couldn't do it any more.

The short service was soon over. Vanessa Rose, looking beautiful in a cream lacy christening gown that had once belonged to Tori's grandmother, was noisier than she'd been at the rehearsals.

She wasn't keen on having water splashed over her and voiced her disapproval loudly, but, other than that, things went without a hitch.

'Penny for them,' Sam asked Phoebe when they were outside the church again. 'You've gone all quiet and reflective.'

She told him and he caught her hand and squeezed her fingers. 'We'll be doing this one day.'

'I hope so. We can ask Tori and Harrison to be godparents for our child.'

'We can.'

She wondered if he minded about being passed over for the job of being godfather to Vanessa Rose in favour of Rufus. He'd certainly never mentioned it. Sam was so stoic. So wonderfully calm and accepting of what life threw at him. She had never seen him get really angry about anything. Or really upset. He just took everything in his stride.

The expression, 'It is what it is,' could have been made for Sam.

'Right, everyone, listen up!' Harrison's call to attention hushed the buzz of chatter outside the church. 'We're heading back to ours for nibbles. Does anyone need directions?'

Maggie and Eddie excused themselves from the nibbles on the grounds they had to get back to the animals. But Maggie came to speak to Phoebe before she went.

'Just over a year till you and Sam tie the knot. Do you think you should send out save the date cards?'

'Shush, that's supposed to be a secret.'

'I'm speaking really quietly.' Maggie beamed at her.

'Not that quietly. But yes, maybe we should.'

Louella, who was within earshot, came across too. 'I've been thinking about Jan,' she told her daughter. 'Surely if you spring a wedding on her at the last minute it will be even more pressure than if she has a year or so to get used to the idea. And you will have to plan it all, Phoebe. You can't do all of that in secret. Jan wouldn't want you to either. Not if I know Jan.'

And her mother did know Jan, Phoebe thought. Their friendship went back to a time before she and Sam were even born. 'I think you're probably right,' she said. 'I'll have a chat with Sam over the weekend. See what he thinks. We still haven't booked a venue, but it's clearly not a secret anyway now. So maybe we should just get on with it.'

'That sounds sensible.' Louella looked relieved.

Maggie and Eddie said their goodbyes.

'See you on Monday, love.'

'Have a good rest of the weekend,' Phoebe said. She knew her family were right. It had been a mad idea wanting to keep their wedding date a secret when all she actually wanted to do was to shout it from the rooftops and start planning everything. She hugged her grandmother and Eddie goodbye. She was feeling all emotional again.

During the service, a WhatsApp message had come through on her phone. The dalmatian puppy group she was on along with the owners of Roxie's siblings were inviting her, Sam and Roxie for a one-year celebration of the pups' first birthday. No one knew exactly what date this was, as they'd arrived in a box at Puddleduck Pets minus their mother, but the party date was the last Saturday in July.

She showed Sam as they got into their car to drive to Tori and Harrison's.

'That's a nice idea,' he said. 'Yes, that sounds lovely. Count me in.'

* * *

'I enjoyed today,' Sam said, when they were finally home again and snuggling on the sofa with a delighted Roxie. 'It was a lovely christening. Really warm and personal. That vicar was good.'

'I agree on both counts. Although it was a shame Frazier and Alexa couldn't be there with the twins.'

They hadn't stayed too long at the party afterwards, because they'd wanted to get back for Roxie, but that had been lovely too. Balloons, party nibbles, and a lot of laughter.

Just before they'd left, Tori had given Phoebe a box-shaped gift-wrapped package. 'That's to say thank you for being a godmother to Vanessa Rose,' she'd said, her eyes shiny. 'We've had such a lovely day.'

'I've loved it too,' Phoebe had said. 'I feel really honoured that you asked me. Thank you.'

Remembering the present now, Phoebe opened her bag and retrieved it. 'Did you see what Tori and Harrison gave me?'

'What is it?'

'Let's open it and see.' Phoebe ripped off the Noah's Ark wrapping paper and discovered the box contained a bottle of her favourite scent. 'That's perfect timing. I ran out about a month ago. Tori is so thoughtful.'

Liberating the bottle from its box, she sprayed it liberally on her wrist and Sam sniffed the air appreciatively. 'That's such a Phoebe scent.'

'Isn't it? I love it.' Phoebe felt suddenly queasy. Frowning, she got up from the sofa and dashed towards the loo with her hand over her mouth. She only just made it. Flushing the loo and feeling slightly shocked, she splashed water over her face. What on earth had that been about?

'I think I may have eaten something that didn't agree with me,' she said, going back into the lounge to see a concerned-looking Sam.

'That's not good. How do you feel now?'

'I feel fine now. How bizarre. I've usually got a cast-iron stomach. Nothing upsets me.'

'I know,' he said, raising his eyebrows. 'What did you eat?'

'A couple of little sandwiches, cheese I think, and I had a samosa and a couple of other spicy Indian snacks.'

'I ate most of those things too.' He stood up and came across to her. 'Can I get you anything? A glass of water?'

'I'm fine, Sam, honestly. Maybe it was over-excitement. It's been a full-on day. I've felt quite emotional.'

She decided now wasn't the time to tell him what Maggie and Louella had said about weddings. She was really tired too. They could talk about all that properly tomorrow.

'I'll have an early night. I'm sure I'll be right as rain tomorrow.'

* * *

To Phoebe's relief, the sickness didn't recur. She woke up the next morning feeling a little bit fragile, but she wasn't sick. Maybe her body had got rid of whatever it had been that had upset her stomach. That was a relief. She was rarely ill. She'd always been blessed with the constitution of an ox, which Maggie had put down to being brought up on a dairy farm and living on a diet of home-cooked food and plenty of fresh air. Not that Phoebe and her brother Frazier had actually been brought up on the farm, but they'd spent huge amounts of time there. Frazier wasn't ill very often either.

Mind you, neither were the twins usually, and they'd obviously had some kind of bug which had stopped them going to the christening. Maybe she had somehow caught that.

Phoebe didn't think anything more of it. But then on Monday

morning, just as she was changing into her scrubs for work, it happened again. She was overcome with nausea and had to rush to the cloakroom. When she came out, she bumped into Jenna on her way back from an examining room.

'You OK, love?' Jenna's motherly face was creased up with concern.

'Um – yes, I'm good. I don't know what's going on. I was sick at the weekend. I thought it was something I'd eaten...'

'You're not pregnant, are you?' Jenna quipped.

Phoebe felt a blast of shock. Oh my God, was that even possible? She and Sam were really careful. She was on the pill. She was on the type that had to be to be taken at the same time each day but her out-of-hours calls meant that sometimes she'd been late and very occasionally she missed one. She didn't think that had happened lately. Oh, crap. Her mind raced with possibilities.

Jenna was backtracking quickly. 'Sorry, it's none of my business.'

'I... er...' It wasn't often that Phoebe was lost for words. 'I don't think so but... blimey, anything's possible. I know it sounds completely mad, considering what we do, but that hadn't even occurred to me.' She took a deep shaky breath. 'Please keep this conversation to yourself.'

'Of course I will. I won't breathe a word,' Jenna said, her face sobering. 'Do you know when your last period was?'

'No. I need to check my diary. It's on my phone.'

'Is that in your bag? Shall I go and get your bag?' They could hear voices in reception. Marcus and Max must have just arrived.

'Yes, please. Thanks, Jenna.'

Phoebe closed her eyes and tried to steady herself with deep breathing while Jenna disappeared to fetch her bag.

22

It seemed to take ages. Phoebe paced the small corridor. She could hear Jenna saying good morning to the guys and then her footsteps coming back along the corridor. Every sound was louder than usual. Phoebe decided she must be in shock – and that was just at the prospect of being pregnant. Oh my God, what if it wasn't just a possibility but was actually a fact?

Jenna arrived with her bag and handed it over wordlessly and Phoebe thanked her. It took her about thirty seconds of diary checking to establish that she was actually six days late.

She told Jenna quietly. 'I know that doesn't necessarily mean anything, does it? It could be something else.'

'It could.' Jenna nodded vigorously but her eyes were doubtful. 'I take it you and Sam haven't been trying.'

'Jeez, no. There's too much else going on at the moment. What with work and trying to decide where we're going to live, and stuff...' She threw her hands up in the air in a gesture of overwhelm. 'Crap. I don't know what to do. I need to take a test.'

'And I'm guessing you want to do that as soon as you can?'

'Yes. Do you know what my schedule's like this morning?'

'Quite busy. Do you want me to shift things around? Or I could nip out to the chemist and get you a test if you like?'

Phoebe thought fast. 'No, don't worry. It's OK. If I am, I am. Nothing's going to have changed by lunchtime. I'll nip out then.'

Jenna patted her arm in a gesture of sisterly solidarity. 'It'll be OK. It'll all be fine. You'll see, love.'

The utter kindness in her voice made Phoebe want to burst into tears. Blimey, being pregnant would also explain the emotional overwhelm she'd been feeling for the last few days. The slightest little thing had been setting her off. She swallowed hard. 'Thanks, Jenna. Thanks for being so lovely. I'd better get my professional head back on.'

'Absolutely. I'll go and get the coffee on. Have you gone off coffee at all? That was one of the first signs for me. I couldn't stand the smell. In fact, it wasn't just coffee. There were loads of smells that made me feel sick.'

'I haven't gone off coffee.' Phoebe felt a dart of hope before she remembered that Tori hadn't gone off coffee either when she was pregnant. She'd drunk decaf all the way through with Vanessa Rose.

Jenna headed back out into reception and Phoebe went back into the cloakroom so she could gather herself for a few minutes. On Saturday night, the scent of her own favourite perfume had set off her nausea. All of the signs that she might be pregnant were there. She just hadn't realised what they meant.

'Stop it,' she told her reflection in the cloakroom mirror, as her hazel eyes stared anxiously back at her. She couldn't be pregnant. Please don't let her be pregnant. Much as she and Sam wanted a family, now would be very bad timing.

She wasn't sure quite how she managed to switch into professional mode, but she did it. That morning, she diagnosed an ear infection in a rabbit, talked to an owner about the pros and cons of spaying a house cat, and did an elderly dog's health check. She managed to join in with the usual office banter with Marcus and Max and she talked to Seth about his cases too. It was actually easier to have something to distract her. Every time there was a break, her head ran into 'what if?' mode.

But finally, morning surgery was over and she clipped on Roxie's lead and told her staff she was heading off for a walk and that she might have to nip home.

Jenna had fixed it so that she didn't have another appointment until 2.30 p.m., which meant she'd have time to get the test and nip back to Bridgeford to do it, before having to head back into the fray. She decided to go back to Sam's for a bit. Then, if she did find she was pregnant, she had the option of calling by Hendrie's to let him know.

Everything went according to plan. Phoebe bought a test at the supermarket to avoid the dilemma of who she might meet at the pharmacy. She knew one of the pharmacists quite well, whereas the supermarket was nicely anonymous.

Finally, she was at the maisonette, sitting on the closed loo seat with the pregnancy test in front of her on the edge of the bath. She'd bought a pack of two. They'd had a special offer and she figured she might need more than one. Although modern pregnancy testers were amazingly sensitive and could pick up the presence of the hCG hormone about a week after fertilisation, she supposed she could mess up the test, and she couldn't bear to go through a single extra minute of not knowing one way or the other.

The test, apparently, took three minutes to work. Phoebe tapped her fingers on the side of the bath while she waited. She'd bought the kind of test that said pregnant or not pregnant. An idiot-proof test.

Pregnant or not pregnant. The words alternated in her head.

What was Sam going to say? Would he blame her for missing a pill? Would he be cross? No, Sam didn't do cross. Not with her. She wasn't totally sure he'd be delighted either. This was definitely not in their five-year plan. They didn't have a five-year plan. OK, their one-year plan.

What would she do about work? She'd need to stop – at least for a little while – as she couldn't take a baby to work. How was that going to pan out? She couldn't just abandon the practice either. They'd only just established a routine with Seth. And until they moved into Tori's old rental, which they couldn't until Tori and Harrison moved out, she and Sam still didn't even have anywhere permanent to live. A flight of stairs was hard enough with Roxie. It would be harder still lugging a baby and a buggy up and down every time they wanted to go anywhere. She thought of the reams of baby paraphernalia that Tori carted about everywhere for Vanessa Rose. The practicalities were overwhelming. Her head hurt with thinking about them.

The three-minute timer she'd set on her phone hadn't gone off, but she sneaked a glance back at the test. There was a word on it already. She grabbed it and saw what every instinct she had had known to be true. She was pregnant.

She waited the extra thirty seconds of the timer, just in case the word 'not' materialised in front of the word 'pregnant', but it didn't happen. However hard she looked at the test, the result was definitely the same. Phoebe stayed where she was on the loo seat, her feet drawn up in front of her, ensconced in a little bubble of shock.

It was the sound of Roxie whining on the other side of the door that galvanised her into action. She gathered up both tests and went to see to her.

'Oh, my darling, I'm sorry. You must wonder what on earth's going on. You thought we were going for a walk, then you had to sit in the car, then we got back and I didn't even take you in the garden. I'm so sorry.'

Roxie wagged her tail, utter adoration in her eyes, and Phoebe bent and kissed the top of her soft head. 'Let's go in the garden, eh?'

A few minutes later, she and Roxie were in Sam's long back garden. It may be a faff having to walk around the side of the house before being able to let Roxie off the lead, but it was a beautiful garden, Phoebe thought, as she walked along the path that ran down the middle of it. The grass was too long, Sam hadn't had time to mow it for a couple of weeks, which meant it was scattered with dandelions, buttercups and daisies. The rose bushes that Sam loved were in full bloom. Their velvet petals glowed in the sun and their sweet scent drifted on a tiny breeze. Phoebe was relieved to find they didn't make her sick. So it wasn't every smell then. Instinctively she cupped her hands around her tummy. It was hard to believe there was a new life in there. She tried to imagine how big it would be – the size of a lentil, maybe? Or a pea? She realised she had no idea. She still couldn't quite compute what had happened. Maybe every woman felt like this. Every woman who hadn't meant to get pregnant, anyway. Every woman who had thought that it might happen one day but had still assumed that 'one day' was at some far-off point in the future.

Roxie was sniffing around a tree at the foot of the garden when Phoebe heard the small back gate clang behind her. She and Roxie both turned at the same time, and then Roxie was heading in a streak of waggy-tailed joy to greet the new arrival. It was Sam, Phoebe saw, wondering what strange synchronicity had brought him home for lunch today too.

'Hey, Pheebs,' he called across to her. 'I just saw you out here from the kitchen window. Everything OK? Did you just fancy a break from work? You're not still feeling sick, are you?'

'No. Oh, Sam.' She went to meet him at a slightly slower pace than Roxie had done. 'I came home because I wanted to take a pregnancy test. In case I might be pregnant – you know – after Saturday night. I was sick again this morning, you see, and I checked my diary and...'

'And have you?' His face was suddenly very still. 'Taken a test, I mean?'

'Yes... I'm pregnant. That's what the test said. I'm still trying to get my head around it, Sam. I only did it about ten minutes ago.' She searched his eyes and saw shock there – the same shock she'd felt when she'd realised what the cause of her symptoms might be. It was gone almost immediately.

'Bloody hell,' Sam said. 'That's – wow – that's amazing. You're actually pregnant.' He held out his arms. 'Oh, wow, Pheebs...'

'You're not cross.' She went into his arms slowly, and he held her for a second and then stood back again, holding her at arm's length.

'Why on earth would I be cross?' He frowned. 'I'm blown away. Shocked, yes, but no, of course not cross... How do you feel about it?'

'Pretty much the same. But I don't have a clue what to do. I'm still trying to process it, to be honest.'

'I bet. Do you know how much pregnant? How late are you?'

'No more than a week, which means it's really early days. We'd have to work it out to be precise. My head's spinning too much to think about it at the moment.'

'Of course it is. Come here. Let me hold you.' They hugged again and she leaned against the warm solidity of him, breathing in the faint smell of aftershave, the familiar smell of him until Roxie gave a small bark, anxious to be part of the action too.

They broke apart and Sam bent to stroke the dalmatian.

Phoebe crouched down and stroked her too, and they looked at each other again over their dog.

'I've got to get back to work,' Phoebe said. 'I've got an appointment at 2.30 p.m.'

'I should get back too.'

'We can talk about this properly later. Don't say anything to your mum yet, will you?'

'No, of course not.' He kissed her. 'Everything will be all right. I love you.'

'I love you too, Sam.'

23

Phoebe didn't feel quite as positive as Sam about the fact that it would all be OK. But she managed to get her professional head on for the afternoon. She was working with Jenna and when they had a moment alone in the examining room between clients, she told her the result of the test.

Jenna nodded. 'At least you know what the score is now.' Her eyes were soft. 'Are you OK?'

'Yes, I am, thanks. I saw Sam at lunchtime. We'll be fine. But we need to keep it to ourselves until after the twelve-week scan.'

'I won't breathe a word to anyone.'

Phoebe knew she wouldn't. Jenna's middle name was 'dependable' and like the rest of her team, Phoebe would have trusted her with her life. It was hugely important to her to work with people she liked, respected and trusted, and she was really glad of that today.

As she left the practice just before the end of the day, having arranged to go slightly earlier than usual, Marcus, who was a natural empath and not just with the animals he adored, asked her if she was all right.

'I'm fine, Marcus. Why?'

'You just seemed a bit down. Not your usual bubbly self.'

'I think maybe I'm a bit tired.'

'On a Monday. That's not good,' he chided gently.

'I know.' She gripped her bag a little tighter, feeling vulnerable, even though the test kits were no longer in there and no one could possibly have seen them but her. Swiftly, she changed the subject back to him. 'How are you and Natasha doing? We haven't had a chance to catch up lately, have we?'

'We're good, boss, thank you.' He paused. 'Did Tori tell you we're hoping to buy Woodcutter's Cottage? We've just put in an offer.'

'Oh my goodness. No, she didn't.' Phoebe looked at him in amazement, shocked they could afford a place like Woodcutter's. It might be only a tiny two-up, two-down cottage but it was in a fabulous location and the price reflected it.

Although, come to think of it, she did have a vague memory of Natasha mentioning they were looking for a house together last year.

It had been around the time when she and Sam were contemplating taking on Roxie, who'd been one of four puppies dumped at Puddleduck Pets. The conversation had stuck in her mind because Natasha had said she and Marcus were going to get settled with their own place before adopting any animals that needed a home.

They were doing things in the right order. The sensible order, Phoebe had thought at the time, whereas she and Sam had leapt in and rehomed Roxie before they were even living in the same place. And now they were going to have a baby too and they still hadn't found a suitable home together. Talk about topsy-turvy.

Interpreting her silence as curiosity, Marcus added, 'Natasha's

Uncle Roger died back in January, and he left her some money, so we've got a great deposit.'

'Gosh. Wow. I mean, that's sad for Natasha, but great about the inheritance.'

'Yup. He was a nice old chap – loved animals, same as Natasha, and he didn't have any kids of his own. He stipulated in his will that Natasha use some of the money to help animals in need. Which of course she would anyway.' Marcus looked animated. 'The first thing we're going to do when we've bought Woodcutter's is to rehome Saddam.'

'Oh, how brilliant.' Phoebe clapped her hands together. 'That's the best news ever. When will you find out if your offer's been accepted?'

'Today, hopefully. Tori's phoning us later.'

'Well, fingers crossed,' Phoebe said. 'I'd better go before my early finish turns into a normal time finish.'

'Sure. Sorry, boss. See you tomorrow.'

'See you tomorrow, Marcus.'

Having told Jenna to keep the pregnancy news to herself, which Phoebe knew she would, Phoebe realised there was no way they were going to be able to keep it a secret from everyone for three months. If Marcus had sensed that something was wrong with her in just one day then Maggie would work it out as soon as they had a conversation, Phoebe thought guiltily.

Sam had arranged for someone else to sort out Ninja tonight so they could sit down and discuss things properly, but Phoebe discovered she'd beaten him back. Unable to settle, she took Roxie for a walk straight from the house. It wasn't the same as walking from Woodcutter's, where there had been a handy woodland at the back of the house, but they weren't far from a recreation park which abutted the river and once there, Phoebe let Roxie off the lead to play.

Roxie was great with most other dogs now despite her shaky start at dog training and before long she'd found a friendly Red Setter to play with. The woman who owned it was pushing a buggy and Phoebe fell into conversation with her.

'How old's your little one?'

'Six months. Aren't you, trouble?' The woman smiled as they both peered into the pram.

'He's gorgeous,' Phoebe said automatically because that was what you were supposed to say, wasn't it? Even when the baby was grim-faced and scowling.

'She's a she,' the woman corrected. 'Her name's Daisy. She's my little flower.'

'Sorry,' Phoebe said, despite the fact she'd never seen a baby who looked less like a little flower. The baby glared at her and started to cry.

'Hello, sweetie.' Phoebe tried again.

The baby cried louder.

'She's teething, I expect.' The woman produced a tube of something from her pocket, squeezed some onto her finger and rubbed it on the baby's gums, which seemed to settle her.

'Teething gel,' she told Phoebe happily.

Phoebe gulped. It was a whole new world she knew nothing about.

'We're off to feed the ducks in a minute, aren't we, poppet? Daisy loves the ducks. Do you have any children yourself?'

'Er, no, not yet. We're still in the, um, planning stages.'

'Don't rush into it. They tip your life completely upside down.' She glanced over at Roxie and her Red Setter, who were still playing. 'Dogs are much easier,' she added.

Phoebe forced a smile as her newfound companion recalled her dog, fastened its lead and said goodbye. Daisy had stopped crying now and they walked off into the evening sunshine, towards the river.

Roxie ran back towards Phoebe when her playmate had gone and Phoebe gave her a treat. *We're in the planning stage.* Why had she said that? She and Sam certainly hadn't done any planning. Earlier on she'd found a date of birth calculator online and she'd worked out that her due date was 15 February. They'd have a baby before they were married. Not that this mattered to Phoebe in the slightest. But it would be much better if they had somewhere permanent to live first. If they weren't doing that topsy-turvy thing again.

Phoebe clipped on Roxie's lead and they walked home over the bridge that spanned the river that gave the market town its name. If she and Sam stayed in Bridgeford, they could take their baby to feed the ducks too. They could push him or her in a buggy and Roxie could run alongside and they would be a family. Like all the other families around.

Maggie would be absolutely delighted when she heard the news. Mum and Dad would be thrilled too. And Phoebe knew that their baby could grow up with his or her cousins – Alexa's third baby was due in July – and Vanessa Rose. There wouldn't be that many months between any of them. Just as she had grown up with Tori and Sam.

Maybe it wasn't such terrible timing after all.

'Hello, my two favourite girls,' Sam greeted them when they got back. 'I was wondering where you'd got to.'

'I'm sorry. We went for a walk to the park and I got chatting to this woman with a baby and I lost track of time.'

'I'm not telling you off.' He caught her hands. 'I haven't been back long either. I bought us celebration doughnuts, and I've put on some coffee. Is coffee OK?'

'Decaf coffee's fine. Are we celebrating, then?'

'I think so.' Sam's eyes met hers. 'Aren't we? Let's sit down and chat it all through.'

A few minutes later they were sitting on Sam's squashy comfortable sofa with Roxie alongside them and a plate of doughnuts on the table.

'How are you feeling?' he asked. 'Are you still in shock?'

'I think I probably am. I... I just... well – it was the last thing on my mind. Us having a baby. I thought we'd have years. Well, not years because I'm thirty-seven and I know that's not exactly young to start a family. I'm not a spring chicken. But we didn't plan it and we haven't even got anywhere sorted out properly to live.' A well of emotion rushed into her throat and she burst into tears and for a few moments she couldn't stop.

He was beside her in an instant, his arms wrapping around her. 'Hey, hey, Pheebs. Don't cry. It'll be OK. We'll be fine. Maybe it's a good thing. Mother Nature giving us a prod to get on with it – huh? Have you thought of it like that?'

'I don't know what I think. I'm sorry, Sam. I'm all over the place.' He was stroking her forehead and she leaned into his embrace, feeling like a child herself. She wanted to suck her thumb. 'Baby hormones,' she said.

'Of course – they must be swilling about all over the place.'

'I feel like my brain isn't my own.'

'I bet.'

For a few moments, they stayed close together on the sofa and slowly Phoebe started to feel better again. She sat up.

'Sorry, this is all about me. How do you feel, Sam?'

'I was shocked too. Obviously. But now I've had a chance to let the news settle, I think I feel pleased. You're right. We're not spring chickens. Why not now?'

'Because our lives are chaotic and busy. Because we don't have anywhere to live. Because we haven't even planned our wedding yet.'

'We're busy. I'll grant you that. But we do have somewhere to live. And the fact that we haven't planned our wedding down to the last detail could be a bonus.' His eyes were questioning.

'Because we can change it, you mean?'

'Exactly.'

'We can put it off until later in the year.' Her heart sank a little at the prospect. 'Or we can do what Rufus and Emilia did and bring it all forward,' he murmured. 'Have a secret wedding. Tori told me they actually got married in a tree house. They had virtually no guests because they couldn't get them up there. And their wedding car was a yellow cherry picker. How romantic is that?'

His eyes were shining with expectation and Phoebe was pretty sure he was talking about the yellow cherry picker being romantic, rather than the tree house, but even so, his enthusiasm was infectious.

'Oh, Sam. You are lovely. And I would marry you tomorrow, you know that. But I think if we did what Rufus and Emilia did and didn't tell anyone we'd be in serious trouble.'

'We'd be in serious trouble with Maggie, you're right there. And to be honest, I think my ma would have something to say about it if we didn't invite her – agoraphobia or no agoraphobia. Besides…' He swallowed. 'I'd got this romantic notion of us riding off into the sunset on Ninja's back.'

'Both of us? Poor Ninja.'

'Well, I thought we might have a horse each. Although that wouldn't be a good idea. Not now you're pregnant. We'd be better off in a carriage.'

'Yes, I agree. Actually, I'm surprised Rufus let Emilia climb up a tree in her condition.'

'She didn't. She was in the cherry picker.'

'Oh my goodness. I see. Was that any safer?'

'Apparently it was. I was chatting to Harrison at the christening. He was explaining the logistics.'

Sam would never cease to surprise her, Phoebe thought, shaking her head. 'I don't mind if we get married before or after we have our baby.' She cupped her hands around her tummy. 'Who is due, by the way, in the middle of February. And as we're not planning to get married until 21 June, it could still work. I'll have about four months to lose my baby weight. Celebrities do it all the time.' She frowned. 'But that's me being vain.'

'You'll look beautiful regardless. You always look beautiful.' Sam put his hand over hers on her tummy. 'I can't believe we're going to have a baby, Pheebs. I can't believe I'm going to be a dad.' His voice cracked a little. 'I can't wait. It's the most wonderful, fantastic news I've ever had.'

There were tears in his eyes and Phoebe felt a lump in her own throat so big that she couldn't speak either.

He kissed her and she breathed in his familiar scent and closed her eyes and laid her head on his shoulder.

Sam stroked her hair. 'We don't have to decide the whole future today. Let's just enjoy now for a little while.'

24

Phoebe and Sam agreed they wouldn't tell anyone they were pregnant until after the twelve-week scan, which would be sometime around the end of July or beginning of August.

'Not even Tori or Maggie?' Sam had asked her curiously.

'Well, I might not wait for the whole twelve weeks, but I'll definitely wait a little while. Just because I don't want to tempt fate.'

And as the last days of June went by and July began, Phoebe felt glad they hadn't told anyone. Being pregnant was something that was never far from her mind, but she loved the fact that it was her secret; hers and Sam's.

Jenna, who also knew of course, didn't mention it again, apart from occasionally, when there was a quiet moment, to ask her how she was feeling.

'I'm feeling great,' Phoebe usually told her, and it was true. To her relief, the morning sickness, which didn't restrict itself to mornings, eased off after the first month, or maybe she just got better at managing it.

Coffee didn't trigger it either, although she was careful what she ate and drank now and she did become a fan of ginger tea, which was very stomach settling.

Phoebe got into the habit of talking to her baby, telling it things every morning about where they were going and what they were doing.

'Today we're going to go food shopping and get things that are good for you to eat. Well, I'm going to be eating them, but you're going to be eating them too because you're inside me and you have to eat the same as I do.'

She found a chart which showed the growth rate of the tiny life growing inside of her. At seven weeks it was the size of a blueberry, at eight weeks the size of a raspberry, and at nine weeks the size of a grape.

So this became part of their conversations too. 'Today we're going to a farm to see a cow with mastitis. Cows are big black and white animals that go moo. You're only the size of a grape. I don't suppose you can imagine something as big as a cow but one day I'm going to show you one for real.'

Phoebe had no sense of whether her baby was a boy or a girl. She'd wondered prior to being pregnant if it was possible to know this on some level, if your body could somehow tell and your mind could then work it out – she'd always been very intuitive – but she didn't know. At least not yet. She swung between boy and girl with equal certainty. Maybe when the baby was bigger it would become clearer.

Neither she nor Sam minded what the gender was. 'As long as he or she is healthy,' Sam said. 'That's all that matters.'

That's all that mattered to Phoebe too, although she was aware that at thirty-seven she was an older mother. This wasn't as scary a prospect as it would have been a few years earlier, although her doctor had told her there was a slightly higher risk of chromosomal conditions and miscarriage.

'I wouldn't worry too much,' he had added. 'You're fit and healthy and about 25 per cent of babies are born to mothers older than thirty-five, these days.'

So Phoebe didn't worry too much. There was no reason to suspect she'd have any serious problems. She was more concerned about how she was going to cover her maternity leave. Maybe she could employ a locum vet. It was something she'd plan after the twelve-week scan. Everything would be much easier when they could tell everyone she was pregnant.

In the meantime, she and Sam talked through how it would work. He had already offered to be a stay-at-home dad, but neither of them could see how that was going to work out with Ninja. Sam had mooted the idea of selling his horse, but Phoebe hated the thought of him giving up Ninja. In the end, Sam had agreed to wait until they were a bit further down the line before making a final decision. They'd also agreed they would delay their wedding date, and Phoebe had cancelled the church and cited family reasons to the vicar.

Fortunately, none of her family had mentioned the wedding lately, largely because Phoebe hadn't seen any of them. She'd even managed to avoid Maggie, which hadn't been hard, as she and Eddie had been on a summer holiday to Italy, while Natasha covered things at Puddleduck Pets. At least she and Sam were both happy with the prospect of moving into the Bridgeford rental as soon as Tori and Harrison had vacated it.

While Maggie was away, Phoebe had a surprise visitor in the form of Archie, who appeared at the practice one lunchtime.

Phoebe was clearing up after her last client of the morning when Jenna came to tell her Archie was sitting in the waiting room, and Phoebe dashed out to see him.

'Hello, Archie. Is everything OK? None of your animals are sick, are they?'

'Nope.' He jumped up from his seat and she saw he'd been reading a leaflet, entitled, 'Your new puppy.'

She glanced at it questioningly. 'I didn't know you were getting a puppy?'

'We're not. We're going to rehome a dog. That's if Maggie's got one suitable. I've okayed it with Dad, don't worry.' His eyes sparkled. 'Dad agrees with me that it's better to get a young dog that really needs a home than buy a new puppy from a breeder who might not be kosher.'

'Is that right?' It was a rhetorical question. Phoebe knew where that was coming from. Rufus had once bought Archie a lop-eared rabbit from a very dubious breeder, although she had to admit she couldn't imagine Rufus ever saying the word 'kosher'.

Her heart swelled with warmth. This was so like Archie too – wanting to help an animal in need.

'So have you seen one you like?'

'No, I thought you might like to come and have a look with me. If you've got time?'

'Of course I've got time.'

They spent a happy half hour walking up and down the kennel block and Archie stopped and read several of the cards Maggie had attached to the front of each kennel.

His favourite was a young lurcher bitch with a soft grey coat and dark trusting eyes. Her name was Chloe and before very long, they'd got her lead from Natasha and had gone up to the neddie field to walk her around.

'Who's the new donkey?' Archie asked as they paused at the five-bar gate.

'His name's Richard. The woman who rescued him named him after her late husband, apparently.'

'Poor thing.' Archie screwed up his face, which Phoebe assumed was a reaction to the donkey having an odd name, rather than the woman losing her husband, although you never could tell with Archie.

Casey's Girl whinnied a greeting when she saw them. It was a shame she was still here with just the neddies for company. Phoebe wondered if she was lonely.

Chloe pricked her ears at the sound of the horse and Archie stroked the dog's head. 'She likes horses then. That's a result. I'm hoping I can take her riding with me.'

'I'm sure she would love that,' Phoebe said, as they strolled around the field with Chloe behaving like an angel, walking sedately on a loose lead and stretching out her delicate pointy snout to sniff the occasional patch of grass.

Casey's Girl ambled over to say hello and she and Chloe touched noses.

'Look at that,' Archie said in delight. 'They like each other.' He stroked Casey Girl's neck. 'Doesn't anyone want her? I thought she would have gone to a good home by now.'

'I did too. But she has some issues.' She told Archie how Casey's Girl had once belonged to a film company and had been taught to rear on command. 'Marcus has done a lot of work with her, but I think it still puts people off.'

'My friend Jack is looking for another horse,' Archie said thoughtfully. 'I'll tell him about Casey's Girl. He's super experienced and so are his whole family.'

Phoebe nodded, remembering when she'd gone to do a vet check on Archie's mare, Enola. She'd met Jack and his parents then and Archie was right, they were very experienced horse people.

'Thanks, it would be great if you could mention Casey's Girl.'

For a few moments they walked around the field with Chloe, all of them enjoying the sunshine and balmy air. It was Phoebe who broke the silence.

'How's Emilia doing?'

'She's massively huge and she can't bend over. She said she'll be glad when the baby's here. It's not coming till October, though, and it will be too small to be interesting for ages.'

Phoebe smiled. That would be her in the not-too-distant future. She couldn't wait.

They walked back to the kennel block and Phoebe listened as Archie told Natasha he would like to provisionally reserve Chloe.

'Dad says he's got to approve my final decision,' Archie said solemnly. 'So is it OK if we come back later?'

'Yes, of course it is. But is Chloe your final decision?' Natasha asked equally solemnly. 'You don't want to take another dog out to try?'

Archie shook his head. 'I don't want to get their hopes up, although I do like Spot, too,' he confessed, gesturing to a small black and white terrier in the pen next to Chloe, 'and it says on the card that she and Chloe are best friends, but I'm not sure Dad will let me have two.' His eyes narrowed speculatively. 'I suppose I could ask.' His eyes brightened as if he'd just thought of something. 'I'll sound things out with Dad.'

* * *

A couple of days later, Archie and Rufus came into Puddleduck Vets to buy flea and wormer treatment and to register their new dogs.

'Dogs?' Phoebe questioned, glancing at Rufus.

'Mmmm, dogs,' Rufus said. 'Trust Archie to get two dogs that needed to be rehomed together. Although Harrison said a dog like Spot will be very handy to have around – terriers are excellent ratters. And he does have the summer holidays to train them.'

Phoebe glanced at Archie, who threw her a look that begged her not to contradict this manipulation of the truth, which she didn't. And she didn't feel too guilty. The two dogs in question would have a wonderful home up at Beechbrook House.

It didn't get more rags-to-riches than that. They'd be going from life in an animal sanctuary kennel to getting their paws under the table at the house of a real-life lord.

'And I told Jack about Casey's Girl,' Archie said, looking very pleased with himself. 'He's coming to see her tomorrow. I'm coming too.'

True to his word, Archie, Jack and Jack's parents arrived the next day to look at Casey's Girl. Phoebe, Maggie, Natasha and Marcus all watched as both Jack and his parents put Casey's Girl through her paces. The little horse behaved impeccably and at the end of it, Jack's father told a delighted Maggie that not only would they like to rehome the mare, but that he would make a sizeable donation.

'She's a valuable horse,' he told Maggie. 'I know you've been reluctant to sell her on the open market, but she'll be a fine addition to our stables, so it's only fair we pay a proper price for her.'

Both Archie and Jack were beaming in delight. In fact, everyone was smiling. Phoebe didn't think she'd ever seen such a happy-ever-after rehoming take place.

* * *

In the middle of July, Natasha and Marcus bought Woodcutter's and, as promised, they adopted Saddam as soon as they got the keys.

Another rags-to-riches story, Phoebe thought with affection. The half-feral cat, who Marcus had almost tamed, but not quite, would have a field day prowling in the woods around the house. Then, after a long day's hunting, he could curl up by the wood burner in the little lounge where Phoebe, Sam and Roxie had spent so many happy nights. Saddam could not have gone to a better home.

Also in mid-July, Tori and Harrison found a house in Burley to buy. It wasn't unlike the house they'd rented in Bridgeford. A spacious three-bedroom detached with a modern kitchen, a garden office where Tori could work and quarter acre full of apple trees and space in the loft just in case they ever wanted to expand their family. 'That's still under discussion,' Tori had told Phoebe. 'Getting married is the next thing on our "to do" list.'

It would be a little while longer before Sam and Phoebe could take over the tenancy of the Bridgeford house because the sellers of the Burley house had only just found something they wanted to buy. But the two sales were progressing, Tori had told Phoebe happily. Their exchange date was scheduled for 2 October. Phoebe was keeping her fingers crossed this happened because that would be perfect timing for her and Sam.

Alexa's baby came a few days early and it turned out that Flo had been right. It was a boy. 'We're calling him Jake,' Alexa told Phoebe and Sam when they visited Alexa and Frazier at home a few days after the birth, bearing gifts, a cuddly black and white snuggle dog that had a look of Roxie about it and a pamper pack for Alexa which included de-stress almond body oil, which Phoebe knew Alexa loved.

'Thank you so much, I feel totally spoilt,' Alexa said, as she put the gifts on the lounge table and introduced them to a sleepy Jake, who was in his cot.

'Say hello to your Aunt Phoebe and Uncle Sam,' Alexa said to her newborn as Sam and Phoebe both cooed over the tiny baby, who already had a thatch of brown hair and was a big boy despite the fact he'd come into the world a week early.

Phoebe stole a glance at Sam, knowing that, like her, Sam was studying the infant with new eyes. Knowing your own baby was arriving in the not-too-distant future certainly focused the mind.

'Are they always born with that much hair?' Sam was asking Frazier now. 'I've always thought babies were bald.'

'Some are.' Frazier, who was an old hand at babies now he was a father three times over, grinned at him. 'But lots are born with hair. I think the world record is 14 inches.'

'Fourteen inches of hair. No way.' Sam's eyes were wide.

'It's true.' Frazier's superpower was an almost photographic memory for trivia.

'I had long hair, didn't I, Daddy?' This was from Flo, who'd been sitting surprisingly quietly for Flo on her father's lap as he lounged in an armchair.

'Not that long, darling.' He smiled consolingly at her.

'Longer than Bertie's,' she pushed.

'Oh, yes, longer than Bertie's.'

Flo poked her tongue out at Bertie, who was playing with a toy car on the lounge carpet and wasn't looking at her anyway. Flo and Bertie might be twins but they were worlds apart in character. Flo was as active and extrovert as her brother was calm and laid back.

'We must be crazy having another one,' Alexa said, her voice full of laughter. 'Three under four years old feels like a world record to me.'

'We're way behind on that one,' Frazier said knowledgeably. 'I think "a lot" in World Record terms is eight babies born at the same time.'

'Oh my God, poor woman,' sympathised Alexa.

'What's the biggest baby ever born?' Phoebe asked Frazier, although only half of her actually wanted to know.

'Twenty-two pounds,' Frazier said. 'Although sadly he didn't survive.'

'Ouch,' Alexa grimaced. 'I'm surprised his mother survived.'

'Me too,' Phoebe said with feeling.

25

The third week of July began with a visit from Knickerbocker Gloria, who'd rescued, she'd once told Phoebe proudly, a hundred and one guinea pigs. Knickerbocker Gloria was her stage name, she'd been a pole dancer in her youth, a fact that she was immensely proud of and told anyone who'd listen, but her real name, the one that was registered on the Puddleduck Vets system, was Mrs G. Brown. Phoebe had always assumed the G stood for Gloria, but had recently found out from Marcus that it didn't. It stood for Gertrude.

Gertrude Brown – hmmm, no wonder she'd taken a stage name. Knickerbocker Gloria was definitely more eye catching, like the ex-pole dancer's crimson red hair.

On a previous visit, Gloria had confided that she'd given up the pole dancing in the nineties and had turned her focus towards rehoming guinea pigs. When Phoebe had first met her, she'd brought them into the surgery in batches of five for health checks and claw clipping. On this particular morning, to Phoebe's relief, she'd only brought in one, whose name was Frisky Fred according to a grinning Marcus when he'd booked him in.

'What seems to be the problem with, er, Frisky Fred?' Phoebe asked Gloria, who was dressed as usual in a cymbal clash of colours – today she wore a turquoise sequinned jacket over lime-green flared trousers and a pink beret sat on top of her crimson hair. You almost needed sunglasses to look at her.

'He's scratching his belly a lot. I'm wondering if it's fleas,' Gloria said. 'Although goodness only knows where he'd have got them. They don't have contact with other animals and I'm always very careful about the quarantine period when I take in a new one. I don't want to be shelling out on flea treatments for my lot. Can guinea pigs even get fleas?'

'They can, but it's not fleas,' Phoebe said, after doing a swift examination. 'He has mites, I'm afraid. But don't worry, it's easily treatable. Although you will have to treat all of the pigs he's been in contact with.'

'Frisky Fred's a very social chap. He's been in contact with all of them. How much is that going to cost? I am a pensioner, you know. And a charity.' She blinked hopefully at Phoebe. 'I'm guessing there's also a discount for bulk-buying of the treatment as well. It's a lot cheaper to buy in bulk, isn't it? And that's what you'll be doing, after all, so you can afford to pass it on to little ol' me.'

'I think we already give you a discount of 20 per cent to reflect your charity status,' Phoebe said, determined to stand her ground. They barely broke even with Knickerbocker Gloria's animals as it was.

'Twenty-five and you've got yourself a deal,' Gloria said.

'I can't drop that much, I'm afraid. It's not just the medication costs. You also get your consultation fees cut.'

Gloria frowned and scratched her arm pointedly. 'Good heavens, do these mites bite humans? I'm feeling a touch itchy.'

So was Phoebe, even though she knew that was very likely just the power of suggestion.

'How about 23 per cent. I'll meet you halfway,' Gloria said, removing her beret and scratching her head.

Phoebe caved in, aware that she was being played but unable to bear the thought of Frisky Fred, or Gloria for that matter, being in her examining room a second longer.

'OK, tell Marcus that's what we agreed. And maybe you could put Frisky Fred back in the car while you settle up,' she called after her as Gloria smirked and exited promptly.

As soon as she'd left, Phoebe grabbed the disinfectant spray and gave the examining table an extra-thorough wipe down. When she popped her head into reception, Marcus was chatting to Jenna, but he looked at her questioningly.

'Did you really just increase Gloria's discount to 23 per cent?'

'Yes, I did, because she was buying the mite spray in bulk. It's a one-off, though – she'll be back on a smaller discount next time.'

'The thing is she only took the one can in the end,' Marcus said. 'I know you'd done the prescription for more, but she said she'd come back if she needed the rest.'

'Did she indeed?' Phoebe shook her head in exasperation. She scratched her arm, convinced she was still itching. 'Oh, well, she is a pensioner, and she does rehome those guinea pigs out of the goodness of her heart.'

'You're too soft,' Marcus said. 'I bet she's richer than us. Jenna reckoned that coat she had on was designer.'

'Yep,' Jenna said. 'Or a very good copy. It looked Prada to me.'

'I wouldn't know a Prada from a Primark. But never mind. She's gone now. Who's up next?'

'Max wants a second opinion on a beagle's rash,' Jenna said. 'I was just coming to find you.'

'And Maggie came in,' Marcus added. 'She said can you pop by and see her before you go home tonight.'

'Of course I can.'

Phoebe went and saw the beagle and confirmed Max's diagnoses of sarcoptic mange. What was it with all these 'itchy' consultations today? She was never going to be able to stop scratching!

Fortunately, the afternoon passed by without any more of them. And after she'd locked up, she headed up to Puddleduck Farmhouse with a delighted Roxie at her heels.

Roxie's favourite place was Puddleduck Farmhouse because she saw her mates, Buster and Tiny, and her third favourite person, who was Maggie, although Phoebe sometimes wondered if Maggie topped herself and Sam on the favourite person chart. Roxie was always so delighted to see her.

'Hello, darling,' Maggie said, bending to stroke Roxie when they arrived in her kitchen. 'And hello, Phoebe.' She grinned as she straightened up. 'My darling dalmatian and my darling granddaughter, aren't I lucky.'

'You're in a good mood,' Phoebe said. 'I take it you didn't want to see me about a sick animal then?'

'No, I didn't. Touch wood. Sick animals aren't the only reason I want to see you, you know. Have you had a good day?'

Phoebe told her about the mites cases and Maggie immediately began to scratch. 'Lord, what is it when someone mentions mites, I immediately feel itchy. Natasha did it to me the other day. We had an infestation of duck mites in the coops and she was telling me all about it. Seth wrote us a prescription.' She shuddered. 'I think they're all gone. How is Seth getting on anyway? He seems very happy.'

'He's in his element. Not that we get the chance to talk that much. He's been doing most of the call-outs, which frees Max and me up in the surgery. We're pretty busy.' She paused and looked at her grandmother suspiciously. 'I take it you didn't summon me for an update on Seth either?'

'Do I need a reason to see my favourite granddaughter?'

'Your only granddaughter,' Phoebe pointed out.

'All right, all right. I do have a reason for "summoning you", as you put it. Shall we sit down?'

They sat opposite each other at the end of the great old oak table nearest the Aga and Maggie put on her serious face.

'Now then,' she began. 'I want to discuss something with you – well, actually I want to ask you something and you don't have to answer straight away, OK?'

'OK.' Phoebe couldn't keep the smile off her face. It was so obvious that Maggie was going to ask if she was pregnant and she was ready to tell her she was. She was eleven weeks pregnant. Her baby was the size of a fig. They were almost at the twelve-week scan anyway. The safety cut-off at which she and Sam were going to tell everybody. There was a big part of her that was amazed Maggie hadn't said anything before.

She was so astute and perceptive. Although they hadn't seen each other alone much lately. There had always been other people around. Maybe Maggie had been being diplomatic.

Phoebe was so convinced she knew where the discussion was heading that Maggie's opening few sentences didn't make a lot of sense.

'Eddie and I are very much in our dotage. As you know...' Maggie rested her elbows on the table and leaned forward expectantly. 'We've both been feeling decidedly creaky lately and we want to step back a bit, so we have something we want to run past you. A retirement plan.'

'You want to run your retirement plan past me?' Phoebe caught up with difficulty. 'Er – OK. What is it? I'm all ears.' She frowned. 'Where is Eddie anyway? Shouldn't he be here too if this concerns him?'

'He doesn't need to be. We've already talked it through.' Maggie beamed. 'Eddie's 100 per cent behind me on this one. As are the rest of the Dashwood family. Don't you worry about that.'

'Right.' Phoebe was now completely mystified and this must have shown on her face because Maggie continued briskly, 'Now, promise me you'll hear me out before you say anything.'

'OK. I promise.'

'We've decided we want to downsize to a smaller place. A nice bungalow. Preferably one with a small garden. Or at least something more manageable. We're thinking of looking in the same area as your parents. There's not much for sale around there, but they do come up. We'd like one within walking distance if we can manage it.'

'I see. Um, OK.'

'And we want you and Sam to move into Puddleduck Farm. I know you need somewhere bigger to live and I know you're going to be scuppered on that front until you've got enough accounts, and I know that—'

'But we can't afford...'

Maggie put up a hand. 'I haven't finished yet. You promised you'd hear me out.'

Phoebe shut up again.

'We're not expecting you to buy Puddleduck Farm. Not right this second. We're thinking long term. Some kind of agreed payment plan until you can get your own finance. Part of it will be yours one day anyway – and part of it will go to your parents and part to Frazier. So they're the other interested parties, so to speak. Now, we have already spoken to them, neither of them want to live in this old house, as you can imagine, and so we've come up with a possible way forward. A way that you can bit-by-bit buy out their share of the place. And we are just talking about the house. The animal sanctuary bit is mine to bequeath, Phoebe, and I've always known that I'll bequeath that to you. Someone has to look after the animals when I'm not around to do it any more and I can't think of a better person for the job. That's if you were crazy enough to want the job, that is...'

Maggie paused. Her voice had become a little husky and her eyes were glittering with unshed tears. 'What do you say, darling? I know it's a lot to take in, but are you up for this?'

For a few seconds, Phoebe felt too overwhelmed to speak. It was the answer to all of their prayers – hers and Sam's – but it was so out of the blue she was blown away with the shock of it too.

She finally found her voice. 'Oh my goodness. I don't know what to say. That's such an amazingly generous gesture. Are you sure, Gran? Are you sure everyone else agrees? When did you ask them?'

'It's a gesture I can quite easily retract. Especially if I hear any more of that Gran nonsense,' Maggie said in as brusque a voice as she could manage. 'You know perfectly well how much I detest that word. And as for asking everyone else, it's an idea we've been kicking about for a while between us. I thought I'd run it past you first, but obviously you'll need to discuss it with Sam and see how he feels too.'

She blew her nose. 'There will still be a few financial details to sort out, but your parents agree, as do Frazier and Alexa. They're all very happy with the arrangement, they think it's a great plan.'

'Won't you need to sell Puddleduck Farm to buy your bunga-low, though?'

'No. You're forgetting Eddie had three houses when we got married. We've sold one but he wants to sell the others. In fact, life will be a lot easier if we do sell them. Having tenants in them is quite stressful. There's always something or another that needs sorting out. Eddie's sick of the hassle, frankly.'

Phoebe's heart felt too full to speak. And when she didn't say anything, Maggie carried on talking. 'Living here would be a great practical solution for you. You'd be close to work, and if anyone needs to be on night duty there's a spare room for them here. Sam could move Ninja over here too – save him doing all that traipsing back and forth over to Brook every day. There is loads of space for Roxie and Snowball and one day, when you start your own family, you'll have room to expand. Imagine it, Phoebe.'

Phoebe burst into tears. The picture Maggie was painting was idyllic, but it was the mention of family that had pushed her over the edge. She rummaged blindly in her bag for a tissue.

'Have one of mine.' Maggie pushed a box towards her and Phoebe grabbed a handful.

'Thank you. Oh, Gr... Maggie. I don't know what to say. It's such a lot to take in.'

'I know.' Maggie smiled happily. 'But it's a very good plan, isn't it?'

'It's amazing. If you and Eddie are sure you want to move nearer to Mum and Dad's. And we can work it all out, financially, I mean, because Sam and I – well, we wouldn't want you doing this just to help us out.'

'It would be a mutually beneficial arrangement that would suit us all,' Maggie said, sitting very upright in her chair and putting on her best business voice. 'I'd keep my hand in over here, but I wouldn't be here every day. I don't need to be. I don't do much on the day-to-day running of the place any more. Natasha oversees the paid part-timers and we have an army of volunteers, as you know.

'Eddie would carry on doing the financial side of things – he deals with all the adoptions and donations. I'd carry on doing the home checks. So all you and Sam really have to do is be here at nights, just in case. Or get cover on the days when you can't be. Then Eddie and I can have a nice quiet life in our bungalow, with maybe just a couple of dogs and a cat.' She glanced at Tiny and Buster, both dogs had opened their eyes at the mention of 'cat' – Buster was now wagging his tail and Roxie, who'd never been taught the word cat, wagged her tail in solidarity.

'You're going to need quite a big bungalow if Tiny's going to be in it,' Phoebe said.

Maggie dismissed this with a wave of her hand.

'It's a common misconception that wolfhounds take up lots of space. They can curl into a very tiny ball.'

They both looked across at Tiny, who yawned, and then as if to disprove Maggie's words utterly, stretched out all four paws to their fullest extent, which meant Buster had to move out of his way, before thumping his great head back down again on the warm flagstones with a sigh.

'I can see you're right,' Phoebe said, aware that Maggie was looking back at her again, her eyes tender.

'So how about you tell me your news now, love,' she continued softly.

26

Of course Maggie had known she was pregnant, Phoebe thought, as she'd met her grandmother's gentle hazel eyes.

Maggie never missed anything important, however busy she was, but the same intuition that had enabled her to pick this up had also told her that Phoebe would share her news when she was ready.

'Does Mum know too?' was Phoebe's first question.

'I don't think so, love. She certainly hasn't said anything to me. But maybe she's just been keeping mum too. Mum being the operative word.' She winked. 'How are you feeling? Not too much sickness? You must be tired, though.'

'I am tired. But actually, I'm feeling really good.' Phoebe cupped her tummy between her hands. 'I still have trouble some days myself, believing I'm pregnant, I mean. Did you know that this little one is already the size of a fig? Even though there's nothing to see on the outside. There isn't, is there?'

Maggie shook her head. 'Not yet.'

'Not telling anyone has given me the chance – us a chance – to get our heads around it. We didn't plan for me to get pregnant.'

'No, I don't suppose you did. But babies have a way of taking us unawares. I wasn't planning to get pregnant when I had your mother, as it happens.'

'I didn't know that.'

'Neither does she. I'm not sure I hold with this newfangled idea of parents telling their offspring they weren't planned. No one wants to feel like their whole existence was a mistake.'

'Gosh, no.' Phoebe looked at her in horror. 'That's not a brilliant start.'

'That's not to say I wasn't thrilled to bits once I'd got my head around the idea. And as it worked out, I was also very pleased she appeared when she did. We tried for a brother or sister for her, but we never did manage it.'

'Wow. I didn't know that either.'

'I don't tell you all my secrets.' Maggie looked reflective for a second. 'Anyway, I always think it's much easier to deal with things in life as they appear, rather than to waste time doing too much planning. Because the only guaranteed thing about life is that things will appear – whether we like them or not. Now then. Having said that, what are your plans for your little fig's arrival?'

For a while they talked about the pros and cons of home births and hospital births, and their parenting plans and Phoebe told Maggie she was relieved Sam was very much up for sharing everything. Changing nappies, doing night feeds. He said he was looking forward to it all.

Up until now, every time she and Sam had talked, Phoebe had felt that a shadow of uncertainty hung over everything. The uncertainty of not starting off with their baby in their forever house, but now, as she spoke to Maggie, the conversation was threaded through with light. Bringing up their baby at Puddle-duck Farm was a dream come true. A heady cocktail of happiness and excitement was rushing through her veins. She'd just have to hope that Sam agreed with the plans because his pride was the only thing that stood between them and their dream home.

Phoebe and Roxie finally left Puddleduck an hour later. There wasn't a massive rush to get back to the maisonette because Sam had a riding lesson scheduled for tonight, but she wanted a little time to process things before she saw him.

'Let me know what he says, as soon as you've spoken to him,' had been Maggie's last words to her.

Phoebe pulled out through the five-bar gate at the front of Puddleduck Farm with her head full of dreams. Maggie's proposition was a massive game changer and she felt as if her head had spun into orbit. But in a good way. A very good way.

As she drove past Beechbrook House, Maggie's neighbour, one day to be *her* neighbour, she saw that the lavender was at its peak. The purple fields that rolled out on either side of Rufus and Emilia's drive shone in all their lilac glory. A sweet-scented rolling lavender sea. The epitome of romance, Phoebe had once thought. And it was true that Rufus and Emilia had found their happy ending. Just as she and Sam were finding theirs.

If Rufus and Emilia's defining flower was lavender then hers and Sam's were sunflowers. They both loved them. Sam loved them because he'd once grown some from seed and had confessed to Phoebe that they were the only plants he'd managed to keep alive for longer than a week.

Phoebe loved them because of their beautiful childlike simplicity. Also, they reminded her of college days, of a time before everything had got too serious, and life was more carefree. Once, when they were teenagers, she and Tori had climbed through the barbed wire fence that surrounded a field of sunflowers and had posed amongst them taking photos. Even in the days before phone cameras and selfies were invented, Tori had always carried a camera and they'd got some amazing shots. Tori had later framed one of them and given it to Phoebe for a birthday present. Phoebe didn't remember seeing that picture lately, but she must have it somewhere, still.

Directly between Puddleduck Farm and Bridgeford, Phoebe had to drive past a field of sunflowers. There was a layby opposite them where passing motorists often pulled in to take photos. Today it was empty and on impulse she stopped.

Leaving Roxie in the car, she crossed the road. It was amazing how the sunflowers all faced the same way. An army of yellow heads with their darker middles all facing in one direction. All facing the sun. She'd heard somewhere that they moved throughout the day in the direction of the sun. Or was that a myth? She had a feeling she'd also once read a more scientific feature that professed bees preferred flowers that faced east, so when the sunflower seeds got to a certain ripeness they all remained facing east. It was all to do with bees and pollination and so had its roots in science.

The sunflowers were all in full bloom, even though it wasn't yet the end of July. They must be an early-flowering variety. They were enormous, especially close up, she realised as, taking care not to snag her clothes, she climbed through the barbed wire and into the field.

They dwarfed Phoebe. Some of them were over eight feet high, she discovered, as she threaded her way between the great stalks. There wasn't much smell. A mild earthiness that drifted on the evening air.

She got out her phone to take a selfie and at the precise moment she aimed the camera, the sun moved out from behind a cloud and the field was washed with evening sunlight. In that moment, it seemed to Phoebe that every flower brightened a little, its petals becoming more luminous, haloing its centre with burnished yellow, so she felt as though she was standing in a great sea of gold.

The photo when she looked at it was a snapshot of happiness. Her face, surrounded by the faces of sunflowers, glowed in the sunlight against a dark blue backdrop of sky. She felt full up with joy. As though every part of her was alive with the feeling. Brimming over. Almost spiritual. Phoebe wasn't a big believer, but it was moments like these that convinced her of the existence of some higher power.

* * *

Phoebe and Sam arrived home at pretty much the same time. He was parking his car on the road, just as she reached the maisonette. Sam always parked outside so she could have the off-road space. It was one of the myriad of ordinary things he did that showed his love for her.

'Hey, you,' he called, as he walked up towards her. 'I didn't know you were working late. Did you have a call?'

'No, I popped in to see Maggie. Don't worry. I haven't eaten.'

'I wouldn't have minded if you had. I'm always capable of knocking up some toast.'

'I know you are. We might end up with that tonight. Or maybe we could go out if you're not too tired. I've got some really exciting news.'

She had an urge to jump up and down on the spot and blurt it out now, she was so excited, but she also wanted to gauge his reaction and it would be easier to do that when they were sitting down facing each other.

'Okaaay,' Sam drew out the word as he looked at her. 'That sounds very intriguing.'

A few moments later, they were upstairs in Sam's kitchen. Snowball and Roxie had been fed so they wouldn't have four pleading eyes looking at them as they faced each other across the breakfast island.

'Go for it,' Sam said.

'Promise me you won't interrupt until I've finished.'

'Cross my heart.'

He didn't interrupt either, while she poured out what Maggie had said. And even at the end of it, when she'd finished and had said, 'OK, you can talk now,' it was a few seconds before he spoke.

'I'm not sure we can do that, Phoebe.' His eyes were shadowed.

'But why not? It would be perfect.'

'Because that place must be worth a fortune. The farmhouse alone is worth megabucks. And all that land. We couldn't pay it off if we lived there for a hundred years.'

'That's not true. I'm sure we could. Anyway, we're not buying the whole thing.' Frustration sharpened her voice. 'Sam, have you actually been listening to a word I've said?'

'I've been listening.' He got up and shrugged his chair back from the table so it scraped on the kitchen floor. 'It's not just the buying bit, Phoebe. It's the upkeep and maintenance. That house must cost a fortune to run and the maintenance on the land is a full-time job. As Maggie says, it's too much for her and Eddie and they're retired. We both work full-time. And we've got a little one coming. Where are we going to find time to do it all?'

'I don't know. We can hire someone.'

He'd paced to the other end of the kitchen and now he ran his hand through his hair in a gesture of impatience. 'We can't afford to hire someone if we're paying off that kind of mortgage. Even if we are doing it bit by bit, it'll be insanely expensive. We'll be under too much pressure. I don't earn that much.'

'I do, though, Sam.' She said it without thinking she might make things worse. 'I'm a vet. That's why I trained for all those years. That's why I set up my own practice.'

'I know you're a vet. I know you've got the potential to earn ten times my income. I don't need reminding.' His voice was harsh now and Phoebe flinched.

She had never seen him so angry. The animals could feel it too. Snowball had just fled from the kitchen in a streak of black velvet and Roxie had crawled between her legs and had put her head on her knee. Her melting dark eyes were anxious, as she looked to Phoebe for reassurance.

'It's OK, darling...' She stroked the dog's head. 'But Sam—'

He cut across her. 'And you still owe your family money for that, don't you? We can't borrow any more from them.'

'Sam, please. You're frightening Roxie.' She stood up too, but Sam was already striding across the kitchen. Then he was out of the door and she heard his feet thundering downstairs, and then the final slam of the downstairs front door behind him.

Phoebe stayed where she was, shocked. What on earth had just happened? She'd suspected he might not be quite as enamoured with the plan as she'd been, but she'd never expected him to react so strongly. She had no idea how their discussion had escalated so quickly into this row. The first row they had ever really had.

Still comforting Roxie, she looked around the familiar kitchen. The fridge with its haphazard collection of quirky magnets, the calendar on the notice board with all the things they needed to do circled in red, the loaf of bread on top of the breadbin because no one had thought to put it away. Or had had the time.

The air smelled faintly sweet. There was a pot of fresh mint on the windowsill behind the sink. It needed watering, Phoebe noticed, getting up to do it. She felt like bursting into tears again – for entirely different reasons than she had earlier. Today seemed to have been one long rollercoaster of emotion. But she was too numb now for tears.

27

Phoebe walked in the forest when she needed to think things through. Sam rode his horse. He was halfway to Brook Stables, his knuckles almost white on the steering wheel, he was gripping it so hard, before he really paused to think.

He had no idea why he was so angry. He'd just known that what Phoebe was suggesting was impossible. As soon as she'd started talking, with her eyes all lit up and shiny, Sam had known he was going to have to pour cold water on her dreams. Maybe that was why he'd felt so angry. Because he knew he'd be the bad guy then.

Although he was heading for Brook, he realised suddenly he couldn't ride Ninja while he felt this angry. Horses were sensitive animals and he couldn't justify passing all this rage onto Ninja. It wasn't fair. Besides, it would be dark soon, and he needed to be alone, not around people. There were always people at Brook. He needed to get a handle on where his head was. As he hit the main forest road, he slowed automatically to the speed limit.

On either side of him, purple heather stretched into the distance, mirrored by the pink clouds above it where the sun had already set. Ponies dotted the heathland and Sam judged there would be another half hour of light before the sky began to properly darken.

His heartbeat was starting to steady a little, the familiar much-loved surroundings soothing him, beginning to work their magic. He didn't even remember the last time he'd felt so angry, so pressurised. It was crazy. He pulled over into a layby that was empty apart from one car with no one in it. He turned off the ignition and sat, looking out across the purple heather, trying to gather his thoughts.

There had always been the four of them. Himself, Phoebe and her younger brother Frazier – Sam couldn't remember a time before Frazier was around – and Tori. They'd been what his mum had called 'thick as thieves' back in the day.

They'd had the occasional fallout, but mostly they'd got on well. Partly because they'd been different enough to complement each other perfectly.

Tori had been the curious, impulsive one. She was the rule breaker, the maverick, the one who'd always pushed the boundaries – it had been Tori who'd suggested they have a picnic in the cow field at Puddleduck Farm one long ago day and they'd set out a blanket and eaten their sandwiches while Phoebe had fed bits of bread to some calves. She'd always loved animals.

Frazier had broken them a hazel stick from the hedge, 'Just in case any of the mother cows get uppity, and we need protection,' he'd said.

Frazier had always set himself up as protector, even though he was the youngest. But then, Frazier had always been older than his years. The archetypal father figure.

Phoebe had been the planner. It had been Phoebe who'd persuaded Maggie to let them take sandwiches and crisps and bottles of fizzy drinks, while also managing to avoid any difficult questions about where they might be eaten.

Sam hadn't protested, even though he'd been aware that a picnic in the middle of a field of dairy cows might not be the most sensible idea they'd ever had. Sam had a support role in the group. Which meant he almost always went along with what the others wanted. Sam was the steady reliable plodding one of the four. The stalwart and occasionally the peacemaker. He didn't argue with anyone. He didn't create a stir and he was OK being the fall guy if that was required.

They'd been halfway through their picnic when Farmer Pete, Phoebe's grandfather, had come charging over with a shotgun, threatening to shoot them for trespassing. Phoebe had sworn blind he hadn't realised it was them, but Sam had been certain he had known and had just wanted to frighten the living daylights out of them so they'd never do it again and risk getting trampled by a herd of cows. He'd certainly succeeded. They'd been in so much trouble that day. Even though Sam had tried to take the blame as usual, both Farmer Pete and Maggie had insisted the four children were equally responsible. With the possible exception of Frazier because he was the youngest and didn't know any better. They'd put themselves in untold danger. Cows with calves were not to be messed with. *Ever.*

It had been a bittersweet ending to a fantastic day.

Sam shook his head to clear the memory.

He had been in love with Phoebe for as long as he could remember. For most of his life, he had loved her from afar because he had always known she was out of his league.

For their entire lives, Phoebe had been the girl who was going places. Focused, determined, academically brilliant, Phoebe had what it took to do whatever she wanted, and she'd always known what she wanted. She'd wanted to be a vet. Phoebe was on a trajectory straight to the stars. Sam hadn't been a bit surprised when she'd been offered a place at the prestigious London Vet School.

He hadn't really been all that surprised when she'd hooked up with Hugh, another brilliant vet whose parents were both in the medical profession. It was a world that Sam didn't understand and couldn't compete with.

His parents had ordinary jobs. Ma had the Post Office and Stores and Pa was a kitchen fitter. His parents were great, but they were no more ambitious for Sam than they'd been for themselves. If there was such a thing as destiny, Sam thought now, then his was to travel the low road, while Phoebe was fast-tracked ahead of him, racing along the high.

Sam rubbed his head. He rarely got headaches, but he had one now. He lowered the window to let in some fresh air. Maybe he would go for a walk after all. His shoulders were tight with tension and he badly needed to unwind.

This was a part of the forest he didn't often walk in. Midway between Bridgeford and Brook. Not near enough to his house to take Roxie and not near enough to Brook to ride Ninja. But it was a lovely spot and clearly popular. A wide sandy track led up through the heathland towards a distant belt of trees.

As he set off along the track, with only the sounds of birds and the dull thud of his boots on sand, Sam wished he had Roxie with him. You were never alone with a dog. He wished he hadn't upset Phoebe too, but he was glad she wasn't with him. He needed to assimilate his thoughts. Work out where all that anger was coming from.

Sam knew that on the surface of things, it was a fantastic offer. It was their dream come true, a smallholding, with loads of space around them. A place where their children could grow up, safe and secure, playing in the same fields, walking in the same forest – oh my God, it was such a tantalising prospect.

Keeping Ninja at home had always been a dream too – not having to travel miles to see to him and riding straight from the house. It was the stuff of fantasy. When Phoebe had first suggested it, Sam had felt his heart soar.

But he'd barely had a chance to register the excitement before the stark voice of reality had come crashing in.

'Who's paying for all this?'

Maggie and Eddie? The thought of Phoebe's grandparents subsidising his future so heavily had smashed the moment. But the thought of Phoebe paying for everything out of the Puddleduck Vets practice was even worse. He would be a kept man. And he couldn't handle that.

The one thing that had always kept Sam's self-esteem at a healthy level was that he was independent. Like his own parents, he was a self-made man. He had bought his own place early on. He had never needed to accept financial help from anyone. Nor did he ever want to. Certainly not from his wife-to-be and her family.

Sam was so deep in thought he didn't see the dog until it had run right up to him. It was a brown and white cocker spaniel with the characteristic long feathered ears of the breed and brown spotted nose and it was very friendly.

'Hello, fellow. Where did you spring from?' Sam bent to stroke it, before realising there were another two on the path ahead of him, also coming his way with wagging tails. Then he saw a figure, presumably their owner, in the distance and heard two sharp blasts of a whistle.

To his surprise, all of the spaniels, even the one he was petting, responded instantly to the whistle and ran back in the direction they'd come from.

Oh, if only they could get Roxie to react as instantaneously as that, Sam thought, temporarily distracted from his dark thoughts.

'I hope they weren't bothering you,' called a woman's voice. She'd not put any of her dogs on the lead, Sam saw, but they were all walking in a group around her, clearly waiting for her next command.

'They weren't bothering me. I love dogs.'

He and the woman recognised each other at about the same moment. For him it was the hair – not many people had hair that colour. White blonde, which glowed in the soft golden light of the evening.

'Destiny!'

'Sam Hendrie.'

'I was just thinking how wonderfully obedient your spaniels were,' he said. 'But now I know why.'

She laughed, showing her dimples, and her amber eyes warmed with pleasure at the compliment. 'They're in training actually. All three of them. They're not mine. Are you, my loves?' This was directed at the spaniels, who were hanging on to her every word.

'Well, it looks like you're doing an amazing job.'

'Thank you.' She glanced around. 'Where's Roxie?'

'She's at home with Phoebe. We had a stupid row.' He felt immediately disloyal, but he'd spoken without thinking, and it was too late to retract it.

'I'm sorry to hear that,' Destiny said. 'Are you on your way out or on your way home?'

He glanced at the sky. 'It'll be dark soon, so I guess I should be getting back.'

'I'm guessing we're going in the same direction then. Do you mind if I walk with you? Or would you rather be alone? I'm easy either way.' She waited for him to answer, and suddenly the prospect of company didn't seem too bad.

'It'd be good to walk together. I meant to get in touch with you anyway – to apologise for missing the last couple of lessons. We had a lot going on.'

'It's no problem. Doing the training at home is more important than turning up once a week to a class.'

'Yes, that's kind of what we figured.' Sam felt guilty that they hadn't done much of that either.

For the next couple of minutes, they walked in silence, their feet crunching on the small gravel and stones that made up this part of the path. It wasn't an awkward silence at all, considering they barely knew each other.

The spaniels ran ahead of them, trotting along the edges of the path, pausing occasionally to sniff something or to run along one of the deer tracks off into the heather. It was incredibly peaceful. Even the birds had gone to bed now and they only saw the occasional shadows of ponies in the distance.

It was Destiny who spoke first.

'If it helps to talk, Sam, I'm a very good listener.'

Her words hung between them in the twilight air and Sam glanced at her serene face and he thought, yes, I bet you are.

Haltingly at first, but gaining in confidence as he spoke, and she did as she'd promised and just listened, Sam explained what had happened. Some instinct told him not to mention the baby, because hardly any of their immediate family knew about it yet, so he just talked about their failure to get a decent mortgage, ending on the statement that he could never accept financial help from Phoebe or his in-laws to be.

At the end of it, there was another small silence before Destiny said thoughtfully, 'Are you the type of person who just needs an ear or would you like me to offer you any solutions?'

'I'm definitely up for listening to a solution,' Sam said.

28

Phoebe had phoned Sam twice and twice the mobile's voicemail had kicked in before she'd realised that he wasn't going to pick up. Either he was driving and it was on silent – Sam's car didn't have any kind of Bluetooth system – or he just didn't want to speak to her.

Either way, she was very pissed off with him. And that feeling mounted as the numbness of shock wore off. She hadn't expected him to be grateful. Well, not at first. She'd expected there might be some misplaced pride. Sam could be ridiculously stubborn about money and she definitely shouldn't have reminded him that she earned more than him. Maybe that had been rubbing his nose in it a bit, but surely he could see that living at Puddleduck Farm was the answer to their prayers.

Obviously he couldn't. Well, there was one thing that she was certain of and that was that she wasn't going to sit around waiting for him to come back and apologise.

She put on Roxie's lead. It was getting a bit late for a walk, but she needed to offload to someone and the only person she could think of was Tori.

She phoned her from the car and her friend answered almost straight away.

'Are you in, Tori? I really need a chat.'

'We are, as it happens. Harrison's here too, though. What's wrong, honey? You sound awful.'

'I've had a row with Sam. I'll tell you when I get there.'

'OK. Drive carefully. Take deep breaths.'

Ten minutes later, she was pulling up outside the semi she and Sam had planned would be their next address as soon as Tori and Harrison vacated it. Her, Sam and their baby. Not that Tori knew about the baby yet. Unless, like Maggie, she too had guessed. Phoebe didn't think so. They hadn't seen each other in person since the christening.

Tori met her at the door and ushered her and Roxie through to the kitchen and Phoebe realised they'd already started packing things up. There were boxes in the lounge and more in the kitchen.

'We've made a start, as you can see.' Tori acknowledged her glance with a wave of her hand. 'We're packing up all the stuff we don't use very often. We've thrown loads out too. It's very cathartic. I'm using the yardstick – if I haven't taken it out of the cupboard since we've been here, or we have more than one, it's not going with us. Sorry, it's not about me. What's going on with you and Sam, lovely? Was it a serious row?'

'Yes, it was. The biggest we've ever had.'

'We can talk in our bedroom,' Tori said. 'Harrison's packing stuff up from the kitchen/diner room and Vanessa Rose is asleep in the nursery. I'll take the baby monitor up but we should be able to hear her from upstairs anyway. Shall I bring wine and chocolate?'

'Just chocolate,' Phoebe said. 'Can Roxie come up too?'

'Of course. And yes, I forgot you're driving. Sorry.'

'I'm not just driving. I'm pregnant.' Phoebe blurted out her news before they'd even got to the threshold of Tori's bedroom.

'Oh my God. That's amazing. That's really wonderful. You haven't fallen out with Sam about that, have you?'

'No. No, I haven't.'

'How much pregnant?'

'Eleven weeks.'

'Bloody hell, how have you managed to keep it to yourself all this time?'

They were talking in stage whispers, which were getting louder, and Tori seemed to be suddenly aware of her sleeping baby. She ushered Phoebe and Roxie into the main bedroom.

'Excuse the mess. I haven't got time to be tidy. We can sit on the bed.' She straightened the duvet as she spoke, sat down and patted the space beside her. 'How are you feeling? Oh my God, I'm so excited for you.' She hugged her arms around herself. 'It's fantastic.' Her eyes sobered. 'But what have you argued about?'

Phoebe told her and Tori listened until she'd finished, even though she was clearly desperate to interrupt. She was fidgeting and frowning.

'What?' Phoebe said. 'What are you thinking?'

'I'm just surprised you're surprised if that makes sense. Sam's always been so incredibly proud and stubborn about money. You can't as much buy him a coffee without him buying you one back the first chance he gets. He always had a chip on his shoulder about being the "poor friend" when we were younger.' She mimed the inverted commas around the phrase.

'That was ages ago, Tori. He's not like it now and I don't remember him being like that when we were at college either. He was always splashing the cash then.'

'Yes, but that was the only time in our adult lives he had more money than we did. He was working then, remember, and we weren't. We were studying.'

'That's true.'

'And the whole time you were away in London he was on an economy drive. First he had a mortgage, then he had Ninja. That horse must cost a fortune. Isn't that why he works at Brook Riding School, so he can subsidise his keep? He wouldn't do that if he didn't have to.'

'That's true as well,' Phoebe said thoughtfully. 'But he also loves teaching.'

'You love being a vet. Doesn't mean you'd do it for free.'

'Fair point.'

'He'll come round. He's probably at home right now wondering where you are.'

'Well, he hasn't phoned me to find out,' Phoebe said, checking to make sure and finding she was right.

'Maybe it's not him who needs to apologise,' Tori said slowly.

'What? Me? But I'm not the one who had a hissy fit and stormed out.'

'I didn't really mean you should apologise. I don't think you should. I'm just thinking all this can be fixed by a bit of smooth talking – what I'm saying is that if you can persuade Sam that it isn't his sole responsibility to provide the family finances but also give him enough space to make his own decisions, if you know what I mean, then he'll probably come round to the idea. Male egos and all that. Sam's old-fashioned, isn't he. He was brought up in an old-fashioned family where the men do the hunter-gatherer bit and the women cook the meals.'

'His mum works. She's got Hendrie's.'

'She also cooks, though, doesn't she, and does the housework and I bet she did all of the child-rearing thing too. Which brings me back to...' Tori's eyes gleamed with excitement and she bounced up and down on the bed so the springs creaked.

'Your little one. I'm taking it this wasn't in your plans. When did you find out?'

'No, it definitely wasn't.' Phoebe felt much better having unloaded to Tori, who she knew in her heart was right. Telling Sam she earned more than him when he was already feeling oversensitive, which he clearly had been, hadn't been very diplomatic. Even if it was true. She should have been much more sensitive about the whole thing. But she'd been so excited.

'I found out soon after the christening. I threw up when we got home that day and then it happened again a couple of days later at work. It's eased off now. I'd been feeling really emotional on that day too. Which I'd put down to the fact that christenings are emotional. Well, being trusted to be a godmother is emotional. Oh, Tori, I was flaming shocked at first, but once I got used to the idea, I was thrilled. Am thrilled.' She cupped her tummy gently. 'I can't believe how much my feelings have changed.'

'It was like that for me,' Tori said, her eyes misting. 'And I know it probably feels like crap timing but in some ways it's perfect timing. Our children won't be that far apart in age. They can grow up together like we did. It'll be like history is repeating itself.'

'I know.' Phoebe felt her eyes filling with tears again.

Tori grabbed a box of tissues from the bedside table and offered it to Phoebe. 'Baby hormones,' she said sympathetically. 'They swirl around and make you feel like a blubbering wreck, don't they?'

'Mmm.' Phoebe blew her nose. 'When does this bit stop?'

'I'm not sure it ever did. I think I was emotional all the way through with Vanessa Rose, but it definitely wasn't as bad in the second trimester,' she added hastily, catching sight of Phoebe's expression. 'It's really great news about Puddleduck Farm. Do you think you'd be able to move in before the baby comes? Is that what Maggie meant? I take it she does know.'

'She does. I told her today, but she'd guessed anyway.'

'I would have guessed if I'd seen you properly,' Tori said confidently. 'You definitely look blooming.'

'Do I really?'

'Yep.'

Phoebe picked up her phone again, which had just pinged with a message, but it wasn't from Sam. It was a message cancelling the puppy party she and Sam had been invited to, which had been due to happen on the forthcoming Saturday.

The host was ill apparently and needed to reschedule. Phoebe sighed, then she remembered the selfies she'd taken in the sunflower field. 'I don't usually like selfies that much,' she told Tori, handing her phone across, 'but I really like this one.'

Tori gazed at it for a few seconds. 'I'm not surprised. It's beautiful. You look like a Renaissance painting. You're just glowing.'

'I love it too. It reminds me of the one you took of me way back. Do you remember?'

'Yes. Didn't I get it framed for you? That was beautiful too. But this one is more so. You look like you're "with child".' She had emphasised the words 'with child', and they both giggled. 'Truly,' Tori added. 'I think anyone would guess if you showed them this photo. You should get this one printed out and framed too. You could build up a collection. Sunflower moments in Phoebe Dashwood's life. But even if you don't do that, this one is definitely one to show bubba when he or she's older. Don't leave it mouldering on a cloud somewhere. Get it up on the wall.'

'Thank you for listening,' Phoebe said softly. 'I know you're really busy, what with moving and stuff.'

'We've both been really busy lately,' Tori said, her face growing serious again. 'But I've always got time to listen to you, honey. You know that. God, you've listened to me often enough. It's usually about men, isn't it – or at least it was in the olden days. Not so much now.'

'Until today,' Phoebe murmured.

'You and Sam will be fine. I'm sure you will. He loves the bones of you. He always has, Pheebs. And now you're having his child. I bet he's over the moon. And going back to this whole money thing, have either of you considered that Sam could be a stay-at-home dad, and you could work?'

Phoebe frowned. 'We've touched on it, but there's Ninja to consider. Although if we did live at Puddleduck Farm...' She broke off thoughtfully. 'Maybe now, though – and you're right, he is over the moon. I think I was a bit tactless over the whole Puddleduck Farm thing. You're right about that too. I need to go home and talk to him. Before I do, though, I seem to remember you said something about chocolate earlier.'

'I did.' Tori produced a bar of fruit and nut from a pocket in the long smock she was wearing. 'Good job you reminded me. Or I might have had to eat it all myself!'

They smiled at each other and Phoebe couldn't believe how much better she felt. 'Thank you,' she said again. 'I feel amazingly lucky having you as a friend. If that's not too schmaltzy.'

'It's totally schmaltzy. But it's allowable, being as you're pregnant.' She broke the chocolate bar in two and handed half to Phoebe. 'Anyway, I feel the same. And I'm definitely not pregnant.'

* * *

Sam was also feeling a lot better than he had when he'd started off on his lone walk. Destiny had been a surprisingly good listener. And what she'd said to him afterwards had made a lot of sense. He no longer felt angry. All he wanted to do was to see Phoebe. He definitely had some humble pie eating to do. He'd stopped on the way back and had bought flowers. Only petrol station ones but the best they'd had. One of the things Destiny had said was that he should really show Phoebe that he was sorry. Show her that he meant it and that flowers were a good way to do it – if flowers were the kind of thing they did. It wasn't really. Sam was aware that he didn't buy her flowers often enough. But that was one of the things he was determined to change. She deserved flowers.

As he drew up into a parking space on the road, he saw her pulling into the space on their driveway. So she'd been out too then. He wondered if she'd been walking. It was dark so probably not until now, although she did have Roxie with her, he realised, as she opened the hatchback to let the dog out.

'Hey, you two,' he called to them as he caught up, clutching the bouquet of flowers which smelled sweet beneath his nose.

Phoebe turned towards the sound of his voice and he saw her face in the streetlight. She looked like she'd been crying. Sam felt more of a heel than ever.

'I'm so sorry,' he said, reaching her and stopping a pace short, unsure of his welcome.

'Oh, Sam, I'm sorry too.' She came towards him and moments later they were in each other's arms, the flowers getting squashed between them, while a delighted Roxie wagged a welcome, clearly pleased her humans were together again.

'Let's go up,' Phoebe said. 'Maybe we can start this evening again.'

'It's nearly half past nine.'

'You know what I mean.'

'I do,' he said. 'I really do.'

29

A few moments later, they were upstairs in the kitchen.

Sam made them both hot chocolates and put in the chocolate sprinkles and miniature marshmallows that Phoebe loved. Comfort food.

'Shall we take these to bed or have them in the lounge?' he asked her.

'Lounge. We can snuggle up on the sofa with the animals.'

'Shall I put the flowers in water or did you want to do it?'

'Can you do it, please?' She hadn't had morning sickness lately, but sometimes strong smells could set her off again.

He looked tired, she thought, her heart going out to him. She carried the mugs through and put them on the coffee table and sank into the familiar contours of their sofa. It was going to be all right. She could feel it was. Sam's whole demeanour had changed since earlier. He'd relaxed into his normal cheerful, laidback self. She wondered if he'd been at the stables. Horses were Sam's happy place.

She heard him running the kitchen tap and getting out their one vase from beneath the sink, and the clink of glass on the drainer as he did the flowers. Then the musical ting of a pet dish as he refilled Snowball's cat biscuits. Not that Snowball was anywhere to be seen. He wouldn't be hungry. He had a bowl of biscuits left out permanently on the window above the radiator where Roxie couldn't reach them.

When Sam came into the lounge, his face was peaceful.

'I shouldn't have gone off on one earlier,' he said as he sat beside her. 'My stupid pride. I'm sorry, Pheebs.'

'It's OK. I was so gung-ho about living at Puddleduck Farm I didn't think it through. Of course it would be too expensive if it was just normal circumstances... And we'd never in a million years be able to afford a place like that...' She paused, trying to choose her words carefully. She didn't want to backtrack completely and give him the idea she didn't want them to accept Maggie's offer because she really, really did, but she needed to give him space to make his own decisions, as Tori had put it. Sam needed head room. He didn't need to feel that she was controlling the whole show and that he was being financed by her family.

There was a little pause as he looked at her. 'Go on,' he said.

Phoebe took a deep breath. 'I would really love it if we could find a way to live there, partly because it would help Maggie too. I know it's all getting too much for her and Eddie, and while they're on site, they'll always be doing too much. But I do get it if you'd rather not do that. If you're totally against the idea then I'm not going to force the issue.'

'I'm not totally against the idea. I know I probably sounded like I was earlier but that was before I had a chance to consider all the practicalities. Finances do come into it. Of course they do. I know we couldn't afford somewhere like that as an outright purchase and I guess I just...' He blinked a few times and rubbed his nose. 'I just hated the thought that I couldn't provide for you – you and our little one.'

He shifted along the sofa and reached for her hand. Taking full advantage of the space he'd freed up, the sofa squeaked as Roxie climbed up on the end closest to Sam.

'And the rest of our family,' Sam said with a soft smile as he stroked Roxie absently with the hand that wasn't around Phoebe's. 'It's partly the way I've been brought up,' he said. 'I know things are different these days and wives and girlfriends can be the major breadwinners, but that wasn't what happened in our house. Pa's always made most of the household income, which is just as well because the Post Office and Stores have never been massive earners. The shop's always subsidised the Post Office, which sometimes doesn't do much more than break even.'

Phoebe nodded, liking the way his fingers stroked hers.

'Pa used to say if you could see inside him, he'd have the words "provider" tattooed through his middle, and to be honest I've always felt the same. Even though my head knows I don't have to be that person with you, I guess, well, I guess that knowledge hasn't quite worked its way down to my heart.'

'Wow,' Phoebe said quietly. 'You really have thought this through.' Sam was always so practical, so nuts and bolts and sensible. She'd never known him to come out with words like that. 'You're right, Sam, you don't have to be that way with me. I'm an independent woman too, remember, and in my family it's always been a more equal partnership between the men and women. Maggie worked every bit as hard as Farmer Pete – she took care of a lot of the finances too, she was always good with money – and my parents have always both worked.'

'Yes, I know. I didn't see the full picture. I was too blinded by stupid pride. It's got me into trouble before.'

'Talking of the full picture,' Phoebe said quickly. 'There could be some savings to offset the cost of a purchase. You wouldn't have to keep Ninja at Brook. We could have him in the neddies' field. With or without the neddies. And there's Five Acre field. And there's the stable that Casey's Girl used to use so he can come in when he needs to. We could maybe one day think about building another stable and getting another horse so we could go riding together, which would be amazing. I know I'm leaping ahead, but it's all possible, isn't it? And it would save so much time.'

To her relief, he was nodding.

'Was that where you went earlier?' she asked. 'To the stables?'

'No. I was going to – I was headed there – but then I decided to go for a walk in the forest instead. I was feeling way too grumpy to mix with any people. And you know what horses are like. Poor Ninja would have picked it up.'

'Yes, bless him. Shame you didn't take Roxie. She'd have loved it. And she'd have been good company.'

'I know. I thought that when I got there. We'd have had the place to ourselves. There was no one around. Well, hardly anyone. On the way back I bumped into Roxie's trainer, Destiny. Do you remember her? She was out doing some behavioural work with three cocker spaniels. You wouldn't believe how well trained they were. They were literally hanging on to her every word.'

'Were they?' Phoebe hated that she felt a twinge of jealousy. She'd almost forgotten about the divine Destiny Dolittle. She pressed it down, determined not to react. 'You got the chance to speak to her then.'

'I did. We ended up walking back to the cars together. We had quite a good chat. She's a great listener.'

Phoebe felt chilled. 'You didn't tell her about our row, did you, Sam?'

He didn't answer straight away, but she saw a flash of guilt in his eyes and she knew that he had. While she'd been crying on

Tori's shoulder, he'd been talking to another woman. Sharing the intimate details of their argument. Not just with any woman, either, but with the last woman on earth Phoebe would have wanted to know about their life.

'I don't believe you, Sam,' she snapped. 'How could you share our stuff with her? It's private.'

'She won't tell anyone. I'm sure she won't. She's not that type of person.'

'You don't know her well enough to know that about her, and I certainly don't. I expect she gave you some advice too, didn't she? Buy her some flowers, apologise.' She remembered his words, 'that knowledge hasn't quite worked its way down to my heart', and she knew suddenly beyond all doubt that they *weren't* his words. Sam never said stuff like that – she knew he didn't – Destiny must have said them. Sam had just quoted them back to her.

Pain and jealousy ricocheted through her as she snatched her fingers from Sam's and leaped off the sofa.

So much for not being emotional. She'd gone from calm and peaceful serenity to ragingly jealous anger in ten seconds flat. Which was about the same time it took her to get across the other side of the room. Half blinded by tears, she stormed into the kitchen, not really knowing where she was going but intent only on getting away from him.

'Phoebe – where are you going? You're being ridiculous,' he called after her, but he didn't immediately follow, and the words 'You're being ridiculous' wound her up even more. How dare he say that when he'd just been having a heart-to-heart about their private affairs with a virtual stranger?

She grabbed her coat from the back of the chair where she'd left it earlier and her car keys and bag from the table. Seconds later, she was through their front door and running down the steep stairs to the main front door. A little voice in her head was saying quietly that storming out might be overreacting, but truthfully she couldn't bear to be around him for a second longer.

Then suddenly she had missed her footing on the stairs, and she was sliding, and she had that awful gut-wrenching feeling you get when you know you're going to fall and you can't stop it. In the next moment she was falling, tumbling over and over on the long flight of stairs, unable to stop herself, just tumbling in a haze of pain and bumping until she hit the floor at the foot of the stairs. For a split second, there was nothing except the stillness of shock. She lay where she was, aware of pain stabbing in several different parts of her body. She was aware of a voice – Sam's voice – calling from the top of the stairs. But it was as though she was wrapped in a bubble of shock, like a circle of clear plastic film that separated them from each other, and Sam sounded far away.

'Phoebe. Oh my God. Phoebe. I'm coming. Don't move. I'm coming.'

She heard the panic-stricken edge to his voice, even through the clear plastic film of shock. Then she must have lost consciousness because for a while there was nothing. Nothing at all.

When she came to, she wasn't sure whether seconds had passed or minutes. But she felt sick, terribly awfully sick. And flicks of pain were kicking off all over her body. There were stabbing knitting needles of red-hot pain in her stomach and her back and her neck. She could hear moaning, but it took a while to realise that she was actually making the moaning sounds herself.

The next part of the evening was hazy. She was aware of time passing, but it was in snatches with no coherence or sense to it. She was lying on the floor at the bottom of the stairs, and there was wetness that turned out to be blood, but she wasn't sure where it was coming from. She must be cut, but her hands when she lifted them to her face were white and uninjured. Then she was sitting up, and Sam was asking her questions, and then she was lying down again alone, so she wasn't sure if she'd ever been sitting up. Perhaps she'd imagined that bit. The next time she was fully aware again, there was someone bending over her. She thought it must be Sam, but it wasn't. It was a woman with kindly eyes.

'Can you hear me, love? I'm Rachel. I'm a paramedic. Can you tell me your name?'

'It's Phoebe.' She wanted to add, I'm not stupid, but she couldn't think clearly. There was something important she needed to ask but she couldn't remember what it was. Until all at once it came crashing back. The dreadful, dreadful horror that her mind seemed to have blocked out for a while was now back with a vengeance.

'My baby. Is my baby OK? My baby.' Oh my God, she'd fallen and she was bleeding and she was crumpled up and there was so much pain, like a twisting in her stomach, two giant hands inside her stomach wrenching and squeezing.

'We're taking you to hospital to get you checked out,' the woman said. 'Try not to worry, Phoebe. We're just going to get you onto a stretcher.'

She didn't argue and say she could walk because she felt too ill and sick and cold. Why did she feel so cold? She let them lift her carefully onto the stretcher, aware of the motion as they carried her out to an ambulance. She was aware of cool night air on her face and of blue flashing lights in the darkness. The thrum of an engine. Then there was the motion of the ambulance as they sped through the streets. Sam was in the ambulance, white-faced, holding her hand. He kept telling her it was going to be OK. Everything was going to be fine. Phoebe clung on tight to the hope of his words, and even tighter to his fingers, even though she didn't see how it could be all right. The fall, the tumbling over and over. The awful hardness of those stairs. The red-hot pokers of pain. How could it possibly be all right?

Then finally they were in a room at the hospital and a kindly nurse with a scanner was leaning over her, but by now Phoebe already knew. There had been too much blood. Too much pain, too much shock. Her baby, her precious little fig, was no more.

30

One of the strange phenomena about life was how your mind and body were not in such perfect synchronicity as you believed. When things happened to your body, your mind could take a while to catch up with the consequences of these things. At least this was how it seemed to Phoebe.

She had lost her baby, but the terrible crashing awfulness of that took a while to properly sink in.

The counsellor at the hospital, a gentle, soft-voiced woman called Linda Baines, told her this delay was because of denial.

'Denial is like a sticking plaster for the soul,' she said. 'Its function is to protect us until we're ready for the truth.'

'I know the truth,' Phoebe said sadly, linking her hands in her lap, although she did also know exactly what Linda Baines meant. For the first few days after she'd lost her baby, she had still cupped her stomach protectively, even though there was no longer anything there to protect. The hollow space of emptiness where there had previously been a burgeoning new life was just too big a deal to get her head around. So she blocked it out. Her mind was just not ready to deal with the loss yet.

'And when we grieve, we don't just grieve for what we have lost,' Linda told Phoebe. 'We grieve for what we never had. We grieve for the future.'

They had done that too, she and Sam. They had cried together, and they had talked a lot about the future they had lost.

Their baby, it had been a boy, would never now grow up big and strong on Puddleduck Farm, learning to love animals, to kick a ball about, to walk in the fields with his parents and Roxie, to pick apples and blackberries and go camping. He would never now learn how to love nature, or how to ride a bike, or how to watch out for Bruce Goose's sharp beak or feed Ninja carrots on the flat of his hand. He wouldn't get to pet the neddies and stroke the farm cats. He'd never now get bossed around by Vanessa Rose and his cousins. He'd never have his first day at school or graduate from uni. The list went on and on. Phoebe hadn't realised how many plans she'd made and how many dreams she'd had until that moment on the stairs when they'd all been snatched away.

Straight after the event, they had both blamed themselves.

'If only I hadn't been so stupidly jealous and stormed off,' Phoebe had said. 'It wouldn't have happened.'

'It wouldn't have happened if I'd kept my big mouth shut,' Sam had countered with deep pain in his eyes. 'You were right. I should never have shared our private stuff with a stranger. I'm so sorry, Phoebe.'

'I'm the one who should be sorry.' They had cried in each other's arms. Nights of crying. It was always worse at night when the darkness settled.

There had also been a brief while when Phoebe had thought the miscarriage might end their relationship. Because after they'd cried, they'd got angry. They'd sniped and shouted at each other, but mostly they'd been angry with themselves. And at least with the anger there was energy.

They hadn't bought much baby stuff, they'd been waiting for the twelve-week scan, but what they had bought, Sam had packed up into a box and put out of sight. Phoebe had ripped their calendar from the wall, scrunched it up and thrown it in the bin because she'd been unable to remove the red rings around the dates of her antenatal appointments.

Neither of them had said 'next time'. It was too early to talk about next times.

Maggie was amazing. She had held Phoebe tightly, briefly, and had said, 'Oh, my darling, how utterly devastating.' She had held Sam too. 'It'll be OK,' she'd kept saying. 'You'll get through it. Just look after each other.'

'Do you think Mum knows?' Phoebe had asked and Maggie had shaken her head.

'She hasn't said anything to me. Neither has Frazier nor Alexa.'

'Then please could we not say anything to any of them?' Phoebe had begged. 'I might tell them one day, but I can't bear to tell them now and then have to immediately un-tell them. If that makes any sense.'

'Of course it does.'

'Ma and Pa don't know either,' Sam had said, sticking his hands in his pockets. 'We were just waiting for the safety margin to be over.' His Adam's apple bobbed.

'No one need know, until you're ready,' Maggie had reassured them both. 'Or never if you're never ready. It's totally up to you, my loves.'

Tori came round with wine. She left Vanessa Rose with Harrison and she spent the evening with Phoebe and they both cried a little.

'I know there's nothing I can say that will help,' she told Phoebe. 'But just know that I am here for you. Day or night. If you need to offload, just call me.'

'Thank you.'

'And I love you,' she added.

'I love you too,' Phoebe had told her.

* * *

Phoebe didn't go into work for ten days. She told everyone at Puddleduck Vets, except for Jenna, who knew the truth, that she'd been struck down with horrendous flu and didn't want to risk passing it on.

Seth stepped up to the plate, despite the fact he didn't know the truth about what was going on. Not only did he cover Phoebe's full-time role, but he also arranged for his nephew, Aiden, to cover farm call-outs. Aiden would do all of the calls that Seth usually did himself.

Seth explained all this to Phoebe on the phone. 'Hasn't Aiden got a full-time job in Salisbury?' she asked him anxiously. 'What about that?'

'He's taken some annual leave, so it's not a problem.'

'Most people take annual leave to go on their holidays, not to work at other practices,' Phoebe protested.

'Aiden's a workaholic so don't you worry about that,' Seth had told her. 'Besides, I think he's trying to distract himself from some kind of woman trouble, so you'd be doing him a favour.'

Phoebe wondered if the woman in question was Jade, but she didn't ask. She was grateful that Aiden was able to help out. Seth obviously trusted him, which was good enough for her. As Maggie had said once before, other people's love lives were definitely none of her business.

Routines and normality were a great antidote for grief. Life moved on whether you wanted it to or not. For other people, the sun still shone, the rain still fell, and milestones still came and went.

Marcus and Natasha had settled into Woodcutter's and Saddam was apparently in his element, so much so that they'd now taken on another cat, a young female they'd named Petra, and also one of Maggie's long-term kennel dogs, Biscuit, who was eleven years old and only had one eye. He and Saddam had always had an understanding, Natasha had told Phoebe. He was one of the few dogs that Saddam had never terrorised. Or maybe Biscuit just didn't see him coming and therefore wasn't scared of him so Saddam had given up.

Tori and Harrison's Burley house was still on schedule for 2 October. They were really looking forward to moving into a home of their own with Vanessa Rose.

Phoebe was really happy that they had found their happy ever after, but she couldn't help wondering if she and Sam were ever going to truly find theirs.

One positive thing that had happened since the miscarriage was that Phoebe and Sam had agreed they would accept Maggie's offer and they would move into Puddleduck Farm as soon as Maggie and Eddie had found somewhere else to buy and had moved out, which Maggie had assured them was likely to be this side of Christmas. They'd decided not to move into Tori and Harrison's rental in the meantime. That move now seemed superfluous.

'A change of scenery will be good for you both,' Maggie had said, and this was the only oblique reference she made to the miscarriage after they had discussed what had happened.

Phoebe and Sam had come to a compromise on the finances that they were all happy with. Sam had put aside his pride about letting Phoebe's family help out. Losing their baby had put things into perspective. Nothing outside of that had seemed important any more. All of the things that had seemed such massive obstacles were now right-sized again.

Good things came from even the most painful of events, Phoebe had concluded. Even if all they did was to give you some perspective on what was important in life.

* * *

When she went back to work, Phoebe discovered that Archie had also started coming over to Puddleduck Pets to help out with the dog walking. She spotted him tramping around the field with the other dog walkers and when he saw her, he came across.

'I'd have thought you'd have had enough on your plate what with walking Chloe and Spot,' she said to him. 'And riding that pony of yours. What are you doing here walking this lot as well?'

'Spot's out with Harrison today,' he said cheerfully. 'And Chloe's in the barn asleep. We went riding first thing, she's worn out.' He put his head on one side. 'I didn't realise how much work dogs are until I got two of my own. You can't just leave them like you can leave guinea pigs and rabbits, can you? They want to be with you all the time.'

'That's right, they do.' Phoebe thought about Roxie, who'd been her constant companion while she'd been off work, and to a lesser extent, Snowball, who'd deigned to come and curl up on her lap if she was sitting in a sunny spot on the sofa.

'Are you enjoying them, though?' she asked Archie.

'I really, really am. We go to two training classes with a woman called Destiny Dolittle. Dolittle's such a cool name for an animal trainer, isn't it? Have you met her?'

Phoebe said she had and then changed the subject. She wasn't sure she'd ever be able to hear the name Destiny Dolittle without feeling an ache of regret.

The emotional healing took longer than the physical healing. Phoebe was hardly aware that it was happening until one day she woke up and realised her first feeling of the day hadn't been pain. Going back to work had helped a lot with this part. Jenna was amazing. The others still didn't know the truth about what had happened, which was how Phoebe wanted it to stay, but Phoebe was aware that Jenna was protecting her, in a dozen little ways.

Making her drinks, being cheerful, buying her favourite biscuits. And one morning, Phoebe noticed that one of her scheduled appointments to see a regular client had been changed. Then later she'd caught a glimpse of Jenna ushering a heavily pregnant woman and her dog into Max's examining room instead of hers.

Bless her. Jenna had always been so very kind.

31

Tori and Harrison were getting married on the last Saturday in August.

A few days before the hen night, which was the week before the wedding, Tori came over to see Phoebe. 'If you're not up to coming to the wedding, I do get it, you know. Being around people when you're dealing with grief isn't so good, I know.'

'Of course I'll be there,' Phoebe said. 'I wouldn't miss my best friend's wedding for the world.'

'Are you sure? Does that include the hen night?'

'Yes, it does,' Phoebe had said firmly. 'I can't just stay at home wrapped in sadness, Tori. Doing normal things actually helps a lot.'

The hen night, to Phoebe's relief, wasn't going to be a massive affair. Tori had opted for a posh meal out with just a few family and friends at the Rhinefield House Hotel, which was set in forty acres of private grounds in the heart of the New Forest.

It had been one of the venues used by the New Forest Diners, a singles club that Tori had been very involved with before she'd met Harrison.

'I think the Rhinefield House Hotel is very apt,' she'd told Phoebe cheerfully. 'For one thing they do great food, but it'll also feel like one last hurrah if you know what I mean.'

Phoebe had smiled wryly. She'd been to New Forest Diners there once too – on Tori's advice – and while she hadn't met a man in the romantic sense, she'd got into conversation with a vet who'd known Seth, and through him had in a roundabout way employed Marcus. So Phoebe had fond memories of the hotel too.

Phoebe hadn't been there since, but she agreed with Tori, it was the perfect place for an upmarket meal. On the evening of the hen night she booked a taxi so she could leave when she wanted to – and as the car sped up the long drive between rhododendron bushes, she realised the place was every bit as grand as she remembered.

The drive opened out to reveal the magnificent grey building with mock Tudor turrets and a crenelated parapet.

'This used to be a private house,' the taxi driver remarked as he dropped her at the front entrance. 'How the other half live, huh.'

'I know. That's what I was thinking.'

'Have a good night, love. I'll pick you up when you're done. Just call the number on the card.'

'Thanks. I will.'

Tori had invited Maggie too, who she'd always seen as a surrogate grandma because she'd been around more than her own grandparents when she was small. They'd spent a lot of her childhood out of the country. Phoebe felt slightly guilty that she hadn't offered to drive herself and pick up Maggie en route but she still felt fragile, and she wanted a quick exit route if she needed it. There was no sense in spoiling Maggie's evening too, if she did need to get away. Phoebe was also relieved that Emilia had decided not to go to the hen night due to tiredness. She was heavily pregnant and it would have hurt to spend an evening with her – to hear her excitedly discussing her imminent arrival.

The hen night was in the orangery and their long table, set up with sparkling cutlery for ten, was positioned beside one of its glass walls so they had a great view of the grounds, especially as it was still daylight when the hen party arrived. The orangery over-looked a man-made oblong water feature that looked a bit like a very long oversized swimming pool. Beyond that were acres of formal gardens – topiary and lawns. The plush surroundings were beautiful.

Tori's grandparents had come back for the wedding, of course, and her gran was at the hen night. Luckily Phoebe felt comfort-able around Tori's family and the few girlfriends they had in common.

She sat between Maggie and Tori and felt herself slowly relaxing.

'How are you doing?' Tori asked her about halfway through the evening. 'You coping OK?'

'I'm good,' Phoebe murmured. 'I really am. This is perfect, isn't it? I'm so thrilled for you. Harrison's the man of your dreams, isn't he?'

'He is. Although I had to kiss a lot of frogs to find him.' Tori glanced around them at the glass room with its framed black and white prints and mood lighting. 'A lot of them were in here as it happens.'

They both giggled.

'How's Sam doing?' Tori added, her green eyes darkening a little. 'Is he OK? Are you two really OK now?'

'It's been tough, but yes, we are. Thanks. We're going to be fine. Truly we are. Enough about us, this is your evening. Are you going to be doing anything outrageous like dancing on the table?

Going skinny dipping in the pool – or whatever they call that water thingie outside?'

Tori gave her a look of mock outrage. 'Phoebe Dashwood, I don't know how you could even suggest such a thing. I'm a respectable mother and wife-to-be these days. I've totally grown up and got past all that nonsense. There will be no dancing on the tables and definitely no skinny dipping in that oversized rill.'

'Is that what it's called? A rill?'

'That's what they're called in smaller gardens. Anyway, I'm definitely not going in there with or without clothes.' She shivered. 'Although I am planning on having too much wine.' She picked up her glass. 'And I very much hope you're going to join me.'

'I am.' Phoebe picked up her own glass and clinked it against Tori's.

'Here's to better things ahead,' Tori said. 'A fabulous future for us all.'

'I'll drink to that,' Phoebe said, sticking out her chin determinedly.

* * *

On the same night Phoebe had gone to Tori's hen night, Sam had gone to Harrison's stag night, which had been held at a private men's club in Salisbury. Sam knew he'd been invited because of the close relationship between Tori and Phoebe but he felt like a spare part. He only knew Harrison and Rufus and he didn't think he'd ever exchanged more than a few sentences with either of them.

Sam had decided in advance to have a couple of soft drinks, wish the groom all the best and then leave, and on the night that's exactly what he did. He breathed a sigh of relief as he climbed back into his Subaru and headed for home. He was looking forward to a quiet night on the sofa with Snowball and Roxie.

When he got back, he saw he had a missed call, which turned out to be from his pa. That was odd. Pa very rarely called his mobile and when he did, it was usually a trouser call. But this time he'd left a message.

'Hi, Sam. Get in touch, lad, when you get this, please.'

Sam called him. 'Hi, Pa – is everything OK?'

'Er, no, not really. Are you at home? I was hoping you might be able to nip by. Your mother's having a mini crisis. I think you might be able to help.'

'I'm on my way,' Sam said, and with a small sigh of disappointment that his planned night on the sofa was not now going to happen, he gave Roxie an apologetic stroke and headed back out again.

The Hendrie household was quiet when he arrived and he let himself in with his key to the flat above the general stores where his parents had always lived and ran up the stairs.

Pa had clearly heard him because he met him at the top. 'Sorry to drag you out.'

'It's OK, I wasn't doing anything.'

'She's in here.' He gestured Sam through to the lounge, where Jan was sitting on the sofa, crying quietly.

'I've tried to talk to her,' Ian Hendrie whispered as he looked at his son apologetically. 'But I don't really know what to say. You're better at all this stuff than me.' He raised his voice. 'Here's Sam now, love.'

Sam pulled up the footstool and sat next to his mother without invading her personal space. 'Hey,' he began quietly. 'What's going on? Did you have another attack?'

She stopped crying and blew her nose with a handful of

tissues she was already holding. 'Oh, hello, Sam. I'm sorry. I told your pa not to call you. It'll pass. It always passes.'

'Is it the agoraphobia? What triggered it?'

She nodded. 'It's so stupid. I feel so stupid. We were going to go out, love, weren't we? We were all set and the table was booked and we got there and we walked in and I just – well, I just... I couldn't breathe.' She paused. 'Ian, make yourself useful. Go and put the kettle on and make Sam a cuppa.'

'He doesn't understand,' she said, as Ian left the room. 'He thinks I should be over it and he gets impatient and it makes it worse.'

'It's OK. And you're not stupid. Are you still seeing the counsellor?'

'No, I'm not, love. It got too expensive.'

'Didn't she give you breathing exercises to do when an attack comes?'

'Yes, I think she did. But I was panicking too much to remember about those.'

'Weren't you on that agoraphobia forum too?'

'I was doing it, but I got out of the habit. Besides, I was coping fine. I hadn't had an attack for ages.' She looked a bit shamefaced. 'Your father shouldn't have dragged you over. I shouldn't need to be offloading on my son. It's pathetic.'

'Oh, Ma, it's not, it's really not.' The defeat in her voice brought out every protective instinct he had. 'We all need help with stuff sometimes. Life can be pretty painful sometimes. It's good to talk.'

'I suppose so.' She looked at him properly for the first time. 'Are you all right, son? You look like you've lost some weight?'

'I have a bit. We've had a rough patch, Phoebe and me.'

'Oh?' She sat up a little straighter in her chair. 'Why's that?'

He hadn't been planning to tell her about the pregnancy that had come to such a painful end, but before he could stop himself, it all came pouring out.

At the end of it, she grabbed both his hands in hers. 'Oh, my lovely boy. Why didn't you tell me? You shouldn't have had to shoulder all that alone.'

His father, who'd come in midway through the story with the mugs of tea on a tray, cleared his throat. 'No, lad, you shouldn't. Tough times. That's when families get together. Talk things through, like, you know.'

Aware of the irony of this statement, his family had never been one for talking things through, at least not emotional things, Sam swallowed.

'There was nothing you could have done. That's why we didn't share it. But to be honest, I do feel better for telling you.'

'Good.' His ma was on her feet now, bustling around, getting chocolate biscuits, the paleness and despair he'd seen on her face when he'd arrived had gone. She had purpose now, and Sam realised with a sense of slowly rising wonder that although he'd always paid lip service to talking things through and he didn't do it as much himself as he should, apart from that time when he shouldn't have done it with Destiny, it was true, it really helped.

Talking about the way he'd felt when he'd lost his unborn child had opened some kind of gateway between him and his emotionally buttoned up family.

For the first time in ages, Sam felt something akin to hope for the future.

32

By the time Sam got home, Phoebe was home too and he told her where he'd been and what had happened. She nodded thoughtfully.

'I hope you don't mind me telling them.' He took her hand. 'I know we said we weren't going to say anything.'

'I know. But that was in the early days when it was all so raw. I thought it would make me feel even worse going through it with more people than was necessary.' She grimaced. 'It would have been different if they'd known I was pregnant.' She looked so sad he could have kicked himself.

'Have I mucked up again, sweetheart?'

'No, of course you haven't. Especially in view of how it turned out. I think sometimes focusing on other people's problems can help with our own.'

'Yeah. It certainly seemed to help Ma. She was lost in a black fog when I got there.'

'Bless her. I'm glad you told her. She won't say anything to my mum, will she?'

'No, I've sworn her to secrecy, and she agreed with me that

news like that should come from you, not her. And you know what Pa's like – he never tells anyone anything.'

'That's true. I will tell Mum some time.' She touched her stomach. 'I'd hate her to think I didn't trust her or anything. But it was such a sad time. I'm getting there, though. I feel a lot better than I did. I'm actually getting round to thinking that sometimes really awful things happen in life, but if they don't destroy you completely then you end up eventually getting to be a stronger person.'

'What doesn't kill you makes you stronger,' Sam summarised.

'Precisely. How was Harrison's stag night?'

'Pretty much as I'd expected. A meeting of old boys who all knew each other and were as relieved as I was when I left them to it.'

Phoebe gave him a half smile. 'Oh, well, you went, that was the main thing. And as it turned out, it's just as well you didn't stay very long. A blessing in disguise.'

'That's a very positive way of looking at it.'

She smiled. 'And I went to the hen night and survived. We're getting there, Sam, aren't we? We're going to be OK.'

'We're OK now,' he said, kissing her forehead softly. 'Like I told Ma earlier, we just have to take things one step at a time. And then one step will lead to another and then another and before we know it, we'll have run a marathon.'

'Very profound.'

'And we need to focus on the positive. That was the other good thing that happened tonight. Ma's promised me she's going back on her forum – she was doing much better when she was regularly talking to other people in the same situation.'

'That's great news.'

'She's also planning to come to Tori's wedding next week. Even if it's just to the church bit for half an hour.'

'Wow, progress indeed. I'm actually looking forward to that. Which is a bit of a turning point.'

'Me too,' Sam said, squeezing her fingers. 'Turning points all round by the sound of it.'

* * *

August had been a month of clouds, strong winds and rain with only the occasional patch of sunshine, and on the day of Tori's wedding it was no different. Phoebe sent Tori a good luck message and Tori replied:

> Flaming weather

> I hope you've got your raincoat.

> It's going to clear by midday, hopefully.

> I'm not really worried. We've got contingency plans for the weather.

Phoebe guessed the contingency plans were marquees. Tori and Harrison's reception was being held on the lawns of Beech-brook House, what with Harrison being Rufus's best friend. She hoped they were sturdy marquees and had the guy ropes knocked in nice and tight.

The wedding was taking place at 11 a.m. At ten it was still raining hard, so Phoebe and Sam headed outside with umbrellas to protect their finery. Sam was wearing his one and only wedding suit and Phoebe was in a new dress. To their dismay, they discovered the Lexus had a flat tyre.

Normally this wouldn't have mattered, they'd have just gone in Sam's Subaru instead, but he'd lent it to his father because his parents' car was in the garage having some work done.

This meant Sam had needed to race back inside, get changed into old clothes, fit the spare tyre, before getting changed back again into his suit. The spare tyre had also been slightly flat, although thankfully not punctured, so they'd gone via the fuel station to pump it up and in the end they hadn't got to the church until two minutes before the start of the ceremony.

The usher, who neither Phoebe nor Sam recognised, gave them a sharp look. 'What happened? Did you forget the time? Get in quick. The bride's due any second.'

Apologising profusely, they rushed inside and found space on a pew and it was hardly any time before the pianist launched into the wedding march and everyone in church craned their necks to get a glimpse of Tori as she came down the aisle on her father's arm.

The classic cream dress looked amazing with her red hair, which was pinned up with diamante clips – she wore a simple lace veil that half covered her face and she seemed to glide like some ethereal angel rather than walk on her proud father's arm.

'Doesn't she look amazing?' Phoebe whispered to Sam as she passed them.

She'd seen Tori's dress before – she'd helped her choose it – but there was something extra-special about seeing it on the actual day. Maybe it was just the sheer radiance of the bride. Tori looked so happy.

'It'll be our turn next,' Sam whispered back, nodding, and Phoebe squeezed his hand.

As the service began and the bride and groom said their vows, Phoebe's mind drifted off to thoughts of her own wedding. Since they'd cancelled the wedding date with the vicar, the whole thing had gone back on hold. But maybe they could reschedule it for June once more. Maybe it wasn't too late. They would have to do some serious planning soon. She and Sam could do it together. It would give the future some focus.

'In celebration, you may now kiss,' the vicar was saying, and Phoebe realised with a start that she'd been so lost in thoughts of her and Sam getting married that she'd missed most of this ceremony. She forced her attention back to the present just in time.

Harrison and Tori came back down the aisle together with joyful steps. Even the morose Harrison had a smile plastered on his face, Phoebe saw. Harrison was a man of few smiles, that was for sure. But Tori clearly loved him.

By the time everyone was outside again, it had stopped raining and the sun deigned to come out, lighting up a watery grey sky – hopefully it would be long enough for the photos to be taken.

People threw confetti and congratulated the happy couple and the churchyard was full of noise and laughter.

'Typical summer's day,' Phoebe overheard a nearby guest say. 'I'm really not sure why anyone ever gets married in August. Who wants raindrops in their wedding album?'

'You get better photos in cloud than bright sun,' his partner replied. 'Tori knows what she's doing. She's a photographer, after all.'

Phoebe spotted Rufus and Emilia outside the church. Emilia was hugely pregnant now. She must be due soon. Phoebe felt Sam's hand close around hers protectively. At some point during the reception, she knew she'd have to speak to Emilia and make small talk, baby talk, but that wasn't yet. She swallowed hard. She'd deal with that when it came.

'Hey,' Sam leaned in and whispered in her ear, 'I've just spotted Ma and Pa over there, and Ma's smiling. Shall we go and say hello?'

To Phoebe's relief, Jan Hendrie didn't make any reference to the miscarriage, other than to touch Phoebe's arm and say softly, 'I hope my boy's taking good care of you, love.'

'Oh, he is,' Phoebe replied. 'How are you doing? It's lovely to see you.'

'I'm doing better than I thought, thank you. We're planning to go to the reception. I've always wanted to see the inside of Beechbrook House.' There was a new steel in Jan's eyes, Phoebe thought with delighted pleasure.

She could see that Sam had noticed it too.

'We'll look forward to seeing you there, Ma,' he said, exchanging glances with his father, who also looked pleased with the way things were going.

Both the afternoon and the evening reception were being held at Beechbrook House and several cars ferried the guests back there.

Sam's Subaru was amongst them, Phoebe was happy to see when she and Sam got there, so his parents had obviously made it over here.

'Your mum's doing great, isn't she?' she said to him as they walked up to the big house.

Rufus may have only wanted a small wedding and reception himself, but it seemed he was happy to facilitate his best friend having a lavishly big one. Summer blue and white was Tori's colour scheme, and so the front of Beechbrook House was decked out with blue balloons and summer blue and white bunting.

She had quipped to Phoebe as August had unfolded in a blaze of grey that it was just as well they'd have something blue at their wedding, because it certainly wasn't going to be the sky!

There were arrows and signs directing wedding guests to the back of the house and Sam and Phoebe joined the people making their way round.

On the back lawn there was a giant blue and white-striped

marquee, more balloons, more bunting and a string quartet. Luckily the musicians were in the main marquee, because the afternoon weather was a mix of sunshine and showers.

And it continued like that for the next half hour as people milled in and out of the marquees, chatting and being served drinks and canapés by a selection of waiting staff. Tori and Harrison weren't having a sit-down meal, they hadn't wanted anything formal – Tori had said there were too many children to entertain – most of whom were currently watching a Punch and Judy show taking place in another marquee. Tori's mum and grans and her new mother-in-law, Harrison's rather posh mother, were taking it in turn to chaperone Vanessa Rose, and loving it, apparently.

The newly married couple themselves were wandering around chatting to little groups of guests.

'We don't mind what the weather's like, do we, honey,' Tori said, catching hold of her new husband's hand as they reached the group Phoebe and Sam were in. 'We just wanted to get hitched.'

'That's right. It'd be a pretty poor show if the success of your nuptials depended on the vagaries of the English weather.' Harrison smiled at her and then at everyone else. He was really pushing the boat out today on the smiling thing, Phoebe thought. Mind you, if you couldn't smile at your own wedding, it would be a pretty poor show too.

The sun came out for the first dance too, or maybe Tori and Harrison timed the dance to coincide with the moment when it did.

Rufus, who was best man, called everyone to attention by tinging a spoon on the side of a cut crystal glass. 'My lords, ladies and gentlemen,' he said without a trace of irony in his voice, because he and Emilia were the only lord and lady present.

'Taking the dance floor, or should that be the lawn, for the very first time as husband and wife, can you please put your hands together and welcome Mr and Mrs McArthy.'

There were cheers and applause as Harrison and Tori danced to Ed Sheeran's 'Perfect', which had the most romantic lyrics ever, Phoebe thought, as she listened to the words and saw the utter happiness on the new couple's faces. It was so beautiful. When Ed Sheeran sang the line about dancing barefoot on the grass, Tori kicked off her shoes and did exactly that, and everyone cheered, and Phoebe felt a lump the size of a marble in her throat and she had to wipe away a tear.

At the end of the song, Rufus announced they would now have the traditional throwing of the bouquet. Entering into the spirit of things, Phoebe joined the other not yet married ladies amongst the guests and Tori stood with her back to the group.

She picked up her bouquet, and Phoebe saw her glance over her shoulder, catch Phoebe's eye and throw it back firmly in Phoebe's direction. She wasn't quite quick enough to catch it, but it did land at her feet, and she bent to pick it up and to breathe in the sweet-scented, perfect flowers.

Did it still count if you didn't actually catch the bouquet? Did that mean she and Sam were going to have more problems before they actually got to walk down the aisle? She brushed away the thought. Of course it didn't – it was just a silly superstitious tradition. She and Sam had already had their share of bad luck.

She was distracted from these dark thoughts when she caught sight of Spot, Archie's terrier, running across the lawn with something in his mouth. A whole sandwich, by the look of it.

Archie was in hot pursuit. He caught up with Spot, who was busy scoffing the sandwich before his young owner could take it from him.

Archie must have been aware of Phoebe's gaze because he looked up straight into her eyes and put a finger to his lips.

Phoebe smiled and nodded. She and Archie would always be on the same wavelength as far as animals were concerned. They would always be on the animals' side. Archie stuck up a thumb and Phoebe stuck up hers in a return gesture of solidarity.

It would be another couple of years before Archie could do work experience at Puddleduck Vets officially, but she'd already agreed he could come in the following year if he wanted to so he could get a head start. That was something else to look forward to.

The one thing she had been dreading about the reception was talking to Emilia. But when the moment came, it wasn't as difficult as she'd feared. Emilia, who was wearing a beautiful lemon silk maternity dress, looked tired and overheated. She fanned her face with a napkin as she spoke to Phoebe and Sam.

'It's so humid today,' she complained. 'We need a proper downpour to clear this heat. A good storm, not this silly English drizzle, ja?'

'Definitely,' Phoebe agreed. 'But hopefully not until today's over. We don't want the marquee to take off and sail off over the trees.'

'No, we don't,' Rufus said, arriving beside his wife. 'Although it should be OK. Harrison was overseeing the pegging in. How are you both?'

'We're good, thank you,' Sam said, and Phoebe sensed he was desperate to get away. Not from Rufus but Emilia. People often assumed it was just the woman who grieved when a couple lost a baby, maybe she would have assumed that herself once, too. But she knew differently now. Sam may not have carried their child, but he'd been every bit as devastated as she had when they'd lost him.

In the end, it was Tori herself who came to rescue them.

'Hi, Rufus, hi, Emilia.' She glanced at Phoebe and Sam. 'Do you mind if I steal these two for a minute? I need their opinion on something.'

She swept them off across the lawn, which was spongy but not as soggy as Phoebe had thought it might be, considering all the rain they'd had. 'You two doing OK?' Tori said when they were out of earshot. Her eyes were concerned.

'We're good,' Phoebe answered for them both. 'But thank you for being so lovely.'

'All part of the service.' Tori gave a mock bow. 'Are you enjoying yourselves?'

'We are,' Sam said. 'That was a beautiful wedding. The reception venue's not too shabby either. It's all right for people with friends in high places.'

Tori beamed. 'I know. We are lucky. It saved us a fortune as well. Rufus's wedding present to us both. The venue, the catering, and the band. He even offered us a night in the manor house for our first night. We turned that down and I think he was quite relieved. Vanessa Rose still doesn't always sleep through the night.'

'Although he'll need to get used to that, won't he?' Phoebe quipped. 'Seeing as he'll have his own little sleep wrecker soon.' She was surprised to find the words didn't hurt too much. She was definitely getting there. 'More importantly,' she added, 'are you enjoying yourself, Tori? Is your special day what you dreamed it would be?'

'Oh, it is. It is.' Tori spread her hands apart. 'How could I not enjoy being in this beautiful place? Although actually I wouldn't have minded if we'd got married in a registry office, as long as we got married. It's weird, isn't it? I grew up dreaming about being a bride. I know it's not very PC admitting that kind of thing, these days, but it's true. I wanted the white dress and the Rolls Royce, and I got them, and it's been amazing. But I think we'd have had just as good a day if I hadn't had those things.' She paused, her green eyes reflective.

'Do you remember when we were kids and we used to have pretend weddings? You two, and me and Frazier.'

'How could I forget? Those weddings are burned in my memory,' Sam said, pressing a hand against his forehead in a look of mock horror. 'You two bullying me and poor Frazier into putting on suits that were four sizes too big for us!'

'I think they were Dad's old suits,' Phoebe said, remembering. 'It's a good job Mum never caught us.'

'They were great days,' Tori said fondly. 'We were so lucky to have the run of Puddleduck Farm – well, the parts where there weren't cows wandering around in the fields.'

She blinked a few times. 'I'm glad you're going to be living there, you guys. It's such a beautiful place for...'

She broke off and Phoebe said softly, 'It's OK, you can say it, Tori. It's a beautiful place to bring up a family. And we are planning a family. In fact, me getting pregnant was a bit of a wake-up call for us both. We weren't thinking about having a family just yet, as you know, we'd put the idea in a box marked "one day" but now we're both really aware that you can't take anything for granted in life. So our "one day" is now "whenever it happens". We're certainly not going to do anything to prevent it from happening, are we, Sam?'

'Absolutely not,' Sam said.

'I'm so pleased,' Tori said. 'And on that note, I'd better circulate, and rescue Vanessa Rose from my new mother-in-law – or should that be the other way round – I think I can hear her squawking from here.'

'Your mother-in-law or Vanessa Rose?' Sam quipped, and they all smiled.

'Catch up again later,' Tori said, hitching up her dress, and heading off towards the marquee.

'I think maybe we should head for the marquee too,' Phoebe said, as a fat plop of rain landed on her nose. She glanced up at the sky, which was an ominous grey. 'It looks like we may have had our allocated sunshine for a bit.'

'It'll be out again later,' Sam said. 'There's always sunshine after rain. It's a universal truth about life.'

'Oh, is it now? I haven't heard that one.'

'It's true,' Sam promised, grabbing her hand as the rain got harder and they both ran laughing towards the big marquee.

33

In the middle of September, Phoebe got another call-out to go and see Arthur at Acting the Goat.

'He's been doing his Houdini act again,' Fliss explained when she spoke to Phoebe. 'He's cut his face this time. I think it might need a stitch.'

'I thought Arthur had finished doing his escapee routine,' Phoebe said when she arrived and Fliss took her out to see Arthur, who had blood oozing from a nasty cut above his eye.

'Yes, he has pretty much, but it's mating season and young Arthur here was rather keen to get to his intended before we were ready for him.' Fliss gave a rueful shake of her head. 'It was my fault, I should have remembered that he can get out of anywhere when he's motivated.'

'Bless his little cotton socks,' Phoebe said. 'Are you OK to hold him while I stitch him up?'

'Course I am.'

'How's mating season going?' Phoebe asked her while she worked on a resigned but patient Arthur. He really was good natured.

'It's only just started but yes, I think all's going according to plan. In view of what happened last time, we decided to let Mary have one more mating. They'll very likely be Arthur's.'

'They'll be beautiful kids,' Phoebe remarked, as she finished stitching. 'Thanks. I'm done.'

Fliss let go of a relieved Arthur, who shook his head and went a bit cross eyed as he tried to look upwards at his stitches. 'We hope so,' she said. 'Will you come in for a slice of cake?'

'Yes, please.'

Phoebe followed her into the bungalow. After the August showers, the weather had turned nice again and they were having something of an Indian summer.

'It's typical,' Fliss said, as she made coffee and cut Phoebe a slice of delicious-looking Victoria sponge. 'The weather took a turn for the better the minute the kids went back to school. The human ones, I'm talking about,' she said, passing Phoebe a plate. 'All summer I was trying to entertain them in all that rain, and as soon as they go back, we get summer. Shish.'

'You have them here a lot then,' Phoebe asked, before taking a bite of cake that virtually melted in her mouth.

'I do. They're not even my grandchildren. They're my niece's children, but her mother, Eliza – Eliza was my sister – died when she was in her early fifties, so I do everything I can to help out.'

'I'm sorry about your sister,' Phoebe said, looking around the modern kitchen. There were a couple of childish paintings stuck to the fridge with fridge magnets.

'Yes, it was cancer. Poor Eliza. She had it for a couple of years. Fought it off once but then it came back. Sarah, her daughter, got pregnant just before she died and one of the last things Eliza said to me was would I look after her grandchildren? She'd always wanted grandchildren; God rest her soul. It was so sad. Our little

Eliza's the eldest one – they named her after her gran, but my lovely sister didn't even get to meet her.'

'Gosh. That is sad.'

'Isn't it? Eliza would have made a fantastic grandma.' Her face clouded. 'The irony of it is that Neville and I never wanted children. He was always obsessed with work and I had enough of kids at school. If ever you want to be put off being a mother, I'd recommend working as a headmistress for six months. It knocks all of your idealistic notions about kids being little angels right out of the water, I can tell you.'

'I bet,' Phoebe said, fascinated.

'I don't think we'd have made great parents, Neville and I – but actually it's very good fun being a stand-in grandparent.' She grinned. 'More cake?'

Phoebe managed to resist the temptation, but as she walked back out to her Lexus, she remembered the conversation she'd had with Seth last time they'd been here.

He'd been convinced that Fliss and Neville hadn't been able to have children and had been sad for them. It was amazing how wrong you could be, Phoebe thought.

She hadn't chatted much with Seth lately, other than to exchange notes on cases they were dealing with. She decided to put that right. It would be nice to do something social with him and Myra. She would ask Sam how he felt about going out for a meal with the couple.

* * *

Sam agreed that he'd love to see Seth and the meal out was arranged for a couple of Saturdays later.

In the meantime, Phoebe, accompanied by Sam because it seemed only right, went to see her parents and they told them about the miscarriage. 'I don't want to make a big thing of it, Mum,' Phoebe said, 'but we just wanted you to know.'

'I am sorry, my loves,' Louella said to them both, and James patted Sam's shoulder.

'I'm very sorry too,' he added, his face sombre.

'We're OK, we're moving on,' Phoebe said.

'Talking of moving,' James said, in what was for him a surprisingly tactful segue, 'what's happening with your move to Puddleduck Farm? Maggie tells me the paperwork's nearly done for that too.'

'It's getting there,' Phoebe said, 'but I think Maggie and Eddie finding the perfect house is going to take a little longer. They've found three perfect places already and then one or other of them has changed their minds again. Maggie mostly,' she added. 'You thought she was bad about changing her mind on wedding arrangements. Choosing a house is proving to be even more troublesome.'

'It's a big decision,' Louella said. 'She'll get there, love. With a bit of luck, we'll all be settled again by Christmas.'

'And if we're not, we'll have Christmas at Puddleduck Farm anyway, I expect,' Phoebe said. 'That's something Maggie and Eddie do agree on. For a start, it's the only place that's big enough.'

'Roll on Christmas,' James said with feeling.

* * *

Phoebe and Sam had arranged to meet Seth and Myra at an Italian in Bridgeford. That day, Phoebe and Seth left Puddleduck Vets at the same time.

'See you later,' Seth said, tossing his flat cap onto the

passenger seat as he got into his car. 'We're really looking forward to it.'

'Us too,' Phoebe said.

On the way back to Bridgeford, she thought about the sunflower field where she'd sneaked in to take a photo on that day when the whole of her future had seemed so sunny. It seemed an eternity ago. She hadn't looked at that photo since she'd showed it to Tori. She associated it too much with hope and sunshine and her being pregnant and blooming. Since the miscarriage, she couldn't bear to look at it. Neither had she been able to bear taking the route home past the sunflower field. She'd driven a couple of miles out of her way instead. But today, instead of taking the long way round, she drove past the field.

She could see before she got very close to it that the sunflowers had gone. Or to be more precise, they were still standing, but whereas before they'd been a proud army of yellow all facing towards the sun, each one now stood skeletal and lifeless, a thin black shadow of its former self. The yellow petals were yellow no more and their round black centres, the only recognisable part of the flower, no longer proudly faced the sun, but drooped downwards towards the earth. To Phoebe, it seemed as though their tall dead stalks were no longer strong enough to hold them up – they probably weren't.

The layby opposite – not surprisingly – was empty. There were no photo opportunities here today, but for some reason Phoebe couldn't quite fathom, she pulled over and parked. Then she crossed the road and went into the field, as she'd done before.

Close up, she could see the individual seed pods on each black flower head. How odd, she thought, that they hadn't been harvested but just left in the field to die. The whole field looked blackened, the sky was grey, and the air felt full of despair. Phoebe didn't linger.

She told Sam about it when she got home and he shook his head. 'Maybe sunflowers are one of those crops that farmers get subsidised to grow and not harvest. Or maybe they didn't ripen properly or something – what with all that rain we've had.'

'Yes, that could be it.' Phoebe nodded sadly. 'Remind me to ask Seth later. I bet he'll know. He's a mine of information like that.'

The table was booked for seven and Seth and Myra were already in situ when Sam and Phoebe arrived at the restaurant, which was all red and white checked tablecloths, red candles in Chianti bottles and scented deliciously with herbs, hot tomato and garlic.

The two couples exchanged greetings and hugs. Phoebe didn't know Myra very well, they'd met less than a handful of times, but Myra turned out to be one of those women who was very easy to be around. She was warm, smiley and chatty without being over-bearing. They all ordered pizzas.

'A forbidden treat,' Seth told Phoebe in a stage whisper. 'She won't let me have them at home.'

'Don't tell such fibs, Seth.' Myra tapped his arm in gentle admonishment. 'We have them at least once a month.' She winked at Phoebe.

'That's not nearly often enough,' Seth complained, giving his wife a pleading look. 'I thought we'd have them more now I'm retired.'

'Semi-retired...' Myra rolled her eyes. 'How's he behaving himself at Puddleduck Vets, Phoebe?'

'He's wonderful,' Phoebe said staunchly, and Seth filled up everyone's glasses from a water jug on the table and smirked.

'See? Someone thinks I'm wonderful.'

It was all very light-hearted and it was obvious to Phoebe that the older couple adored each other.

'So what do you do?' Myra asked Sam.

He told her and she looked fascinated. 'My Seth was a jockey – back in the day. You did OK, didn't you, love?'

Seth nodded. Horses were still one of his favourite subjects, and for a while they all chatted about horses and the differences and the similarities between racing, show jumping and steeple-chasing.

Their pizzas arrived. Giant things that filled the plates and meant they had to shift wine glasses around on the table.

'Why did you stop racing?' Sam asked Seth as they ate.

'It's a young man's game. You break things more easily when you're older. And only the guys at the top of their game really make any money. Besides, we wanted to start a family.'

'We did,' Myra said. 'But sadly, it wasn't to be.'

'I am sorry,' Phoebe said with feeling. 'You two would have made great parents.'

'Thanks.' Myra was the only one who hadn't quite finished eating, but now she pushed her remaining slice of pizza to one side of her plate and wiped her face with her napkin. Her eyes went a little reflective. 'I had a couple of miscarriages. Three in the end before they established I was unlikely to carry a baby full term.'

'Oh, gosh.' Phoebe met the older woman's eyes.

'Sorry,' Myra said. 'It's not really dinner party conversation. And it was a very long time ago.'

'I had one too,' Phoebe said softly. 'Quite an early one. I was eleven weeks.'

'I'm very sorry to hear that,' Myra said, her eyes holding Phoebe's over the flickering red candle so it was as though the two women were alone on the table. 'But please try not to worry. There are lots of benign reasons for them. I'm sure you know that.'

'Mine was caused by a fall,' Phoebe said, aware that both Seth and Sam were also listening. 'So at least I know the reason for it.'

Aware that Seth was now looking very concerned, she met his eyes briefly and said, 'It was back in July. When I was off with the flu. I couldn't face telling anyone the truth.'

Myra murmured her understanding. 'Bless you. That must have been traumatic.'

Phoebe glanced at Sam. 'I... We're... getting over it.'

'These things take longer than people think,' Myra went on. 'Give yourselves plenty of time. Don't work too hard. Lean on Seth. He'd be happy to do some extra hours if you need him to, wouldn't you, love?'

'Absolutely,' Seth said. 'I'm more than happy to do extra hours whenever you need me. There'll be no charge.'

Phoebe felt her eyes fill with tears at his kindness. 'Thanks, Seth. I'm OK. Really, I am, and you've helped loads already. Having your Aiden in was brilliant. I've always felt a bit guilty that he gave up his holiday to help us out. But it was so kind of him. We couldn't have managed without him.' She hesitated. 'How is he doing now? Did he get over his woman trouble?'

'Yes, I think so.' Seth's eyes warmed with affection. 'Aiden is his own worst enemy when it comes to women. He falls in love too easily and he's always worn his heart on his sleeve. But you can't put an old head on young shoulders, can you? He seemed happy enough last time we talked.'

'That's good news,' Phoebe said.

The conversation moved on but it wasn't until the end of the evening that Phoebe remembered the sunflowers.

'Why would a farmer let a field of sunflowers just wither and die?' she asked Seth.

'Maybe they haven't. Where are they?'

Phoebe told him and he frowned. 'Mmm, yes, I know the field

you mean. It could be that they just haven't harvested yet. Leaving sunflowers in situ can be part of the natural drying process. It saves time and money and preserves the seed quality.'

'I knew you'd know,' Phoebe said. 'So they may still harvest them then?'

'They might do. Or it might be crop rotation. Sunflowers are good at absorbing nutrients from the soil so when they decompose the nutrients go back to the soil.'

'But whatever the reason, it's all a part of the great big cycle of nature,' Sam said. 'A necessary part. Is that what you're saying?'

'I'd say that sums it up perfectly,' Seth said. 'Right, I'm getting the bill. No arguments.'

He didn't win that one, Sam insisted on going halves, but as Phoebe and Myra sat at the table while their men fought it out, Myra said to Phoebe, 'Shall we swap numbers? It would be nice to keep in touch. Even if it's only the odd WhatsApp.'

'I'd like that.'

'If you ever want to talk to someone, Phoebe, about what happened, someone who understands because they've been there – I'm a good listener.'

'Thank you.'

'And Phoebe, just because you didn't get the chance to hold your baby, it doesn't mean you're not still a mum.'

'Thank you,' Phoebe whispered, feeling her throat close, as she looked into the older woman's soft eyes. For the first time, she felt as though there was someone else out there who really understood how she felt. And it helped. It really, truly helped.

34

In October, Emilia and Rufus became the proud parents of Francesca Alfreda Gracie Holt. Archie, who was clearly hugely excited, sent Phoebe a stream of blurred baby pictures on Whats-App. This was followed up by an official announcement from Rufus and Emilia.

Phoebe and Maggie sent them a congratulations card from everyone at Puddleduck Farm and Phoebe told Archie she'd look forward to meeting his new sister as soon as she was big enough to be shown off to the world.

October also became the month of the house move. Tori, Harrison and Vanessa Rose moved into their new house in the first week of October, as planned. Maggie and Eddie found their perfect house on the day before Halloween.

'Are you sure this is the one?' Phoebe asked Maggie when she popped into Puddleduck Vets at lunchtime to tell everyone the news, wearing a black witch's hat covered in silver stars.

'Of course I'm sure. It's perfect.'

'To be fair, that's what you've said about all the others, though, Gran.'

'How many times have I told you not to call me Gran?'

'Why are you wearing a witch's hat, Mrs Crowther-May?' asked Marcus, who was sitting behind reception.

'Oh, lord, I'd forgotten that was on my head. Natasha got me to put it on for some kids earlier who were rehoming a cat.'

'A black cat, I assume,' Phoebe said in delight. 'Were you threatening them with all sorts of dire magic spells if they didn't take care of their new cat?'

'Of course I wasn't,' Maggie said in a voice that made Phoebe think that was exactly what she'd been doing. She waved a sheaf of estate agent's details at Phoebe. 'Don't you want to see our house?'

'Yes, please.' Phoebe spread the details out on the reception counter and everyone who was in reception, which included Jenna and Max, leaned in for a closer look.

The pretty bungalow with the red-tiled roof and blue front door reminded Phoebe of Puddleduck Farm. It had a big kitchen and a square lounge which led into a rather beautiful glass building that was a cross between an orangery and a conservatory. It was on a corner plot so the garden was bigger than Phoebe had expected too and full of what the estate agents called 'well-established shrubs'.

'It's beautiful,' she told Maggie.

'Fabulous,' echoed Jenna.

Marcus was nodding enthusiastically.

'It's within walking distance of your parents,' Maggie added proudly. 'Not that either of us are planning on giving up driving just yet. We still need to come over and keep an eye on your lot, for a start.'

'So you can cast spells on us,' teased Marcus and Phoebe marvelled at how confident he'd become lately from the shy serious youngster he'd been when he'd joined Puddleduck. Natasha was definitely good for him.

'I might cast the odd spell.' Maggie shot him a look and then winked. 'If you don't all behave yourselves.'

Everyone straightened their shoulders a little, even though they all knew she was joking.

'Have you made an offer?' Phoebe asked.

'Not only have we made one, but it was accepted this morning. The current owner's moving to Southampton to live with her daughter so there isn't a chain. Nice lady, actually. She might have to rehome her little cat – it depends on her granddaughter's asthma – but I told her if there were any problems at all, she could just bring him back to us and Eddie and I would give him a good home until the end of his days. I think that's what clinched the deal, actually.'

Later that day, Phoebe and Maggie sat in the kitchen at Puddleduck Farmhouse and chatted about everything, while the dogs lay around on the flagstones, each in their usual spaces. Buster and Tiny by the Aga and Roxie inching as close as she could without ever quite getting in prime position.

'Are you sure you won't be too sad to leave here?' Phoebe asked her grandmother.

'Yes, I'll be sad, but I'll also be relieved that I'm leaving my old home in such good hands. Not to mention the fact I won't really be leaving it. I can come back any time I like – well, presuming you and I don't fall out, and you let me in.' Her hazel eyes warmed.

'I can't imagine us ever falling out,' Phoebe said. 'Not for long. And you can have the spare key to the door. We don't need three.'

'I wouldn't dream of it, but thank you, my darling. How are you and Sam doing now?'

'We're good, or at least we're getting towards good. We're actually going to a party tomorrow afternoon.'

'A Halloween party in the afternoon. Strange time to have one.'

'It's not a Halloween party. Which is a pity because if it was I could have borrowed your hat.'

'Thanks for the reminder.' Maggie took the hat off and put it on the kitchen table. 'I'll stick it back in the pantry with my broomsticks.' She winked. 'What sort of party is it then?'

'It's a puppy party with Roxie's siblings. I know they're not strictly puppies any more – we were going to have one back in August when they had their first birthday, but unfortunately the woman who's organising it was ill so it had to be cancelled. It was rescheduled for this Sunday, which was the next time that everyone could meet.'

'So Roxie will be meeting up with her siblings again – that's a nice idea. I hope they all still get on and don't start squabbling with each other. Although I suppose if they do, they'll have a vet on hand.'

Roxie pricked up her ears at the sound of her name and Phoebe mouthed, 'Good girl,' across the kitchen.

'Where's the party?'

'At Lyndhurst in some posh house. Apparently they have half an acre of garden so the dogs can have a good old run around. We won't be cramped, anyway.'

'Have fun,' Maggie said. 'And make sure you take lots of photos. I'd like to see how those little scallywags are getting on.'

'You can come with us if you like? I'm sure the host wouldn't mind if you came. She used to be one of the volunteers. I think her name's Diana.'

'No, no, it's fine. I don't want to gate-crash any parties,' Maggie said. 'You and Sam go and enjoy yourselves. According to the weathermen, it's supposed to be warm and sunny on Sunday too.'

* * *

The weathermen were right, it was sunny on Sunday, and as Sam and Phoebe pulled into a wide drive where six cars were already parked, they were both in good moods.

'I'm really looking forward to seeing how the others are all getting on,' Phoebe said as they walked across the gravel driveway and rang the front doorbell, which turned out to be unnecessary as it was on the latch.

A cacophony of barking began and Roxie strained forward on her lead when she heard the other dogs.

'Do you think she'll recognise them?' Phoebe said.

'I guess we're about to find out.'

The door was opened by a smiling woman, who Phoebe recognised as Diana, though it had been a while since they'd met.

'Come in, come in, mind the dogs, it's chaos,' she told them cheerfully. 'We're all out the back.'

There weren't just dalmatians, Phoebe realised as they followed her through the house. A couple of cocker spaniels were milling about in the wide hall too, wagging their feathery tails and looking very excited.

There was much sniffing and wagging and then they were outside in a garden, which did indeed look vast.

Two of the other dalmatians were playing around a swimming pool with a dark blue cover on it and the other one was being petted by a man sitting on a garden bench who looked a bit overwhelmed by all the activity. On the far side of the garden, an agility course had been set up. There were several jumps, two tunnels, an A-frame and some weaving poles and at that moment a woman with blonde hair in a ponytail was running alongside the jumps while a black and white collie-cross lookalike jumped them beside her.

An older couple and some teenagers were watching her.

'We got our friendly dog trainer in to give us a demonstration on agility and maybe teach us a few moves,' Diana explained. 'We thought that might be a fun thing to do.'

Phoebe glanced across again and she felt a twinge of unease in her stomach. 'Is that Destiny Dolittle, or just someone who looks like her?' she asked Sam.

'I was wondering the same thing. It does look very much like her.' He glanced at her. 'Are you OK with that?'

'Of course I am.' She wasn't surprised he was asking, though. Her insecurities around Destiny might have been completely irrational with no basis in reality whatsoever, but that didn't stop her feeling blindsided. Especially after what had happened after the last time she'd appeared out of nowhere like a bad penny.

Roxie, who was still on the lead, gave a small whine of excitement as she spotted one of her siblings and Sam bent to unclip it. For a few moments, there was a lot of wagging and bouncing around and all the owners came smiling to watch. Very soon there were four dalmatians and two cocker spaniels running around on the lawn and everyone was comparing notes about their dogs.

The next time Phoebe looked up, the agility demonstration had finished and Destiny was talking to some of the people who'd been watching.

'Let's go and say hello,' Phoebe said.

Sam glanced at her in surprise. 'OK, if you're sure.'

They walked across the lawn towards the agility course and Phoebe swallowed and found herself wondering if today might be the day she finally got the chance to find out what the real

Destiny was like, as opposed to the glamorous rival version she had created in her head.

Destiny spotted them just before they got there.

'Oh, hi, Sam. Fancy seeing you here.'

Over friendly, Phoebe thought, irritated, but before she could say anything, Destiny turned in her direction.

'Phoebe, isn't it? How lovely to see you again. Where's your gorgeous girl?'

'She's around here somewhere.' Phoebe pointed to where the dalmatians were still playing together, racing in and out of two apple trees. 'It's hard to tell the difference between them when they're all together,' she said, feeling surprised that it was so hard. 'But I think that one's Roxie.'

'She's definitely the prettiest of the bunch.' Destiny's amazing amber eyes warmed. 'God, I love dogs.'

'Can I get you two ladies a drink?' Sam intervened. 'Apparently they're serving tea, coffee and wine in the house.'

'Just a sparkling water for me, please, if they've got it,' Phoebe said.

'The same for me, thanks,' Destiny added.

When Sam had walked away to get them, there was a slightly awkward pause. But Phoebe was determined to forge ahead. 'Do you just train dogs or is it other animals too?'

'No, it's not just dogs. I do cats as well, and there is some call for other animals. I've helped people out with horses. Once it was a pet rat. I had a call about a parrot the other day.'

'A parrot with a behavioural problem?' Phoebe gasped. 'What kind?'

'It was a language problem, funnily enough. The guy who owned it wanted some help in retraining it to talk – or more to the point, not talk. It had become such an excellent mimic it was interfering with his love life.'

'It wasn't called Mr Spock, was it?' Phoebe asked, intrigued.

'It was. How did you know that?'

Phoebe gave her an edited version and before long they were both laughing, which certainly broke the ice.

'I'm guessing you started out by training your own dogs, did you?' Phoebe asked.

'I did, yes. I've loved dogs since I was tiny. I had an odd upbringing. My parents were – how do I put this? I guess today's term would be not present. Dad was a scientist and he was always immersed in some field study or another. And Mum walked around with her head in the clouds. I'm not sure she even noticed I was there half the time.' For a moment, Destiny looked reflective. 'My mum's name was Sky. Her mother came from a long generation of hippies and fortune tellers, and I think they thought that would continue with me, hence the name, Destiny, but I turned out to be Mrs Practical without an intuitive bone in my body. Except for dogs. I think I had more in common with Bruno, our boxer, than I had with my parents. I certainly spent more time with him than them.' She broke off. 'Gosh, sorry, you didn't want to hear my whole life history.'

'I'm interested,' Phoebe said, realising that she was and not just because she wanted to feel reassured that this woman wasn't a threat. There was something very likeable about Destiny. Something very authentic and real.

'I don't usually tell anyone all that either. You must be a good listener.'

Her voice was so genuine that Phoebe felt disarmed. She also felt suddenly amazingly grateful that she hadn't had the kind of family Destiny had been born into.

'Are you close to your parents now?'

'No, not really. I mean we haven't fallen out. But we're just not that close either. How about you?'

'Yes, I'm really close to mine.' Phoebe thought about Maggie and Farmer Pete and how amazing it had been to grow up on Puddleduck Farm; and about Louella and James, who'd been great parents, supportive and nurturing. Even Frazier had been pretty cool. The one thing all of them had been, was there for her. She couldn't imagine having family who didn't notice whether you were around or not.

'Do you have any brothers or sisters?' she asked Destiny.

'No. I was an only child. So were my parents, so no cousins either. Gosh, that sounds sad and lonely. It wasn't, though. I always had animals. Guinea pigs, rabbits, pet mice. As well as Bruno.'

'I had guinea pigs too, and rabbits.'

'I count myself incredibly lucky to have grown up with animals,' Destiny said. 'Lots of kids don't have that opportunity and they've shaped my whole life, my whole career. Was it the same for you? Sam said you're a vet. Did you always know you wanted to do that too?'

'Yes, I did. From a very early age I knew it was what I was born to do. If that doesn't sound crazy. I used to do operations on my collection of toy animals, and every time I used to think I'm going to do this for real one day.' Phoebe blinked a few times, surprised at herself. She rarely shared that with anyone, let alone with a beautiful female she'd been highly suspicious of for the last nine months of her life.

'It doesn't sound crazy at all.' Destiny smiled. She had dimples, Phoebe saw in fascination. Gosh, could someone really be that beautiful? And be nice too? She had a vague memory of Tori saying that Destiny had seemed nice when she'd interviewed her for the magazine.

'You could have been a model,' she blurted. 'You are so stunning.'

Destiny flushed but she didn't deny it. 'I don't think I'd have liked the long hours and I'm guessing being a model would be a lonely business. Good looks have their downside,' she added after a moment. 'Nice men admire you from a distance but don't ask you out because they think you're out of their league and women hate you on sight. I should qualify that – women who don't take the time to get to know you hate you on sight. They grab their men and steer them off fast in the opposite direction.'

Phoebe felt guilty. That was exactly what she had done.

Sam arrived back with a tray of sparkling water. 'I see you two are getting on well.'

'We have a lot in common,' Phoebe told him. 'We both love animals.'

'And we're both independent and beautiful women,' Destiny added with no hint of irony in her voice. 'We were bound to have a lot in common.'

A moment later, they were joined by Diana, who wanted to talk about agility, and after that they didn't get the chance to speak much to Destiny again.

'Destiny wasn't a bit like I'd expected her to be,' Phoebe said to Sam when they were finally on their way home again with an exhausted Roxie asleep in the back of the car.

'No?' He left the question mark hanging in the air and took his eyes off the road for long enough to glance at her. 'What did you expect her to be like?'

'I'm not sure really.' She pondered this for a moment. 'Arrogant maybe, sure of herself. But she's not. I really liked her. She has a lovely, genuine warmth.'

'Good,' Sam said. 'I like her too. But not in the way I like you,' he added evenly.

'I know.' Phoebe felt a little shamefaced. 'I don't know why I felt like she was such a threat. It seems ridiculous now.'

'You can't judge a book by its cover. But that's exactly what we all do sometimes.'

'Yes, I know. Seth and I were saying the same thing the other day. We both thought that Fliss and Neville at Acting the Goat had the perfect life. They own a beautiful smallholding in the forest. And then Seth decided that maybe they didn't have the perfect life because they didn't have children and I later found out they didn't have children because they didn't actually want any.' She laughed. 'We'd got that one completely wrong. Another case of you can't judge a book by its cover.'

'Yep,' Sam said. 'But we all do it.' They'd just arrived back at the maisonette. 'We'd better see if we can wake Roxie up,' Sam said. 'She's completely spark out in the back.'

35

Two weeks before Christmas, Maggie and Eddie completed the purchase of their bungalow. They had adopted the previous owner's little cat in the end. Maggie was convinced that had sealed the deal and Phoebe thought she might be right.

It had all clearly been meant to be.

They'd hired professional movers to pack up and transport things from Puddleduck Farm to their new home, but the entire Dashwood family were helping out too.

Phoebe wasn't sure how much they were actually helping and how much they were getting in the way, although Sam, Frazier and their father had done their fair share of the heavy lifting.

Maggie was shouting instructions to everyone, and Phoebe, Louella and to a lesser extent, Alexa, because she had three youngsters to keep an eye on, had made endless mugs of coffee for everyone all morning.

Earlier on, Phoebe had also done a complete animal handover with Maggie and Natasha so the transition would go smoothly.

Louella was in the process of making one final coffee. The

whistling kettle was staying with the Aga so it didn't need to be packed anyway.

'We're going electric in our new home,' Maggie said, when she came into the kitchen to see if there was anything left to do. 'Although I think the hob's actually gas so I could get one of these whistling affairs.'

'You can take this one if you like,' Phoebe suggested.

'No, that definitely belongs here.'

'What about these yummy cookies I found in the cupboard?' Phoebe asked, waving an ice cream tub that had been repurposed as a biscuit tin under Maggie's nose. 'Are they staying here?'

'Yes, they're a moving in present. You're supposed to be saving them for later for you and Sam, not sharing them with the removal men and everyone else.'

'Too late for that,' Phoebe said, prizing off the lid and liberating a cookie.

Maggie shook her head. 'You should be the size of a house the amount of sugar you eat. It's really most unfair.'

'I think stress burns off calories,' Phoebe said happily. 'And we've had plenty of that lately. House moving is very stressful.'

Sam's maisonette had been sold once and should have been coinciding with Maggie and Eddie's completion but then the chain had broken down so the buyer had been forced to withdraw at the last moment.

In the end, everyone had agreed that it would be less stressful all round if Sam and Phoebe moved into Puddleduck Farm anyway.

'That way you can bring everything over at your leisure,' Maggie had said.

So, although they weren't moving into Puddleduck fully that day, they were moving the bare essentials, somewhere to sleep for them and for Roxie and Snowball, and food for the cupboard.

Phoebe and Sam had taken a week off work to do the rest at a more leisurely pace.

It did feel weird, Phoebe thought, watching Puddleduck Farmhouse become emptier and more echoey as the personal effects of years disappeared in boxes out of the door.

The huge kitchen table was staying. It would have taken six men to lift it, even if anyone had wanted to move it, which they didn't. The farmhouse kitchen was its rightful home. The desk and chairs in the room Maggie used as an office were staying. The bedsteads were staying but the mattresses were going.

Even so, by lunchtime, when the last lorry was about to head off, the house was a great deal emptier than Phoebe had ever seen it.

Frazier and Alexa had taken the kids, who were getting fractious, back home and Louella and James had gone ahead to the new bungalow to help out there.

The only cars left were Sam's Subaru, which contained Roxie, and Maggie's old Land Rover, in which Buster and Tiny were sitting on blankets, their heads hanging out of the open windows watching all the activity. At least Buster was still watching. Tiny had given up and gone to sleep.

Now, Maggie, Eddie, Phoebe and Sam all stood in the front parking area, outside the blue-painted front door, and Maggie looked up at the house. The sun was out and she shielded her eyes as she scanned the place that had been in her family for so many years. The house where both she and her father had grown up. The house that had belonged to her outright since 1979. The house where she had loved Farmer Pete and had brought up her family. The house that held the memories of generations.

Scores of seasons had come and gone, and it seemed to Phoebe that it was fitting that it was the last season of the year when Maggie herself left. Red berries dotted the bush by the front door and the December air had a frosty nip. There was no mistaking that winter was upon them.

No one spoke and Phoebe noticed that Eddie turned his head and took a few steps away from his wife, as if he were giving her the space to say goodbye.

Phoebe did the same thing, catching hold of Sam's hand, and squeezing his fingers.

The only movement for the next few seconds was everyone's breath, clouding out in puffs of white against the backdrop of the silver sky.

It was Maggie herself who broke the silence. 'Right then, you lot. We haven't got time to stand around here all day. Onwards and upwards.'

'We've got plenty of time,' Phoebe said softly. 'And if you want to change your mind about going there's still time for that too.'

'I don't,' Maggie said briskly. 'Now is the perfect time for me to go, and I couldn't be leaving the place in better hands. Besides, I'll be back in a couple of weeks. We'll all be here as usual for the Christmas festivities, won't we? Only difference is this year you and Sam will be the hosts.'

'We can't wait,' Phoebe told her. 'We'll have loads to talk about, I'm sure.'

Maggie looked at Phoebe speculatively and then at Sam. 'Well, aren't you going to carry her over the threshold?'

'That's for newlyweds,' Phoebe said. 'And we haven't got married yet. That's one of the things we want to talk to you about at Christmas. Our revised wedding plans.'

'You can do the threshold bit again when you're married,' Maggie argued. 'Anyway, Sam, you might not be able to lift her when you're married. She might be too heavy. What with all that sugar she eats.' She gave Phoebe a very definite wink. 'Isn't that right, my love?'

Phoebe gasped. Sam didn't seem to have picked up on what her grandmother was saying. He and Eddie were both laughing now, in relief maybe, after the poignancy of a few moments ago. Sam broke off and looked across at her. 'Do you want to be carried over the threshold?' He held out his arms.

'I suppose we should humour her,' Phoebe said. 'If you're sure you can lift me.'

'I think I can manage.' Sam swung her into his arms, giving a mock groan as he did so. Then he carried her over the threshold and with a theatrical flourish set her gently down again on the old woven doormat.

Eddie and Maggie clapped and Phoebe felt her throat fill with the emotion of the moment. Or maybe the emotions were the result of something else. Something that Maggie seemed to have already guessed – in that spooky telepathic way she had. Because she couldn't possibly know the result of the pregnancy test that Phoebe had taken first thing this morning.

Phoebe hadn't even told Sam yet. Neither had she told him they might need to reschedule the wedding for the third time – put it back for another few months, but for the best reason in the world. She was pregnant again. It was the first piece of good news she would give Sam when they were sitting at the table in their precious new kitchen... In their precious new dream home... Puddleduck Farm.

ACKNOWLEDGEMENTS

Thank you so much to Team Boldwood – you are amazing. Thank you to every single one of you who works so hard to bring my books to my readers in paperback, audio and digital.

As always, my special thanks go to my fabulous editor, Caroline Ridding, to editors Cecily Blench and Debra Newhouse, and to Alice Moore for the gorgeous cover.

Thank you to Rhian Rochford for her veterinary knowledge, without whom this book would be a lot harder, particularly for her help with chapter one. Thank you again to Liz Meyer, who has generously shared her puppy journey and whose own dog, Darcie, was my inspiration for Roxie. Thank you to Annie Probin, who helped with the Mr Spock chapter, and thank you to the Dunford Novelists.

Thank you to Gordon Rawsthorne for being my first reader.

Thank you, perhaps most of all, for the huge support of my many readers – without whom it would be pretty pointless writing novels. I love reading your emails, tweets and Facebook comments. Please keep them coming.

ABOUT THE AUTHOR

Della Galton writes short stories, teaches writing groups and is Agony Aunt for Writers Forum Magazine. Her stories feature strong female friendship, quirky characters and very often the animals she loves. When she is not writing she enjoys walking her dogs around the beautiful Dorset countryside.

Sign up to Della Galton's mailing list for news, competitions and updates on future books.

Visit Della's website: www.dellagalton.co.uk

Follow Della on social media:

facebook.com/DailyDella

x.com/DellaGalton

instagram.com/Dellagalton

bookbub.com/authors/della-galton

ALSO BY DELLA GALTON

The Bluebell Cliff Series

Sunshine Over Bluebell Cliff

Summer at Studland Bay

Shooting Stars Over Bluebell Cliff

Sunrise Over Pebble Bay

Confetti Over Bluebell Cliff

The Puddleduck Farm Series

Coming Home to Puddleduck Farm

Rainbows Over Puddleduck Farm

Love Blossoms at Puddleduck Farm

Living the Dream at Puddleduck Farm

Happy Ever After at Puddleduck Farm

WHERE ALL YOUR ROMANCE
DREAMS COME TRUE!

THE HOME OF BESTSELLING
ROMANCE AND WOMEN'S
FICTION

 WARNING:
MAY CONTAIN SPICE

SIGN UP TO OUR
NEWSLETTER

https://bit.ly/Lovenotesnews

Boldwood

Boldwood Books is an award-winning fiction publishing company seeking out the best stories from around the world.

Find out more at www.boldwoodbooks.com

Join our reader community for brilliant books, competitions and offers!

Follow us
@BoldwoodBooks
@TheBoldBookClub

Sign up to our weekly
deals newsletter

https://bit.ly/BoldwoodBNewsletter

Printed in Great Britain
by Amazon